The
Secret Library

Essential sensual reading

Traded Innocence

3 sensual novellas

Traded Innocence
by Toni Sands

Cooking Up Trouble
by Elizabeth Coldwell

Migrations
by K D Grace

Traded Innocence – Toni Sands

Sea, sky and smugglers' coves ... paradise for some but despair for beautiful Rebecca. Her father plans to marry her off to a tyrant. Intrigued by a soothsayer's words, she tumbles at the feet of bad boy Jac, an apprentice smuggler, good with women and horses. Desire mounts as powerfully as Rebecca's determination to rewrite her destiny. Is the local witch the answer to her prayers? Mystic Morwenna is Jac's ex-lover. Can she be trusted? Midnight at Half Moon Cove sees scavengers and power-hungry barons struggling for supremacy. The lovers must face greater danger before innocence is traded for passion in the sandy cove where they first met.

Cooking Up Trouble – Elizabeth Coldwell

The good news is that Morgan Jones has landed her dream job, co-presenting the Saturday morning TV cookery show, *Cook's Treat*. The bad news is she'll be working alongside the hottest celebrity chef in London, Scott Harley. Voluptuous Morgan has never forgiven Scott for trashing her cooking style and physical appearance in a magazine article, but when she meets him in the flesh for the first time her reaction is very different. The attraction between the two of them is mutual and undeniable, but she's determined not to fall for his obvious charms. Their chemistry on the show disguises the tension behind the scenes – a tension that grows more sexual by the day. Can she stand the growing heat – or should Morgan get out of the kitchen?

Migrations – K D Grace

Val Hastings, assisted by her do-gooder cousin Sarah Cline, is shanghaied into driving their Aunt Rose across the US to visit her son. What begins as the trip from hell turns into a sexy adventure when they find themselves sharing the interstate with a mysterious, leather-clad biker. Aunt Rose and Sarah are convinced he's up to no good. But after Val catches him pleasuring himself at a rest area, and he offers her some steamy help to make her journey more enjoyable, she's convinced he's her nasty saviour.

Is Hawk, the biker, a murderer, a free spirit, or something else? Whatever he is, animal attraction wins out over caution, as he joins the ladies for a cross-country romp that keeps Sarah and Aunt Rose nervous and Val hotter than her overheating engine.

Published by Xcite Books Ltd – 2012
ISBN 9781908262028

Cover design by Madamadari

Contents

www.xcitebooks.com

Scan the QR code to join our mailing list

Traded Innocence
by Toni Sands

Chapter One
Spies in the Sand Dunes
Wales – 1828

ON THE GOLDEN CRESCENT visible at high tide, a horseman cantered towards the headland. An emerald green bandanna tied back glossy black hair from his face. His white shirt ballooned as he rode, muscular thighs gripping the horse's flanks.

Fingers laced, two young women giggled their way across the dunes above, to scramble into a sandy bowl, sheltered by swaying grass and sea thrift.

'She'll never catch us now,' said Rebecca, fingers raking her copper curls. 'I won't let her spoil our fun.'

'Biddy's only following your father's orders,' said Catrin. 'He wants you to make a good marriage.'

'It's not fair! Marrying me off to someone who's a hundred years old.'

Catrin frowned. 'He's a wealthy lord.'

'Born back in the last century. You do the sums! Once I'm in the old goat's clutches, I shan't see you any more. As for Biddy – she'd chop off her head rather than leave my father. I'll have no one to talk to.'

Catrin looked down at the dry sand trailing through her fingers.

Rebecca's eyes narrowed. 'You know something, don't you?'

But her cousin's attention was elsewhere. On the beach below, a horseman had appeared. The horse's hooves kicked at a wave, sending watery diamonds into the air. Catrin pointed him out to Rebecca and they watched him vanish around the headland.

'He rides well.' Catrin smoothed her skirt around her legs.

Rebecca bent her head towards her cousin's ripe-corn mane of hair and whispered.

Catrin gasped. 'You wanton!'

'Why? I know what you really meant. And you still haven't answered my question. I might be forced to tickle you.' Rebecca knew her companion would confess to murder once subjected to this torment.

Catrin upturned her palms. 'I'm to be married too.'

'What?' Rebecca froze.

'You and I will be wedded and bedded by summer's end. It's what's destined for young women like us.'

Rebecca scrambled to her feet. We'll see about that.' Her defiant cry merged with the mew of the gulls fussing overhead.

The girls retraced their route. Laughter drifted down to the shore where the horseman had turned to ride back towards the opposite cliff. His lips twitched at the glimpse of snowy petticoat peeping from skirts swirled by the breeze. His gaze followed the two slender figures climbing the path snaking through the dunes until it dipped sharply, swallowing the tops of the girls' heads.

'Pretty,' he told his horse. 'A fair milkmaid and a fiery goddess. This peninsula shows promise. Maybe I'll enjoy my stay with my uncle even more than I anticipated.' He pressed his thighs against the animal's flanks. 'Come, Sofia. I need sustenance and so do you.'

'I can't marry him. I won't. I can't bear the thought of his lizard claws on my body!' Rebecca drained her goblet of wine. Slammed it on the table.

Her father rose and paced towards the window, wishing for the umpteenth time his beloved Marion was still alive. But his wife had been burnt out by fever when Rebecca was a child.

Now a lovely young woman, as well as a minx, her bright autumn leaf hair and proud nature were poignant reminders of her mother. Lord Beaumont had seen the expression in men's eyes, watched them contemplate the dew on the bud. Rebecca must be married, and soon. Loyal Biddy was no match for his spirited daughter. And if Rebecca continued wandering off on escapades, even with Catrin …

Hugh tried wheedling. 'Geraint's a good man. You'll lack nothing, Rebecca. Nor will your children.'

'Children?' Rebecca's tone implied he'd suggested a family of polecats. 'How can I marry someone without first loving him?'

'My daughter – that's what your dear mother thought when we became betrothed. She'd convinced herself she couldn't possibly wed a fair-haired man. I had to gain her confidence until, like a shy young filly, she trusted me. After Rhys was born, she thanked me for her flaxen-haired boy.' His voice faltered. 'In the fullness of time, you arrived and we had two fine children.'

'But Father, you're much more handsome than my lord Geraint. While his left eye looks at my face, the right one peers over my shoulder.'

Her father hid a smile. 'Imperfection is God-given, as is perfection. Looks are not of great importance in a man or a woman.'

Rebecca pounced. 'So say you! A handsome man who married a beauty. How can you condemn your daughter to taking a toad to her bed?'

'Hold your tongue, girl. Go to your quarters. You'll find marriage brings its own rewards. And any children of yours will be handsome, of that I'm certain.'

She'd pushed her father enough. Rebecca knew he was deaf to her views. He was also concerned about the local people's obsession with smuggling. The idea of such dangerous doings thrilled her. She and Catrin often whispered in the dark, the whiff of melting candle wax tickling their nostrils. What were they really like, these swarthy sailors bringing fragrant scents, fiery spices and rich tobacco? Which local men patrolled the smugglers' coves?

Rebecca sought out her cousin, startling Catrin who sat dreaming in her room. 'He won't listen, Cat. I'd run away but he'd fetch me back before nightfall. I long for something to happen ... someone to help me.'

'Will you settle for a wager?'

'What?'

'I heard the servants talking last night,' said Catrin. 'I was outside the kitchen door, giving Lol his supper.'

Rebecca nodded. Catrin's little corgi gave her ample excuse to be around the yard. 'Go on.'

'There's talk of a new king.'

'Something's happened to George?'

'No, silly. A smuggler king.'

Rebecca leaned closer.

'Will Bevan from down the coast, is no longer the dominant force. There's a local man, Dermot Maddocks, trying to keep Bevan out. Maddocks has a nephew – a young Irishman, come to keep his uncle company.'

'An apprentice smuggler?'

'Bold but gentle, they say. Reluctant to use his fists or his sword, unless the provocation's too great.'

'Then he's a fool or a coward.' Rebecca knew compassion wasn't a common trait among the smuggling community.

'He's known as a kind man who takes his share of bounty and distributes it. There are widows and old, sick folk thanking God for Jac Maddocks' generosity.'

'I think,' said Rebecca, 'this Celtic Robin Hood sounds dreary. Maybe he's too puny to find a wife.'

'Biddy says he's pretty enough to eat.'

'She said that?'

'Told me she was out walking the other afternoon and saw him riding along the bridleway. Biddy's not so old, you know.' Catrin nudged Rebecca. 'I think she's right.'

'You've seen this Jac too?'

'We both have,' said Catrin. 'Wasn't it only yesterday we ran off to the sand dunes? Remember the horseman on the

4

shore?'

'I recall him.' Rebecca's expression was unreadable. 'So, what's your wager?'

'I wager you can't steal a kiss.'

A smile curved Rebecca's lips.

'Of course, it's only servants' gossip about his kindness,' said Catrin hurriedly. 'You mustn't endanger yourself or risk your reputation for the sake of a little escapade. I don't know what possessed me to mention such a thing.' She looked anxiously at her cousin. 'You're a lady, almost betrothed to a man of substance.'

'If I'm to wed a frog,' said Rebecca, 'surely I deserve to kiss a prince? This is one wager I can't resist, even if the prince is a smuggler.'

'Will you take me with you?'

'Where are we going, Catrin?' Rebecca's full lips parted.

'We know when the prince rides out.'

'So we do, Catrin. So we do.'

Rebecca's curiosity about the handsome horseman fuelled her fantasies later as she lay in bed. There he was, walking along the sea shore. No one else was allowed to ruin their solitude. Jac ran the last few yards towards her, making her heart race. Making her anticipate the touch of his lips on hers. Their first kiss surprised her with its intensity. Holding her gaze, he pulled her close so she felt his excitement as his body pressed against hers. His lips covered her throat with tiny kisses, found her mouth again, his tongue teasing, flooding her body with delicious sensations. Her own hands took on a life of their own, stroking her breasts, seeking out each nipple in turn. Rolling it between thumb and index finger.

Her mind spun an erotic fairy tale in which she and Jac lay on the sand, his hand stroking the soft skin of her thighs. She felt herself melting as he bunched up her skirts. She moved her legs apart. Instinctively. Gently. He murmured her name as he edged closer to her core.

Was this how Jac's touch would feel? She almost called out to him as she found her magic place. She began climbing. Unable to prevent faint moans escaping her lips. Jac was in her mind's eye. Jac inhabited her body. Afterwards she hugged her arms round her, rocking herself, dazed by the emotional torrent she'd created. Reality crept back, an unwelcome bedfellow. How could she give herself to a man incapable of stirring any of her senses except that of distaste?

'The turquoise brocade, isn't it? Oh yes,' said Biddy, holding the gown against Rebecca. 'See how well the bodice fits your shape.'

'The grey taffeta, I think.' Rebecca's eyes gleamed.

Biddy sucked in her breath. 'The low neckline of the turquoise is more becoming, surely?'

'Precisely.' Rebecca dumped the rejected gown into Biddy's arms. 'I can get dressed on my own.' Rebecca stalked to the door and flung it open. 'Thank you, Biddy. I'm sure you've more important tasks than playing nursemaid to me.'

The older woman walked down the corridor, defeat hunching her shoulders. Not for the first time, she wondered what Rebecca would have been like, had her mother not died before her time. Biddy suspected the girl's strong will would have surfaced whatever the circumstances.

That evening, my lord Geraint was to dine at Beaumont Manor on food fresh from the estate. Mutton roasted with fresh herbs, leeks, new potatoes and tiny turnips, filling the kitchen with savoury scents. Creamy goat's cheese would partner flatbread and a slab of salty butter. Pudding was to be trifle, a sweet feast of summer fruits and custard. The meal would be washed down with imported claret and honeyed wine.

Biddy's feelings about attending this dinner were complicated even though her employer expected her presence. Every minute spent in Lord Hugh Beaumont's company was poignant. Biddy sometimes wondered what his lordship would think if he could plunge into the whirlpool of desires played out in her head as she sat sewing or brushing Rebecca's hair at bedtime. The rich copper tresses rippling over the girl's shoulders, always filled Biddy with desire for someone to brush her own still luxuriant hair with loving strokes.

Rebecca's father had visited Biddy's bed once since his

wife died. After an evening's drinking in a house muffled by darkness and sorrow, he'd stolen in like a shadow. She'd pulled back the covers, her nakedness his passport. He'd kissed her mouth then her breasts until she ached for him and he took her with an urgency both shocking and exciting. Afterwards, she'd stroked his hair until he fell asleep, lying motionless, determined to stay awake until he left at daybreak.

Each night for weeks afterwards she'd retired to bed and waited. The dizzying prospect of carrying Hugh's child filled her with enough fear and longing to make her physically sick; convincing her she must be pregnant. But the nausea passed with no further physical consequences of his visit. The door to her chamber remained unopened at night and Biddy continued as mother figure to Rebecca, clinging to her dream of warming his lordship's bed even if he didn't take her for his wife.

Biddy privately considered the motherless girl ungrateful. Geraint was a man of substance needing a wife. Rebecca had known nothing but love and plenty. Marriage to the nobleman would provide entrée to grand houses and estates along the peninsula and further. All she needed do was provide an heir and a spare to his lordship. The nursery established; she could resume her social life, flirting with the confidence of her married status.

Not for one moment did Biddy imagine her own future lay anywhere but within Hugh Beaumont's manor. With Rebecca wed and mistress of her own household then might her lord replicate that single night of passion? Biddy's hunger for him remained unsatisfied.

The dining table was dressed for company. Maids served succulent helpings from steaming dishes. Poured wine into goblets. Rebecca's expression remained demure and she spoke only when addressed by either her father or Lord Geraint. Biddy ate little, sneaking glances at her employer as he conversed with his guest of honour about estate business and affairs of interest only to the gentlemen. Or, so the males perceived.

'That's wrong.'

7

A dog whined beneath the table. Biddy dropped her knife with a clatter. Rebecca met her father's gaze.

'You wish to express an opinion, daughter?' His calm voice sent Rebecca's heart pumping faster.

'Surely, Father, to beat a wife because of one incident of impropriety is unjust. It seems to me harsh beyond belief, my lords.'

Rebecca knew Lord Geraint watched her closely, a gleam of amusement in his eyes.

Her father tapped his knife on the table top. 'You don't understand the circumstances, Rebecca. The woman consorted with a smuggler, a vile and unscrupulous man who battens off the sea like a vulture lives off carrion.'

This was dangerous territory. Rebecca's elder brother, Rhys, died because he tried to intervene in a smugglers' squabble that spiralled out of control. His devastated father had roamed the lanes and coves seeking revenge. What were casks of brandy and twists of tobacco compared with the life of a lovely boy?

It was common knowledge that gentry, innkeepers, farmers and other outwardly respected members of the community were up to their collars in smuggling. She'd heard from Catrin and Biddy how such men dodged the law. She also knew her father, knuckles gleaming pearly as he gripped the knife handle, doubtless wished he could take out the smuggler who'd torn the life from Rhys.

One glance at Biddy showed her anxiety, her slight body rigid as she read the expressions on the men's faces. Rebecca noticed her husband to be wasn't quick to agree with her father. Geraint gazed at her breasts, despite her demure neckline. He took his time meeting her glare.

'A wife's first loyalty must be to her husband. Infidelity, whether practised or considered, must surely deserve punishment.' His tone was silky.

Rebecca seethed. He'd succeeded in making her sound flippant about the rules of matrimony. What was more, he made her sound as though she sided with the smugglers. She wanted to argue but noticing Biddy's warning glance, bit her lip.

'I meant no disrespect, Father.' Rebecca turned towards her suitor. 'I didn't understand the full significance of what was said.'

'Let's speak of more cheerful matters,' said Hugh. 'Your seventeenth birthday has passed. Now we should celebrate your formal betrothal to my lord Geraint.'

Rebecca's mouth dried. Her future husband surveyed her face and figure as though scrutinising a cow for sale at market. At that moment she knew what she must do. If it meant disgrace and banishment, so be it. The means of planning her escape, given Biddy's meek acquiescence to the whole business, was not apparent.

Chapter Two
A Wager and a Knave

'WHAT'S IN THE BASKET?' Rebecca fidgeted with the snowy napkin.

'There's a bottle of Biddy's homemade cordial and some titbits for Mrs Owen and her family. She's confined to her cottage.' Catrin giggled. 'It's an excuse for us to be out walking instead of sewing your trousseau.'

The formal betrothal had been confirmed after the dinner.

'Oh, clever Cat,' said Rebecca. 'I've never suspected such hidden depths. Are we off on a spying mission?'

'We deliver this. Then continue our walk.' Catrin shot Rebecca a sly glance. 'I thought we'd head for the sand dunes ... some fresh air after last night's rich food.'

'Don't remind me.' Rebecca shuddered, recalling the oily touch of Geraint's lips as he kissed her hand before leaving. 'Do you believe in miracles, Cat?'

'I believe in destiny.'

'Does Mrs Owen still read the cards?'

'How much time do you spend listening to servants' gossip?'

'Not quite as much as you. I fancy having my cards read but if Mrs Owen is indisposed, I'd better not trouble her.'

'She's not indisposed, just resting,' said Catrin. 'Her mother's caring for the little ones.'

'A village woman, resting?'

'Her time is near,' Catrin whispered.

The two walked on. Rebecca longed to satisfy her curiosity but it was unlikely Catrin knew much more than Biddy did. There seemed a chasm between married and single women.

Rebecca wondered if what her father said was really true and love could grow between a man and woman, even if it didn't exist before they married.

'Does it hurt?' Rebecca stopped walking.

'Childbirth? Don't you know your bible?'

'I meant ... when the man enters you.' She watched Catrin's cheeks turn pink.

'Hush, Becca. How should I know?'

'Are you looking forward to wedding your clergyman, Catrin?'

'I am.'

'Is he good-looking? Like the horseman?'

'He pleases me.'

'You can't wait, can you? What do you say to a swap? You take Geraint and all his riches. I'll wed nice John Morgan.' Rebecca watched her friend's face. 'There. You're doing just what I did – imagining those hands creeping over your body. Now you know how I feel.'

'Rebecca, you'll be the envy of the peninsula when you become My Lady Geraint. You'll probably be paying me visits, bringing titbits to help us out.'

'You still don't understand, do you?'

'Come on. We're nearly there. Afterwards, we'll have our bit of fun.'

Rebecca doubted they'd get close enough to the young man for her to claim a kiss. With his credentials, he might suspect an ambush and gallop off. At least she could imagine carrying out the wager. Maybe get a better view of him this time. That's if he turned up.

'A dark-haired man – a knave not a king,' said Mrs Owen. 'That's what I see.'

The cottage smelled of cabbage. Rebecca, mesmerised by the woman's pumpkin belly, hardly noticed.

Mrs Owen tapped her top lip with a forefinger. 'He has a heart of gold but he moves in dangerous places. That could be his downfall.'

Rebecca squirmed in her chair. 'But, do you see me? What

11

about my marriage?' She ignored Catrin's sharp intake of breath.

The woman's gaze roamed the arc of brightly-coloured cards spread over the kitchen table's surface. 'My lady, I've heard you're betrothed to Sir Geraint.'

'Yes, but will I marry him? My lord is fair, not dark. He has a beard and one eye awry. Might there be some different path ahead for me?' Rebecca wheedled.

The woman's swollen fingers gathered the cards. Her pumpkin bump bulged when she leaned forward. Rebecca watched, fascinated.

'Choose three,' said Mrs Owen.

'We should go now,' said Catrin. 'We must be tiring you, Mrs Owen.'

The other two ignored her as they gazed at the curious images. A small boy wriggled from his grandma's lap and crawled across the floor to tug Rebecca's skirt. She bent to ruffle his hair.

Mrs Owen sat back with a sigh. 'Lovers meeting. A kiss. A voyage. That's what I see.'

'Soothsayers know what to say to young women, Becca. Don't be deceived. She probably tells that particular tale over and over.'

'Maybe she does and maybe not. Didn't you notice her face? It was as if she saw something different from what she knew was planned and it puzzled her. Why do that if she was repeating the same old story?'

'She liked the basket of goodies we took,' said Catrin. 'Wanted to give something in return.'

'If she's right and I escape marrying that greasy toad, I'll return one day and reward her.'

'You mustn't fill your head with such notions. Wedding preparations have begun. Run away and you face scandal and poverty. You'd hardly be able to return and reward her then.' Catrin stopped to catch her breath.

Rebecca stalked ahead. They were crossing the dunes. The empty provisions basket was hidden under a willow tree Catrin swore made a useful landmark. Hampered by skirts and petticoats, their boots sinking into sand, progress was erratic.

'I hope we haven't missed him.' Rebecca stopped. 'Look – let's climb down here. It'll be quicker.'

'That way's too steep.' Catrin still lagged behind.

Rebecca ignored her, knowing the girl must follow if she wanted to keep her in sight. She began clambering down the grassy slope.

A lone rider on a chestnut horse followed the shoreline. He'd rounded the headland while the girls were talking and continued his progress towards their side of the cove. The breeze caught the jingle of spurs, spinning the sound through the warm air. His horse cantered then galloped. Rebecca halted, watching the man throw back his head and laugh the laugh of a man at ease in his skin. She longed to be on that horse with him, arms wrapped around his waist, her breasts pressed against his back. The powerful image stole her breath.

'Careful, Becca. You might hurt yourself.'

'Come on, slowcoach. Let yourself go ...'

Catrin shrieked. Hand in hand, the two of them toppled down the remaining slope and landed in a flurry of lacy petticoats and linen drawers on the damp sand.

A shadow loomed. 'Are you two young ladies all right? That was quite a tumble.'

The girls peered up at the tall figure silhouetted against the shore. His eyes danced as he looked down at them. He dismounted before they could move. His shirt was open almost to his waist.

Rebecca, cheeks warming, looked straight up at the dark tangle on his chest. A tiny breeze teased her curls. Without Catrin's presence, would she have remained on the sand? She scrambled to her feet. The horseman held out his hand to her. Instinctively she took it, feeling the firm warmth of his fingers. His admiring gaze roamed her body as if savouring every inch. Going where his fingers had gone in her fantasy. She wouldn't have tolerated such insolence had he not been the subject of her night fantasies. A frisson of triumph jolted her.

The mare tossed her mane, whickering as she pawed the

sand. Her rider turned to her, his fingers whispering down the side of her head, making her nuzzle him. Watching this affectionate gesture, Rebecca felt a pang of envy.

'You should have averted your eyes when we tumbled down the slope, Sir,' Catrin chided.

Rebecca stifled a giggle. Maybe Miss Prim was practising for her future role of preacher's wife.

'My apologies. Your servant, Ma'am,' said the stranger, closing his eyes and stretching out both arms towards the girls in mock supplication.

Rebecca was shaken by the impact of his nearness. A shadow of stubble darkened his chin. He wasn't too tall yet topped her by a couple of inches. The strength evident in his frame seemed less potent than the gentleness when he'd cupped her elbow, helping steady her as she rose. She didn't know which was worse. Hot cheeks or the stirring of something indefinable, unknown, and potentially dangerous. This wasn't only a meeting contrived by two young women seeking fun. It was something instinctive. It made her clench her fists at her sides. How easy it would be to run to him and claim that kiss, yet now he was within touching distance, she felt shy. Longing for the touch of his lips, she knew this must only happen because he felt the same. There should be no snatched kiss resulting from a stupid wager.

'Will I look now?' His creamy Irish lilt sent tremors down Rebecca's spine.

'We should continue our exercise,' said Catrin. 'We walk for the sake of our constitutions.'

He opened his eyes and nodded. 'Then I'll detain you no longer, Ma'am. I too consider the sea air good for my well-being.' He smiled at Catrin but it was Rebecca upon whom his gaze lingered. 'Jac Maddocks at your service, Ma'am.'

The horse's whinny broke the spell. Jac placed one booted foot in the stirrup and hoisted himself into the saddle. The mare tossed her head eagerly. Nodding courteously to the young women, the young man slapped the mare's flank and horse and rider cantered back the way they'd come.

Catrin spoke first. 'I think we should declare the wager void

After all, you as good as achieved it. You couldn't take your eyes off him.'

Rebecca didn't answer. She had her back to Catrin, her gaze following the retreating rider, lingering on his tight breeches. Her lips moved soundlessly as, unseen by her companion, she tasted Jac's name on her tongue.

'Come on.' Catrin nudged her. 'We must get back before your father sends a search party. Put the dark-haired knave out of your mind, Becca. Dangerous places are not for the likes of you and me.'

Rebecca turned on her. 'I thought you said Mrs Owen's prediction was claptrap,' she snapped.

Too casually, Jac related the afternoon's incident to his uncle over supper. Dermot chortled at the description of the two girls tumbling down the slope to land in a provocative bundle at his nephew's feet.

'It sounds to me like Lord Beaumont's daughter,' he said. 'I mean little Rebecca and her cousin Catrin. Poor Becca lost her mother too soon for her own good. Though Biddy's tried her best to look after the girl's needs.' He winked at Jac. 'The father's too, I wouldn't mind wagering.'

The innuendo was lost on Jac. 'If that was Rebecca I met, she's no longer a little girl.' His mind conjured up a picture of swirled petticoats. The tantalising glimpse of long legs. Now he knew the redhead's name. She was gentry. Dared he address her, should their paths cross again?

Dermot cocked an eyebrow. 'Not for you to notice. That particular nectar's promised to Lord Geraint. Rebecca's father's estate adjoins the land Geraint owns. Hugh Beaumont has set his stall out. Geraint likes the notion. Who could blame him? He's years younger than Hugh. Rebecca's brother, Rhys, is long gone, poor lad. As is the mother, God rest her soul.'

For a moment, Jac saw something resembling regret flicker in his uncle's eyes. There was history here and Jac wanted to know it.

'They'll be after an heir to the two estates, that pair,' said Dermot.

'Explain to me,' said Jac. 'Who is this Geraint?'

'A well-born, nasty piece of work. I know for sure he's in cahoots with Will Bevan. Geraint's skilled at hiding his true colours. I've always suspected he was behind the killing of Rebecca's brother.'

'Yet you say she's promised to this man?' Jac looked startled.

'Geraint has a pedigree, though I hate to admit it. That, his fortune and his acres have conspired to tip his wick with gold. In the eye of the beholder he's a good catch. But whoever shares his name and bed won't have it easy. They say he's partial to boys, not only girls. Whatever they are, he prefers 'em with the dew still on.' Dermot's face hardened. He grabbed his tankard and drank from it. 'Rebecca can't be more than 17, poor little baggage. That bastard must be slavering at the thought of bedding her. If she was my daughter, I'd be fishing calmer waters to find her a husband.'

Jac felt his skin prickle. Anger and disgust welled up. 'Hell's teeth,' he cried. 'Can you not say something? What if Rebecca's father doesn't know what you know? Is that a possibility?'

Dermot's lips set in a thin line. He rose and walked over to the window. Spread his hands on the sill. With his back towards his nephew, he said, 'Hugh and I no longer share confidences.'

'Then I must say something. We can't let this marriage proceed!'

Dermot turned around to face the room. 'We? Leave well alone, Jac. Don't torture yourself over things outside your control.' He poured more ale into his tankard and offered his nephew the pitcher.

Jac shook his head, his face ominous as the sun-starved sky. His mind saw pictures it had no business conjuring up. Those thighs would feel like silk under his touch. Longing filled his gut. He felt himself stir.

'You're young,' said Dermot. 'You have needs. There are wenches in my mansion would be happy to warm you at night. I imagine you've already tasted some of the local delights …

yes?'

Jac nodded.

Dermot rubbed the back of his neck. 'Steer clear of the married ones. Above all, don't meddle where you shouldn't. By that, I don't mean the witch's cave. In my day – but you don't want to hear an old man's fantasies.'

Jac wasn't surprised his uncle too had once fallen under Morwenna's spell. He got up and in his turn gazed through the window. The calm water reflected dark plum and gunmetal clouds. The sunset, almost too beautiful to bear, matched his emotions. It was easy for his uncle to tell him what and what not to do. Dermot wasn't fighting an insatiable craving.

'Tell me what happened,' said Jac. 'Why do you and Rebecca's father no longer share confidences?'

His uncle's eyelids fluttered. 'As boys we swam together, fished together. Wrestled in the dunes like fox cubs. Then our characters and our backgrounds began to clash.' He sighed. 'I've always had a yen for the dark side, if you like. Fortune hunting … danger. Hugh's father died and as the only son, he inherited everything, including the responsibility.' He looked down at his hands. 'Hugh lost his heart. And so did I. Things turned complicated. Now the love he felt stifles him like a shroud. He's loved and lost twice over, you see. Not long after his firstborn, Rhys, was killed, his wife Marion took the fever. The man's spirit has been broken. His judgement's clouded. No doubt he'd say the same thing about mine.' Dermot's smile was wry.

'If his judgement's in question, all the more reason to step in. If Rebecca goes to this Geraint, her life will be a nightmare. What sort of man would wish that to happen?'

Dermot held up his hand in warning. 'All I know is, if you get involved in this, Hugh's bound to suspect my fingers pulling the strings. Don't go near young Rebecca. If you do, you'll set the hounds of hell baying after your blood. I've no wish to lose my only heir. I've already lost enough in this life.'

'You still haven't explained. You and your childhood friend each fell in love. Why did that separate the pair of you?'

Dermot put his head in his hands.

17

Realisation hit Jac like a punch in the solar plexus. One woman - two suitors. It was obvious Hugh Beaumont with his enviable heritage would be the favourite. But what of Rebecca's mother? Had she married the man she wanted? Or had she gone to her grave still nursing a broken heart?

Sleep eluded Jac that night. He pushed back the covers and stretched naked in the moonlight. His hand explored what nudged his inner thigh and his rueful smile was lost in the darkness. Despite his uncle's earlier warning, the source of Jac's arousal was of course a woman. Not just any woman but a girl woman with pert breasts begging him to trace his finger underneath. Her nipples would be sweet rosebuds between his lips. As for that ivory skin, cool as her hair was fiery, didn't it implore him to stroke it? Didn't it demand his kisses as urgently as her hair made him long to curl his fingers in its coppery depths? He yearned to feel the warmth of her and to breathe her scent, that essence of newly-minted woman.

His mind absorbed the image. His body reacted. Jac groaned, feeling his erection tug him. Taunt him. He slid his right hand down its length, pushing air through his lips.

He had to put Rebecca out of his mind. So which of the women he'd bedded since living with his uncle would he wish to satisfy his need now? Was it the young widow Bishopston with her eager arms, those dimpled cushiony thighs the gateway to her honey pot? Gentle and grateful, she never chided him for disturbing her, whatever ungodly hour. Beneath him, she vibrated like a taut-stringed harp. The more he fucked her, the more she cried for more. She fed him bread and wine afterwards and sent him on his way with a kiss.

Or was it the raven-haired beauty the locals called the witch? Morwenna's hot, sweet as raspberries mouth, her artful darting tongue, could bring a man to the edge. Hold him there, before he plummeted into the great beyond. At first she'd feign reluctance, sharpening her tongue on him until, patience almost spent; his need gnawing his innards and glazing his eyes, she'd allow him into her bed. Snarling or cooing, the temptress' mix of reticence and earthiness excited him beyond belief.

So why would a brief encounter with a virgin urge him to forego such sensual pleasures? The flame-haired girl was a willow wand against the widow's voluptuousness. And how could Rebecca equal the witch's skill in the art of satisfying a man? He knew he could no more kick Miss Bright Eyes out of his dreams than resist saddling up Uncle Dermot's chestnut when the mare whinnied and nuzzled her starry face against him in the mornings. Women and horseflesh fell like ripe fruit into Jac's hands. And here he was, lusting after the unattainable. Like some horny youth desperate to prove his manhood.

Jac had an eye for quality. He'd noticed the cut of Rebecca's gown, the richness of its fabric. This girl was not for him. Dermot's warning rang in his ears. Better to forget her. But she was still there when he closed his eyes. Her curls tumbled round her face as he gave himself up to his fantasy. Let her bend over him to take him in her mouth. How gentle she was. How persistent. Jac groaned. Forbidden fruit. Always the sweetest.

He curled his fingers around his cock and let his dream ride him.

Chapter Three
Half-Moon Bay

THE WELCOME PARTY WAS in luck. The virgin moon was keeping her charms to herself. Jac too, kept himself to himself. His uncle's men, disguised by darkness, lounged nearby with horses and carts ready to whisk away barrels of brandy, packages of tobacco and chests of China tea and coffee beans. Some would risk straining their back muscles to lug a pair of roped casks to the safe house and earn extra coins. Jac hoped for something special among this consignment. Something to bring relief to the old fellow whose cottage teetered on the nearby cliff. The old timer would surely sleep once his gut pain eased.

He wondered if a remedy existed to quell his own growing unrest. But knowing himself so well, he feared it might have the opposite effect. Tuned to danger, he tensed, sensing rather than seeing a movement. The night breeze whipped his cloak around his body as he focused on the cliff's underbelly. Until one of the men swung a lantern revealing a flash of fire against the rock face.

Jac's fingers closed around the hilt of the dagger tucked in his belt. What if this was a trap? He'd be a fool not to expect trouble but he fancied this quarry wanted to be found. And by him. Padding like a big cat over the sands, his stomach lurched as he realised he'd been right. This was someone who'd no business being in the vicinity after nightfall. Relief flooded him and roughened his tone.

'You little fool. What are you doing here? Are you spying for that bridegroom of yours? Does he think a woman's a suitable agent to report back to him what's doing in the cove?'

'How did you recognise me?'

'There aren't too many in these parts with looks like yours, Rebecca. Pull that hood of yours properly over your head.'

'I can assure you no one knows I'm here.' Her voice didn't falter.

Jac shook his head. 'This isn't a bazaar – somewhere for my lady to choose a pair of lace gloves or flask of lavender water. You must go home at once and don't even think of returning again after nightfall. You're fortunate I spotted you when I did. It's asking for trouble, butting in like this.'

'How dare you! Who are you to order me about?'

He grabbed her wrist. Gently but firmly. 'Little fool. If I didn't know your status, I'd have you bundled aboard that boat and let you cruise to Spain. Some good voyage you'd enjoy then, Madam. The sailors would see to that.'

'Why must you try to frighten me?' She made no attempt to disengage herself. Her words hissed into the darkness but she had to wait for a reply. Jac marched her back towards the looming cliffs, away from prying ears.

'You could have got yourself killed! Strike first before someone strikes at you is the rule here.' His tone softened. 'That's why I'm trying to frighten you. Best you go now. Don't say anything to anyone about what you've seen tonight. Understand? Not even that pretty milkmaid friend of yours.'

'Oh, so you find Catrin pleasing, do you?'

The jealousy spiking her voice tugged at his groin. He sucked in his breath, forgetting to release her hand. 'She's pretty enough. But you, Madam, are a beauty. And beauties spell trouble. Especially when they've a mind of their own.'

'I vow not to say a word to anyone. As long as you ...'

'As long as I what? Are you about to blackmail me, Rebecca?' He was more relaxed now. Over his panic at realising how close he'd been to lashing out at a shadow. That loveliness could have been marred. Or worse.

'I won't say a word. You can be sure of that, because I've need of your help.'

'Is that right? How could I help someone who already possesses everything money can buy?' He thought of her father's plans. Jac's impassioned response to his Uncle Dermot still haunted him. What was happening? Standing a whisper away from Rebecca beneath the sheltering rock face, he smelt her warmth … felt his body stir with more urgency this time.

'You're right. I should go back now,' Rebecca said. 'Catrin's a light sleeper. I don't want to compromise her. Will you ride here tomorrow afternoon?'

'Yes. But why take the risk of coming here by night if you know my daytime habits?'

There was a pause. 'It's necessary to take risks,' said Rebecca. 'Otherwise I endanger my soul.'

Before he knew what was happening, she placed one hand on his shoulder, stood on tiptoe and brushed his cheek with a butterfly kiss. He stood watching her slight figure disappear into the gloom. It was clear she'd have no trouble finding her way back. She and her friend probably made a habit of night-wandering. Now the pretty little vixen reaped the benefit of her orienteering skills. He groaned, fingering his face where her lips had been. The men would jeer if they knew how his breeches bulged at that moment.

Jac had a good idea why Rebecca was singling him out. She'd no need to purchase fripperies or contraband brandy. But her betrothal to a rich, odious man might well be what worried her. He could only respect her for that but it would be interesting to discover how she though he could help. For a moment he regretted not having taken advantage of that fleeting kiss. He could have pulled her to him, crushing that soft mouth with his own – pushing his tongue inside while his hands roamed her body. Eager to keep their meeting unobserved, would she have protested? Or did she wish he could caress her breasts as much as he did?

The cart was fully loaded. It creaked as the men moved off. His uncle beckoned. There'd been no need for Jac's vigilante skills that night. Mr Bevan's gang of predators must have been deployed elsewhere, maybe Firefly Cove, just along the coastline. The only visitor had been one who exerted too powerful an impact on Jac's body and his mind, for comfort. He smiled to himself. Comfort was the last thing he wanted. If becoming linked with the redhead spelled danger, as Dermot predicted, then let it.

Rebecca thought her lungs might burst. Holding back her giggles, she flattened her body closer to the wall behind her bedroom door after Biddy's second discreet knock. The door inched open. Any moment …

'Rebecca?'

Biddy sounded puzzled. Surely she must be able to hear the pounding of her charge's heart beyond the door panels? Rebecca's breath hissed from her lungs at the sound of Biddy's retreating feet. Now the woman would assume her charge was somewhere outside. Which, soon she would be.

A door closed at the end of the corridor. Biddy would be climbing the narrow staircase leading to her quarters. She'd take out her sewing, her fingers poised to continue the exquisite drawn thread work she was creating for the bridal trousseau. The gold stripes, the emerald and sapphire, were the colours of the Beaumont family coat of arms, now reflected in a daughter's wedding finery.

The entire household, including Catrin, was in a lather over marriage preparations. What would they say if they knew the bride contemplated twisting her bridal cloak into a rope to aid her escape by night? Except of course, she knew simpler ways of quitting the house.

A few days had passed since Rebecca's nocturnal tryst with Jac. Today Catrin was visiting her mother. It was easier to hoodwink Biddy without Catrin complicating matters, fond as Rebecca was of her. Hugh Beaumont was hunting. There was no one to prevent her from meeting Jac.

Her feet hardly touched the treads as she glided downstairs and into her father's study. He never locked the ante room, liking to let his dogs in and out through the side door. Moments later, Rebecca, darting through shrubbery, arrived at a gate opening on to a footpath. This was the quickest way to reach the sand dunes. And the cove beneath.

Would he be waiting? Or would she be the one sitting on a rock, gaze fixed on the headland. She wished she'd warned him of her difficulties in slipping away. Hoped he hadn't given her up and decided to ride elsewhere.

It was low tide. Soon she saw the expanse of sand, the turquoise sea ruffled by a brisk breeze. She began her descent. Heard the mournful call of a gull as it swooped past her head on its way to the water. It was a predator. Her stomach lurched as she recalled her father's words when he condemned smugglers as vile, unscrupulous men battening off the sea. She was seeking out such a man. Was Jac vile and unscrupulous? It was impossible to believe. Rebecca closed her mind to such thoughts as her feet touched shingle.

Jac was saddling Sofia, the chestnut. The mare nuzzled his shoulder. He crooned love words to her, blew into her nostrils. Women and horses – he could still hear his father's words on the day Jac turned 15. 'They'll be yours for the taking one day, my boy.'

He and his father no longer spoke. They'd never seen eye to eye. But once Jac decided to go and live with Uncle Dermot in Wales, his father refused to say another word to him. Not even goodbye. Jac's liaison with his uncle was proving mutually beneficial but his father couldn't understand why Jac preferred smuggling to farming.

Of course the old man's forecast turned out to be true. But this particular woman was not like the others. Jac marvelled at the speed at which she'd become an obsession. She was too young. She was too beautiful. She was a different status. And this unnerved a young man striving to stay out of trouble in his new homeland. Consorting with a girl betrothed to a wealthy, powerful lord hardly boded well when it came to avoiding mishap.

He wondered if Rebecca would arrive that afternoon. It mightn't be easy for her to go off alone. A young woman of her class was probably surrounded by gatekeepers. But that was her problem. He was keeping his part of the bargain. This was the third afternoon since she'd walked out of the velvety darkness and startled him. Not that it was any hardship riding across the fields and down the gentle gradient to the beach. The cliff path on Rebecca's side of the cove was more challenging. Nor would that worry the pretty vixen.

Jac climbed into the saddle, Sofia's hooves clattering against cobbles as he mounted. He noticed dark-haired Mari, one of the servant girls, watching him from her vantage point of the well.

'Lovely day,' he called.

She nodded. Held his gaze a moment before moving towards the still room door. The swing of her hips and a backward glance over her shoulder told him all he needed to know. Should he stop and make an assignation? She could easily slip into his room once her duties were done for the day. He shifted in his saddle. She was a pretty morsel but maybe it was best to keep his hands off his uncle's staff, in spite of Dermot's suggestion.

Jac had been abstaining for days. The compliant widow had gained a new admirer, a red-faced farmer whose wife, after months of illness, was hardly cold in her grave. Widow Bishopston had declared chastity, putting paid to Jac's erratic visits to her bed. He'd enjoyed the brief interlude since stopping at her cottage one day to request a drink, but had no desire to jeopardise her chances when it came to attracting a solvent new spouse.

As for Morwenna … unseen strings pulled the witch into moods the like of which a man could only contemplate with wonder. Their relationship began after he visited her for a herbal remedy to help heal his finger, damaged in a scuffle soon after his arrival from Ireland. She'd worked a miracle on the wound, fed him a fruit infusion then removed all her clothes, keeping her long-lashed green eyes fixed on his instant erection. His staying-power, normally excellent, had astounded him that afternoon in her woodland cabin.

Folk claimed Morwenna cast spells and brewed potions to elicit passion. He found that easy to believe though he doubted she could reel him in unless he wanted to be caught. There was something much more immediate upon his mind and nothing could deter him.

Hadn't he anticipated Rebecca's next visit to the cove over

the last few days? Each afternoon he'd reined in Sofia after they rounded the headland, scanning the dunes for a glimpse of gown, a flash of bright hair. He'd even wondered if she might send Catrin as an emissary then recalled Rebecca's comment about not wanting to compromise her cousin. Knowing the redhead lacked allies made Jac all the more determined to come to her aid. He fantasised about removing every one of her pretty garments and finding the real woman.

Jac knew Dermot had contacts that could ensure safe passage to Rebecca and her serving woman, to get them out of Wales. Then Jac could sleep easy at night. Explore new conquests and indulge his passions again, without a care. If only he hadn't lost his reason.

'Do you think I'm an eejit, Sofia?'

The mare pricked her ears but continued on her way.

'I have to help her escape from that monster,' Jac told his horse. 'Once she's gone, I won't be tormented.'

But how he would arrange this wasn't yet clear. What was clear was that his insides lurched alarmingly at the thought of her going away.

'So you came at last.'

'There are times when it's easier to sneak away than others.'

Jac slipped from the saddle and stood, holding Sofia's bridle. He whispered into the mare's ear. Gave her rump a gentle smack. She wandered off towards the shoreline.

'Will your horse be all right? Can you trust it?'

He turned towards Rebecca. 'Horses, dogs, women ... you have to know how to handle 'em. Trust's a two-way thing. So, what would your father think about a noble young lady like you consorting with a rogue?'

'How much do you know of me? And where precisely do you come from?'

'Ah, two questions. Well, I know all I need to know about you. And I come from the south of Ireland.'

'I think I know who your uncle is,' she said.

'Is that right? I certainly know who your father is.'

26

She frowned. 'So you're aware how difficult things are for me?'

'Difficult? There's some would kill to be in your shoes, my lovely lady. But I don't mean to tease. I realise something of your, shall we say, predicament.'

She fell into step as he strolled across the sand towards the headland.

'No,' he said as she made to unfasten her hood. 'Keep your head covered, for fear of curious eyes. I'm thinking of your safety.'

Rebecca's hands trembled. Jac's mix of arrogance and tenderness intrigued her. She felt the first tiny spark of hope. Maybe there was a way. Maybe she wouldn't need to marry that toad after all. In all her 17 years she'd never met anyone like the Irishman. What a contrast he made to Geraint. For a start, her despised fiancé was probably old enough to be Jac's father, let alone hers.

'I've heard the servants speak of someone called Jack. Would that be you?'

'Maybe,' he said. 'I'm flattered to be the subject of conversation. Unless of course it's Jack with a K they're saying and not Jac without.'

'You're teasing me again. Jac's a fine name. I prefer it to Jack.' Her eyes danced with merriment.

'Rebecca is a beautiful name,' he said softly.

She shot him a swift glance. 'Thank you. How old are you?'

'Guess.'

She considered. '28?'

The corners of his mouth drooped and he stopped walking. 'Then I must have aged since meeting you. I'm just turned 21.'

'Not so much older than me.'

'But you're still a schoolgirl?'

'I'm almost 18. The right age to be married off.' She pursed her lips. 'Anyway, you look older than you are.'

The sky was darkening. He looked up at it and began walking again. Faster this time. 'You and I move in different circles. I doubt you've seen the sights I've seen.'

Fear of the unknown battled dread of the fate waiting if she didn't find a way out. She increased her pace, almost matching his stride. 'It's for that reason I seek your help.'

His silence made her wonder if he planned to turn her down. But his firm yet gentle clasp on her elbow thrilled her, filling her with hope.

'Will you walk into the next cove with me, Rebecca? Maybe a little further?'

'Yes,' she said. 'I'll walk as far as you want me to, as long as you'll hear me out.'

'Tell me about yourself.'

Rebecca described her childhood, the loss of her brother and her mother. She wasn't to know Dermot had provided Jac with details. She played down her own character, praising Biddy for putting up with so much.

'Biddy was grieving too,' she said. 'Rhys was her favourite. I know she has a soft spot for my father but my mother was always kindness itself to Biddy. She treated her as a younger sister rather than a maid.'

Rebecca spoke of Catrin's companionship and how the spectre of Geraint and the pressure upon both girls of their forthcoming marriages had stolen some of the fun from their lives. Catrin, she said, seemed anxious for Rebecca to accept her father's decision.

'She seems to think I'm the luckiest girl on the peninsula,' she said. 'Why would anyone think fine clothes and jewels compensate for having to wed a man who makes my skin crawl?'

The weather was changing. There was a distant growl of thunder. Jac gestured to some nearby rocks forming a natural sitting place and Rebecca noticed something that had slipped her attention before. The tip of Jac's forefinger was missing. Instead of sitting down, she reached for his left hand and took it in hers.

She saw the uncertainty in his eyes and recognised his vulnerability. She felt a torrent of tenderness. He was beautiful, this 21-year-old Irishman. She didn't care about his chaotic lifestyle. All that mattered was the man. Slowly she raised his hand to her mouth. Her lips closed around the damaged forefinger and she began to suck. Gently and rhythmically her tongue licked Jac's fingertip.

Chapter Four
Tide's Turn

HE PULLED HER TO him, his need to hold her in his arms irresistible. Like a bell clanging in his ears he heard his uncle's warning and cast a look around, satisfying himself there were no peeping toms. The first raindrops fell.

'Quick, I think it's only a shower.' He took her hand in his and led her across the shingle, darting round outcrops of rock, towards the cliff face. There was a hidden cave he knew.

Entering the gloomy interior they ducked their heads. He pulled her down beside him onto a natural shelf. Gently he unfastened the clasp of her hood. Her eyes were so trusting. He shouldn't do this. But he had to kiss her. There was no going back now. His tongue wanted to go where his finger had, and the roaring in his ears was more powerful than the timeless thump of the waves against the shore.

She seemed to be waiting for him, a tiny smile curving that lush mouth. Almost reverently, Jack put one hand behind her head, his fingers caressing her creamy neck and tilting her face towards his. She was so young and lovely, a girl instinctively acting like a woman, exciting him like no other female had before.

He must be gentle. Difficult, when his need was desperate. 'May I kiss you? He whispered the question against her lips.

She parted her lips in response. Their mouths met.

Jac closed his eyes, tasting like a man hungry for honey after a long fast. Was this the first time she'd kissed a man? He'd discount childhood sweethearts. Hadn't we all pretended? He wanted so much to be the first grown man to kiss her now she was a grown woman. Stopped wondering and started to fall

30

in love.

When they broke apart, her eyes were still closed. He dropped a light kiss, first on one eyelid then the other. She opened her eyes again. Their likeness to dark brown velvet perfectly suited her copper locks. He watched in a hazy state of delight as her gaze dropped to his mouth. The tip of her tongue peeped between her lips and the buzz of desire thwacked him between the thighs, robbing him of breath and stealing his reason.

'Rebecca,' he said, holding her arms firmly, to create a safe distance. 'This isn't wise. You are a precious, beautiful young lady but you come with a price on your head. I'll walk you back across the beach now. You must go home before your maid comes looking for you.'

'Biddy knows better than that,' Rebecca said quickly.

He saw the puzzlement in her eyes. She mustn't know how much she affected him. He needed to keep that to himself. He'd never taken a virgin and he didn't intend doing so now, even while he thrummed with longing. He'd better go for a dip in the sea before riding back. Otherwise he'd be tempted to seek out his uncle's servant girl. Somehow he knew that wasn't the right remedy for the way he felt.

'Come on,' he said, stretching out his hand to draw her hood over her hair. Even that proved dangerous. Brushing his fingers against that silken mass of curls dissolved his bones to jelly. He had to swallow hard. Take a deep breath. Then stand up, stooping to prevent bumping his head on a roof honed by countless high tides.

He heard her following him. Heard her boots crunch upon the wet shingle. Walking a few paces in front, he set off around the headland again. 'Hurry,' he urged, calling over his shoulder. 'Tide's coming in fast.'

Still she dawdled.

'I mean it. You can be cut off on the rocks while you're still trying not to get your feet wet.'

She started running. In the wrong direction. Wavelets splashed beneath his feet, a gentle warning of what was to follow.

He swivelled around and chased after her. His boot caught the edge of a pebble and he cursed, losing his balance, arms wind-milling as he sought to regain it. She was yards ahead of him. He set off again, heartbeat booming in his ears, legs pounding like pistons until he came close enough to grab her and scoop her up. Little minx. Once caught, she relaxed in his arms while he carried her round the headland, the incoming tide threatening not just his knees but his thighs. A whiff of her perfume rocked his senses. A blast of cold water at the junction of his trunk and thighs would be almost welcome.

He slackened his pace.

'I'm not a child,' she said, raising her head from his shoulder. 'Please put me down.'

'I'm very aware you're not a child,' he said. 'That's the reason I wanted to get you out of there. Before I did something I'd regret. Don't play tricks like that ever again, Rebecca.'

Only when they reached firm sand did he lower her gently. She stalked ahead. Amused, he followed her. His horse waited patiently by the cliffs. Rebecca halted as the animal pricked up its ears and trotted forward.

'Don't be frightened,' said Jac. He held out his hand to Sofia as she surged towards him, nostrils flaring, then stopped, waiting for them to approach her.

'See? She likes you,' he said. 'She'd never wish to scare you.'

'We're the same colour, she and I.' Rebecca raised a tentative hand to stroke the side of the mare's tawny head.

Jac watched Rebecca mimic a motion he recognised as his own and wondered if she'd watched him. She was a box of sweetmeats all right. But not all of them were what they seemed. His breath caught in his throat at sight of two such beautiful creatures together. One was his to ride when he pleased. As for the other – deciding what to do about that one was the biggest challenge he'd faced in his life so far. Jac knew how to fight. He knew how to survive in unfriendly terrain. He knew how to kill, though hoped he'd never have to.

But did he know how to deal with love? Especially when he'd no business loving a woman whose body, mind and fortune were promised elsewhere.

Wild thoughts battered his brain. What price fortune? He could sweep Rebecca up in his arms again, throw her on the mare's back and clamber into the saddle behind her. One click of his spurs and they'd be halfway to the headland. Despite the incoming tide they'd reach the far side of the other bay. Sofia was strong enough.

But was he strong enough to face his uncle's fury? Jac was no coward but he was a relative stranger to Wales. If Dermot threw them out, where could he possibly take a woman used to a pampered life? With no money, no prospects, Rebecca would have no option but to creep home in disgrace. Her father would probably lock her in a nunnery. Dermot would send his nephew back to Ireland where Jac's father would slam the door in his face too

The moment was gone. While he hesitated, Rebecca drew her cloak round her. 'You're right. I should go.' Her tone was flat.

He ached for her and with her. 'When's your wedding day?' How he hated himself for asking that.

She raised her chin. 'The last day of the month, on the stroke of four.'

Dismay and frustration curdled his stomach. A wedding timed to allow for feasting and ... 'So soon?' Even to himself it sounded a feeble kind of remark to throw a girl in distress.

'Thank you for listening to me,' she said. 'At least I won the wager.' She began walking quickly away from him.

He took a step forward. 'Rebecca ...'

Even if she'd heard, she didn't turn around. He watched her making short work of the rocky outcrop beneath the belly of the cliff. Still he watched as she began climbing the path; her supple body leaning forwards so she ascended more swiftly. What was he supposed to do?

'Stop, damn you,' he yelled, fists clenched at his sides. The words floated on the breeze.

She was about to round the bend that would take her totally from his view. She halted. Yelled, 'Damn you too – Jac without a K!'

In his desperation, he could think of only one option. 'Give me two days. I'll leave a message with Morwenna. You know who I mean?'

She nodded. Then she was out of his sight. But the scent of her, the feel of her body in his arms, stayed with him. Perhaps the witch could brew a potion to calm his body. As for that wager Rebecca mentioned, he'd no idea what the devil she meant.

Morwenna's skills were sought by many folk living on the peninsula. Some, it was said, rode for hours to locate her cabin and procure a remedy for whatever ailment irked them. Regarded with a potent mix of respect and fear, she lived alone but was rumoured to take lovers.

Rebecca arrived in the clearing 48 hours after leaving Jac at Half Moon Cove. In front of a wood cabin, a woman, long dark hair water-falling down her back, stirred something in a pot suspended over a fire.

'You must be Morwenna?' Rebecca moved a little closer.

The woman appeared not to hear.

Rebecca cleared her throat. 'I ... I'm Rebecca.'

'Hah,' said the woman. 'I told the smuggler a chit like you would never find her way. But he insisted you'd navigate a whale's intestines. Let me look at you.'

In one silken movement, she rose from her three-legged stool and stood, hands on hips, eyeing her visitor. Rebecca gazed back. She saw a woman with clear, green eyes, an upwards slant at the corners giving her a feline appearance. Morwenna's lips were fuller even than Rebecca's, her skin far duskier, suggesting a rich lineage. The younger woman had no idea what age she might be.

'So what are you after?' Morwenna folded her arms. 'You think you know all about my powers of sorcery. So, how about a love potion to lure pretty Jac? Or is that too late? Maybe you need something to empty your womb.'

'Neither, thank you,' said Rebecca, wishing her cheeks wouldn't reveal her embarrassment. 'Jac Maddocks told me to visit you so you could pass on a message.'

'Not so much a message as a piece of advice. Come, sit down.'

Morwenna plucked a cushion from the cabin doorway and flung it on the ground beside her. Rebecca hesitated but sensed the woman did things her way. She sank on to the cushion and watched Morwenna fill two beakers with steaming liquid from the small cauldron.

'Don't be afraid. This isn't a magic potion. I often prescribe it for apprehensive virgins.'

Rebecca took the drink and sniffed. 'It smells delicious,' she said. 'Anyway, I don't believe in magic.'

'Then you are a fool, as well as a virgin desperate to escape her bridegroom. When Jac told me of your plight, I knew I must help you.'

Rebecca fingered her silver locket. 'People keep telling me I should be pleased about marriage to Lord Geraint. He's wealthy but he's ... he's ...'

'A toad?'

'Precisely.' Rebecca felt a rush of relief. 'Do you know him?'

'I know far too much about him. For that reason, he hates me. If his lordship knew you were here, he'd probably insist your father locked you up until the hour of your marriage. I despise anyone who intimidates women – forces them into the beds of unscrupulous men.' Her eyes flashed.

Rebecca groaned. 'I can't marry Geraint. I don't care what happens to me as long as he doesn't get his hands on me.'

'Then you should care, Miss. There are worse fates, mark my words.'

Rebecca sipped her drink. The aromatic steam curled inside her nostrils, tangy and sweet. 'I know. I shouldn't have said something so stupid.'

'I think you're seeking drastic measures?'

'Anything to get me away – even if only for long enough to exasperate Geraint so much that he seeks out another bride.'

'You know Jac's at his wits' end? He can't take you to his uncle. There are too many loose threads from the past. Unpick them and blood will be shed.'

Rebecca lifted her chin. 'I'm willing to go further afield. If my father refuses to listen to me, so be it. Let the men do what they will.'

Morwenna raised an eyebrow. 'You'd go to the continent? Would you sail to France, pretty Rebecca?'

Rebecca trembled. She reached once more for her drink, cupping the horn beaker in both hands, aware Morwenna watched every move. 'I'd sail to France,' she said. 'But I have no chaperone. I'm afraid to confide in Biddy.'

Morwenna's deep, rich chuckle disturbed two ring neck doves. Wings whirring, they soared above the trees, cooing a protest. She raised one slender arm, charm bracelets jingling, and the lovebirds glided to a branch, nestling together.

She looked at Rebecca. 'A powerful symbol,' she said. 'Your destiny spelled out.'

'Please, please don't tell me it's to be with that toad.'

Morwenna reached into a small leather pouch hanging from her belt. She took out a handful of small, shiny pebbles. Selected seven and handed them to Rebecca. 'Choose one. Kiss it. Cast all of them on the ground between us,' she said.

When Rebecca threw the stones, they scattered on the grass, two settling together with a tiny click.

'Well, well,' said Morwenna. 'Two people against the world – means you will wait a long time for wealth if you follow my advice. But happiness can be yours if only you're brave enough to fight for it.'

She pushed her hair back from her face and leaned towards Rebecca, bunching her long crimson skirts around her bare, suntanned legs. 'This is what we must do.'

Rebecca's brain should have buzzed with thoughts and images after her visit to Morwenna. Instead, possibly induced by the herbal refreshment, she felt calm, something that had eluded her over the previous few days.

She attempted to sneak through the side door, hoping to avoid the lord of the manor. Biddy often sat afternoons in a parlour leading off the hallway and Rebecca knew her father spent time with her most days, to discuss domestic matters.

And, she suspected, address any perturbing issues posed by the daughter of the house. She ran straight into him as, dogs at heel, he loomed in the doorway.

'Where have you been, Rebecca? Biddy was as elusive as sea mist when I asked her.'

'That's because she'd no idea of my whereabouts.'

Hugh Beaumont frowned. He reached to pluck a tiny twig from his daughter's tawny tresses. 'Walking alone in the woodland? Why is your cousin not with you?'

'Catrin's with my aunt again, Father. More wedding plans.'

He cast his eyes skywards. 'May I remind you, my daughter, you too have a wedding approaching?'

Rebecca cast her eyes demurely to the ground. 'I know, Father. Biddy has everything in hand. I'm to have a final fitting of my bridal gown tomorrow.'

She knew she'd surprised him and decided to surprise him even further by dipping a quick, graceful curtsey. 'Shall I accompany you and the dogs on your walk?'

'I think not. It would be courteous if you spent some time with Biddy, don't you agree? Soon you'll begin a new life.' His face softened. 'We shall all miss you, Rebecca.'

Then why make me leave you? Her unspoken words hung in the air between them. The question in her eyes as she gazed at her father wouldn't receive the answer she longed to hear.

'But we live in unsettled times. I'm no longer young and strong. You need someone to take care of you, and who will give you children.'

'You're saying I need someone young and strong. Why then do you not allow me to find that someone?'

'Stop it, Rebecca. Accept your destiny and be grateful. There is no more agreeable suitor than Sir Geraint. A younger husband would hunt too much, drink too much. Gamble the nights away with his friends. My lands would shrivel.'

'How can you say that? Not every young man fits such a description.'

'How would you know?'

'Dermot Maddocks' nephew isn't like that.' The words were out before she could stop them. The calming properties of that herbal potion had loosened her tongue.

'What did you say?' A muscle flickered in her father's cheek. His words were barely audible but the look in his eyes doused Rebecca's fire.

'I didn't mean ... I only meant the servants say Jac Maddocks is a kindly, generous man. He helps old people and sick children.'

'You are telling me a scavenger who deals in contraband goods is kind and compassionate because the servants say so? Will you tell that to your bridegroom? Will you say you'd rather wed a scoundrel who can't keep his breeches fastened?'

Rebecca knew she hovered close to the abyss. But knowing what she did about the man her father had chosen for her husband, she could no longer contain her anger.

'If that's true then he has much in common with my lord Geraint. Though in the toad's case, he drops his breeches not just for the young ladies but also for the gentlemen. I'm told so by someone who knows.'

Her father raised his hand. She recoiled, horrified at how he'd goaded her and how she'd reacted, horrified by Morwenna's candid disclosures. The pair stood, glaring at one another. Her father's favourite whippet whimpered. He bent to pet it.

'Why do you never place a gentle hand on my shoulder, Father? Why will you not be guided by my mother's spirit? I say again. Marion was not forced to marry a man she despised. You know full well, if she was still alive, I should not find myself in this position.'

'Don't fight me, Rebecca.' His tone was weary. 'You'll marry Sir Geraint and there's no more to say.' Dogs running ahead of him, he walked out of the door but not before Rebecca noticed the tears misting his eyes.

She stared after him. She'd tried to make him change his mind. There was no other option but the promise of a new life in France. That was surely worth a hazardous boat trip. Anger consumed her as she wondered what obsessed her father. Why was he so blinkered that he couldn't think straight?

*   *   *

'What have you learned, Tom?' Sir Geraint leaned back in his chair, squinting up at his young servant.

'I followed her to the wood. She moves like a cat. I needed to be careful so she didn't know I was on her trail.'

'If you want your reward, don't bother me with tiresome explanations.'

Tom nodded. 'She went to the witch's cabin, my lord. The witch was sat outside, brewing a spell.'

Geraint sighed. 'Get on with it, boy.'

'They talked a good while. The witch gave Rebecca a drink out of her cauldron.'

'Tell me what you heard.'

'I daren't go too close. I didn't fancy getting changed into a rabbit.' He chuckled.

Sir Geraint thumped his hand on the arm of his chair. 'So help me, I'll skin you alive like one, unless you do better than this.'

The boy shuffled his feet. 'I heard the witch talking about the Frenchman. The one that brings the onions. She asked Rebecca if she was a good sailor. But ...'

'But what?'

'A rook cawed and I didn't get the next bit. The witch got up and took Rebecca inside. They weren't there long. I couldn't get closer for fear of being found.'

Geraint pulled at his lower lip. 'These blasted French onion sellers. They've started creeping back since the war ended.' He opened the top drawer of a small table. 'Here you are. Now off you go and not a word to anyone.'

Tom took the coin, muttered his thanks, and hurried from the room.

Geraint stared at a wall hanging, its vivid colours depicting a bloody battle. When at last he spoke, it was to the empty room.

'So you think you can outwit me, my little shrew? Ay? Fancy a little voyage do you? We shall see about that. Should we kill Johnny Onions, do you think? Or should we advise your loving father to keep you prisoner in your quarters until your wedding day?'

He began to laugh. 'No,' he whispered. 'Why spoil her fun? Why not let her think she's getting away with it. A little dip in the water will cool her appetite for adventure. It's that bitch Morwenna who needs following.'

He got up from his chair and strode to the open door. 'Tom,' he bellowed. 'Come back here. I've another errand for you. Pick yourself a place near that hovel and stick like a leech. I don't want to see you again till you've something to tell me.'

Biddy smoothed the sleeves of the gown. Rebecca's creamy skin gleamed like fine porcelain against the sea green taffeta. She stood back. 'It's beautiful. You look every inch a princess.'

The girl turned slowly around. 'Even from the back?'

Biddy smiled. 'Yes, even from the back. Your mother would be so proud of you.'

Rebecca nodded. 'Yes, Biddy. I think she really would.' She turned away to hide the excitement she suspected shone in her eyes. After all she'd said; she could hardly expect Biddy to believe she looked forward to marriage.

'Everything will turn out well,' said Biddy. 'You'll learn to love your husband.'

'I expect you're right,' said Rebecca. 'Have you done with me then? I'd like to take a basket of food to Mrs Owen.'

'You're a good girl. I'll help you out of your gown. Shall I walk with you? Catrin's all but left us now. You must miss her.'

'Of course, but I know her mother needs her help more than I do. My uncle isn't well and they've animals to tend. If you want to walk with me, I'll help you down the cliff path – and back up again.' Rebecca held her breath.

Biddy shuddered. 'I'll come with you to the Owens.' She looked down at her swollen ankles and wrinkled her nose. 'But not down to the cove. Must you go so far?'

'I enjoy the freedom. Don't take that from me, Biddy, please. I shall lose it soon enough.'

Biddy busied herself with the heavy swathes of fabric.

40

Rebecca didn't wait for an answer. She was pulling on a pale grey dress. Tying a ribbon around her unruly mop and reaching for her boots.

Biddy followed her downstairs. As the two women left the house the conventional way, Rebecca wondered what Biddy would think if she possessed the ability to read minds.

She linked arms with her companion. 'I hope Mrs Owen likes what we've brought her today,' she said. 'Tell me again about your poor ankles.'

Biddy talked all the way to the cottage. Rebecca handed the basket over and admired the new born baby. Biddy wanted to hold the sleeping infant.

'I'll see you back at the house,' said Rebecca. She wondered if Mrs Owen remembered what she'd seen in the cards but with Biddy there, the question remained unasked. Her head told her she was stupid to hope Jac might have fallen in love with her. Her heart told her their kiss in the cave was very special. Maybe Catrin was right. Maybe fortune tellers always said what they thought their customers wanted to hear. But now the sea voyage seemed a possibility and that resonated with Rebecca.

On her own, her nimble feet ate up the distance far more easily. Soon she was hurrying through the dunes. A bumble bee droned. A butterfly alighted on a pink flower. Tangled foliage brushed against her skirt and the ocean shimmered beneath. She began the steady climb down. Was he near? There was no arrangement. She was to deal with Morwenna now. But Jac invaded her thoughts.

How many times had she relived that kiss? How could anyone expect her to kiss Sir Geraint now she knew Jac's lips? If she fulfilled her father's wishes, she could say goodbye to clandestine meetings with handsome Jac. And if she took flight to France with Morwenna as chaperone, she'd likely never see him again.

In despair, she shielded her eyes against the sun. And there he was, riding towards her. A rushing sound in her ears owed nothing to the sound of the waves cresting on the shore. She didn't hurry the last yards of the grassy slope although she wanted to get down and hurtle across the sand towards him. She wanted him to gather her into his arms and ride away with her. As to where, Rebecca didn't know or care.

Jac too had slowed down. The mare trotted forward, tossing her head as if to say, *I'm as beautiful as you are.*

Rebecca held out her hand palm upward. She'd pulled a carrot from the manor's garden.

'You spoil her,' said Jac, dismounting.

Rebecca looked up at him. 'No more than you do, I fancy.'

He chuckled, eyes scanning the sands, examining the cliffs. 'Let's walk towards the middle of the beach. It's easier to see if anyone approaches.'

'I don't think I was followed,' she said.

He threw back his head and she watched the swell of his Adam's apple, saw the crisp curl of his jet black hair flatten against his collar. The ache to touch him was a physical reflex. She curled her fingers so the nails bit into her palms. As much as she wanted to touch him, she longed for him to touch her.

'What is so funny?' She tried to look stern.

He took hold of Sofia's bridle and they set off. 'Funny is the thought of anyone being nimble enough to keep you within sight,' he said. 'You're a little fox chasing through my dreams.'

She didn't respond; didn't dare confide her own dreams to him.

He looked sideways at her. 'I thought I wouldn't see you again. You were so angry with me last time. I didn't mean to upset you but I needed time to think.'

'I should apologise for being rude. I came today, hoping to see you and to thank you for talking to Morwenna.'

'She has a good heart. I knew she'd help if she could. Did she tell you she faced the same problem as you, years ago?'

'She did,' said Rebecca. 'She escaped on her own, though. She's far braver than me.'

'I have no doubt you're brave,' he said quietly. 'I knew that when you first came at me out of the shadows like a beautiful ghost. I wish I could sail with you but it'd create mayhem if you and I disappeared at the same time.'

She nodded. 'Morwenna told me about her relatives in France. She likes to visit them when she can.'

'That's where you'll stay?'

'I'm to learn how to be a dairy maid. Earn my keep. After Morwenna returns, she has ways of finding out what happens. A message will be sent.'

She heard Jac's sharp intake of breath. 'Wagging tongues can be dangerous,' he said. 'I have a feeling your husband to be has fingers in many pies. He'll want to get you back.'

'Morwenna says the faster we move the better. If I stay here, the marriage will take place. If I go away, the dust can settle and with any luck, Sir Geraint will seek another bride. One that's less trouble! He surely won't suspect I'd leave the country in a French boat?'

'I don't know.' Jac's jaw tightened as Rebecca looked at him again. 'But if anyone reports seeing us together, he'll come looking for me. Not that he'll learn anything. First he has to catch me and I doubt he can.'

She stopped walking. Put her hand on his arm. 'I can't bear the thought of you getting hurt. Haven't we been careful?' She glanced up at the cliffs. 'There's plenty like Biddy who can't even climb down the path.'

'I hope you're right,' he said. 'But I can look after myself. Thing are coming to a head between Dermot and Will Bevan. My uncle's determined to push Bevan back down the coast. Each night a consignment's expected is a big night. We never know when they'll try their luck.'

'Two days from now, Morwenna and I will sail,' said Rebecca, trying not to visualise the scene, 'with the evening tide.' She swallowed hard. 'If anyone asks, I'm the daughter of her friend, going to marry a French farmer's son. My new life will begin. She'll cut my hair when I join her at the cove – bring clothing for me to change into.'

He exclaimed, 'Chop off your beautiful hair?'

They were almost at the headland. Jac stopped so suddenly, Rebecca's foot skidded on a clump of seaweed and she fell against him. He pulled her into his arms and she felt his fingers smooth an errant curl away from her forehead. Gently he pressed his forehead against hers.

She closed her eyes, breathing in the scent of him, longing for him to press his youthful vitality against hers. Very much aware of the consequences. 'Not so sure-footed now,' she said. Her lips were a heartbeat away from his mouth.

'My fault,' he said. 'I'm falling too. Can you stop me?'

'No,' she whispered.

The kiss began in her head. Jac's mouth met hers, telling her it had begun in his head too. This time she was bolder, seeking his tongue with hers, excited by his groan ... his body hard against hers. His mouth moved to explore her neck. His lips found her left ear. She was hit by a torrent of sensation as the tip of his tongue circled her lobe and pushed inside. Tickling her. Sending ripples darting to her core.

'Jac,' she whispered.

'Should I stop?'

'Yes. No.'

'Tell me what that wager was?'

'Can't you guess?'

'Was it something to do with this?'

Intense and sweet, Jac's next kiss deluged her. His hands cupped her breasts and it was her turn to groan. His thumbs drew swirls around her nipples. Each slow, steady movement took her one step closer to an elusive something she craved more than she desired breathing.

Each of them was panting when at last he released her. 'They call Morwenna the witch,' he said. 'But you've bewitched me, my little fox.'

'Would it be safer to go into the cave?'

'Safer? For whom?' He shook his head. 'I don't take advantage of young women, Rebecca.'

'But I like you kissing me.'

'I like kissing you too, sweetheart. But I'm a big, bad smuggler. You're an innocent young lady. You need to save yourself for the lucky man who'll be your husband one day.'

'Is that all you men can think about? Blood rushed to her cheeks. 'Is that all we women are fit for? Why can't I become a smuggler too? Would you marry me then, Jac Maddocks?'

Chapter Five
Secrets and Struggles

HE NEVER KNEW HOW he dragged himself away. Rebecca had posed a question so provocative, so painful he'd opted not to reply. Jac knew he'd hurt her. But he too was hurting. She'd catapulted into his life, all tumbling curls and frilly petticoats tugging at his heart, his mind and other places he daren't contemplate, not when he'd such important business to deal with later in the cove.

'She's too young, Sofia,' he spoke through gritted teeth. 'Too perfect for the likes of me. And what would I do with a wife?'

Despite his tattered emotions, Jac grinned as he pictured Rebecca the Smuggler – in tight breeches and tunic, firm breasts and rounded hips betraying her gender in the most delicious way. He gripped the reins tighter at the thought of her warm skin beneath his fingers. He'd followed the curve of her hips with his hands, delighting in the contours of her thighs. When she suggested visiting the cave, the thrust to his groin was instant and thrilling. How had he pulled himself back in time? She'd never know the agony of his decision.

'She thinks I don't care about her, Sofia.' Jac flung the words into the breeze. The mare reacted to his movements and picked up speed, each lunge of her long legs distancing Jac from the woman he knew he'd give his life for. But he daren't look back. She'd come to him for help. He'd set in motion a plan he'd never have devised, were it not for Morwenna. It was in the hands of the womenfolk now.

Maybe one day, when all this was over, he could discover Rebecca's whereabouts and sail to France to visit her. No sooner had the thought emerged than he pushed it away again. No use wondering and wishing. If he let emotion cloud his judgement tonight, he'd be as much use to his uncle as a case of rancid butter.

He'd be better off finding that little serving girl and bedding her. As Jac felt the ground swell beneath Sofia's hoofs and her pace slow to carry them safely on to the bridleway leading to home, he pondered the possibility. Maybe, he should let fate intervene – challenge himself with a wager of his own?

Aroused by Rebecca's lush body, still seeing the desire in her eyes, could he satisfy his need by bedding another girl? If Mari happened to be in the courtyard when he arrived, should he claim a kiss and judge her reaction? That would place responsibility with her. He could also prove to himself he wasn't beholden to one woman. Love wasn't for the likes of Jac Maddocks. He'd been a fool to think so.

Sofia knew her way home. The mare cantered the last half mile of the journey while Jac tried to convince himself he could quench romantic fancies with honest lust. A hayloft romp suddenly seemed tempting.

When the mare's hooves clattered against the cobbled surface of his uncle's yard and he saw no sign of Mari, he wasn't sure if he felt relief or disappointment. The young lad who cared for Sofia came running to grab her reins as Jac dismounted. The mare was led away and in the sudden silence, Jac heard someone singing.

He walked slowly towards the sound. Why deny himself pleasure if it could be his for the taking? One day, the fiery little fox would thank him for leaving her intact. He hesitated at the door to the barn. Pushed it open. Mari abandoned her song. Wordlessly she moved to the ladder. Placed one foot on the first rung. Jac too began to climb, eyeing the girl's curvy hips swaying above him. This was what he needed, wasn't it? Why then did he wish it was a certain flame-haired beauty leading him on?

Mari stood on the hay-strewn boards, looking at him. She tossed her hair back from her face. Unlaced the top of her blouse. He feasted his eyes on the cleft. She was plump as top of the milk. What more could any man ask for? He pulled her down on the hay. Her pretty billows tasted sweet to his tongue. This was no virgin. She gave as good as she got. Her fingers were skilled and it was Jac who called out as she sought and found. Yet, there was a sense of futility. The love play seemed mechanical. Jac's mind was engaged elsewhere. Flying above the fields and down towards the sea shore. He faltered.

'Jac?' Her voice was heavy with desire.

He knew his passivity must be a disappointment. Mari's eyes were bright, cheeks flushed, lips parted as she looked at him. Taking her hand, he replaced it at his groin. This time he let her explore while he explored her folds, postponing the moment until he could stand it no longer. He heard her coo, seeing his pearl of moisture.

She turned herself around, sticking her lovely behind in the air, inviting him to enter her, needing him to fill her completely. Now he was totally aroused. Heard her moan with satisfaction as he entered. But as he began his rhythmic movements and took what he knew she wanted to give, it was Rebecca's face painted inside his eyelids. If he could only make love to her, it wouldn't be like this. It would be an act of beauty. Not this raw coupling in the hay barn. It was almost shocking when he heard Mari's shrill voice beg him to speed up. Rebecca's voice was very different. Low ... sweet. He closed his eyes and pretended.

And when he lay beside Mari, his heartbeat returning to normal, he wasn't sure if he'd given his feelings away by calling out Rebecca's name. Jac cursed himself for believing a quick tumble could cure his ache.

Sir Geraint's boy, Tom, wandered the woods. In search of the witch's cabin, he'd taken a wrong turning.

The witch also wandered the woodland in search of a particular herb. But she knew her whereabouts as well as her way home. The boy she saw ahead, blundering through the undergrowth, caused her not a little amusement. It didn't take long for her to reach a conclusion. She'd suspected an eavesdropper the afternoon before when entertaining her

47

visitor.

Morwenna missed Jac's regular visits. Missed following the magical path to erotic bliss. To her annoyance, her spells didn't work on him. She'd tried to control him, first pushing him away then drawing him on, flexing her sexual muscles in every possible way. They were good together, recognising in each other a little of the other. He was a lot like his uncle, Dermot. The elder man had yearned for the unobtainable but yielded to Morwenna's caresses on many an occasion. That was in the past. Now it was the nephew longing for what he couldn't have. Until Rebecca quit the peninsula Jac's mind was focussed elsewhere. Morwenna admired the girl's feistiness but she had her own motive in helping her escape. Once my lady was on French soil, Jac would come round again. Looking for solace, wouldn't he come trotting back once Morwenna returned from her visit to Brittany? Or, besotted as he was, would he follow the love of his life?

Morwenna enjoyed power. She didn't need magic in order to cook Rebecca's goose. In the meantime, a young man not bright enough to suspect a trap might provide an hour or two's romp. The better to direct him, she pushed down the neckline of her blouse, exposing the valley dividing her two melon breasts.

Tom fell into her hands like a frightened fawn. Morwenna almost felt sorry for him. She knew who'd put the boy up to this quest. Well, she'd make the young man earn whatever reward the reptilian lord had promised.

'You seem lost, young sir,' she said in her husky tones.

He whirled round, cheeks reddening; eyes wary. 'I must've taken a wrong turning,' he stammered.

'I know these paths well. Tell me where you're heading and I'll guide you.'

'I seek the woman they call Morwenna. I ... I need her advice for my master.'

She watched his eyes rove over her breasts. At once she clasped her hands beneath, pushing them so they spilled above her neckline. 'Then follow me and we'll see if she's at home.' She gestured to their right. 'You're almost there.'

He fell into step. He was eager, blond and smooth-skinned. Broad shoulders filled out his shirt to perfection. He smelt not bad. Geraint didn't tolerate unwashed servants. One thing in his favour ...

Moments later, they arrived at the cabin. Morwenna walked to the closed door and rapped with her knuckles. Put her ear to the wood and tapped again.

She turned to the boy, frowning. 'She's not there. I'm a friend of hers. Do you want to come in and wait?'

She loved the way he hesitated, loved the feeling of anticipation, allowing her eyes to move lazily down, taking in the length of his youthful frame. Morwenna pushed open the door and stepped inside. The boy hesitated upon the threshold.

She held out her hand. 'Come in,' she said. 'It's cool in here. I'll find something to quench your thirst.'

She knew he was hers already. Bewitched by a woman old enough to be his mother but beautiful enough to appeal to a youth who squirmed in his bed at night, dreaming of long-haired temptresses with fire in their veins.

Morwenna poured liquid into a cup and offered it. 'An infusion of woodland herbs will invigorate you. This is the best one Morwenna makes.'

'Aren't you having some?' He accepted the drink and sniffed suspiciously.

She took the beaker back and sipped. 'There you are,' she said. 'Now you know it's safe to drink. Tell me, what is your name?'

'Tom,' he said, first sipping then taking a deep swallow.

'I'm Thalia,' she said. 'Come and sit here with me, Tom.'

He sat beside her on a bunk disguised by a colourful patchwork quilt. His eyes wandered to the ceiling. Festoons of dried herbs and flowers hung from wooden struts. A crescent moon, woven from willow, swung beside dangling strings of beads. Swathes of silk and velvet transformed walls and surfaces. Morwenna watched Tom's gaze take in the purples, the crimsons, the silvers and the gold. Watched his eyes widen in awe. Watched his eyes glaze with desire as she placed one tapering fingernail on his knee and stroked slowly, oh so slowly, towards his groin. The bulge held promise. Her hand began unfastening his breeches and he leapt to meet her.

She chuckled softly. Bent her head. He moaned. His hands gathered her breasts, squeezing them, rubbing them. He was panting. Morwenna liked this. Liked playing the temptress. She wouldn't tease and torture this one, one so young and eager.

'I'll teach you how to please a woman,' she said, lying back. 'Learn from me. Make me wet for you. Then you shall have me.'

She felt him shudder. His manhood rivalled that of the smuggler. My lucky day, she thought. At first he was too tentative. She whispered to him, making dirty words sound like satin and silk. Tom seemed eager to learn. He rewarded her handsomely ... she liked things to happen in threes. She mounted him, sliding him inside her, dipping and tugging at him, using all her witchy skills. Only when they were both sated and sweat-soaked did she allow him to learn one more thing. And watched dismay chase across his face as she enquired, 'Now, Tom. What was that question your master wanted to ask me?'

'You've tricked me,' he said, jumping to his feet. 'You've bewitched me with your magic. I'm still dazed.'

'If you're dazed, it's because you've jumped the hurdle three times. Now, listen to me. You were sent to spy on me – yes?'

He regarded her sulkily then nodded.

'As a reward for pleasuring me, I won't tell his lordship what happened here today. In return, I need you to feed him some information I shall give you.'

'How do you know I'll do what you say?'

She regarded him with amusement. 'What else will you tell him? That I have a heart-shaped mole at the top of my left thigh? That I'm kinder in bed than he is?'

Tom blushed scarlet again.

'If you don't want a beating, you'll tell him what I say. And remember, now I have you in my sights, we are linked, you and me. Betray me and you'll regret it.'

Geraint poured himself a tankard of ale. 'What did you find out? You were gone long enough.'

Tom nodded. 'It was a while before anything happened. The two girls arrived together.'

'Lady Rebecca and her cousin?'

'Yes. The little fair one stayed outside while my lady went into the hut.'

Geraint thumped his tankard on the table, spilling beer over the side. 'Cunning little piece! The witch must have put her up to that. Did you hear anything at all?'

'After a while, my lady came out and the two girls set off together.' He hesitated. 'I know you told me to stay there but I thought if I followed them, I might hear something.'

Geraint sat back in his chair. 'And did you?'

'Before they left the wood they sat down on a log. It was easy for me then. I hid behind a tree trunk. Heard everything they said.'

'Then tell me!'

'She leaves tomorrow night. She boasted how easy it was to creep out of the house and get down to the cove. Morwenna's meeting her on the beach. They sail just before midnight.'

Geraint's eyes narrowed. There was a huge consignment expected the following evening. Bevan's men planned to muscle in on Dermot Maddocks. 'Which cove, you whelp?'

'Firefly.'

Geraint relaxed. 'Nicely out of the way – I don't want to set foot on Half Moon. Not with blood being spilled.'

'The onion seller will be paid well. All he knows is these two women, Mary and Elizabeth, want to get to France. He likes the idea of helping a young girl to rendezvous with her sweetheart. And he likes the idea of the extra reward the witch might give him in return for a safe journey.'

'That lascivious bitch. I shall enjoy watching two treacherous cats frozen with fear at the thought of being thrown overboard!'

Tom frowned. 'Won't that be dangerous? The current could sweep them out to sea.'

'Good riddance to the witch. As for my young bride – she'll be vastly relieved when I rescue her from a watery death.' He smirked. 'You shall head my raiding party, Tom. Aren't you honoured to be so trusted?' He half-closed his eyes and leaned back in his chair, gripping its arms.

He guessed Tom was gazing at him in horror. Geraint was well aware of his young servant's dislike of fighting. The two coves were not far distant from each other. To reward Tom with a poisoned chalice made him feel an anticipatory frisson. And the thought of outwitting Rebecca aroused him intensely. He longed to put her in her place. To make sure her wedding night was one she'd always remember.

Rebecca gazed at her room, knowing she might never see it again. Sitting in those familiar surroundings made her feel more and more as though she was playing a part. Panic seized her as she imagined what would happen should she be caught. Probably she'd be locked up with Biddy until it was time to prepare for her wedding day. If only Biddy wasn't lovesick over Rebecca's father. Things might be very different. Life in a foreign country, living among strangers who didn't speak her language, would be difficult. She hardly knew any words of French.

Everything had happened so swiftly since Jac consulted Morwenna. Her fingers curled around the note the witch had handed her when Rebecca visited her in the cabin. What Morwenna said on that occasion conflicted with the instructions she'd written. But Rebecca realised the importance of keeping her plan secret. She'd longed to confide in Catrin but knew her cousin would be so horrified she'd likely run straight to her mother or even Rebecca's father.

How strange to know Jac wasn't involved now and Morwenna was. Somehow Rebecca had hoped he might work some kind of miracle. Whisk her away to a safe place. Somewhere with trustworthy people around and pleasant countryside. Maybe somewhere on the English border, where, one day, news would arrive that Lord Geraint had taken a bride and her father, anger spent, pined for his only child's safe return. Jac figured in this fantasy though how he'd be transformed into a worthy suitor wasn't clear.

The house had been quiet for an hour or more. Rebecca's few belongings were tucked into a tapestry bag. She'd already parted with precious jewellery to pay her passage. Other pieces were rolled inside a scarf. Poised to escape and wearing her cloak, she sat on her bed, in which a bolster slumbered peacefully, blankets tucked around its sightless head.

So many times had Rebecca relived Jac's last kiss. If she closed her eyes and wrapped her arms around herself, she could see his dark eyes, full of tenderness as his mouth sought hers. His beard grew silkier the longer it grew. She wriggled as she remembered caressing the back of his neck where the hair curled over his collar. Tried to stop thinking of him before her fantasy sent her hands roaming her breasts as his had done that last occasion. He'd never taken the liberties with her she craved. He was a true gentleman. Why, oh why could her father not see that?

She jumped as she heard the signal, even though she'd anticipated the sudden, soft hoot of an owl. It was time to set off. Morwenna would continue making her way to the beach. Each would walk alone. Taking one last look around the room she'd slept in since childhood, Rebecca picked up her bag and tiptoed to the door.

At the head of the stairs she halted. Listened, unsure whether her father sat in his study or not. Moonlight silvered the way to the massive front entrance. But Rebecca's route took her into the sitting-room. For some few years, she'd used this method of leaving and entering the house. If she climbed on to the window seat, she could release the casement catch, slide over the sill and land on the lawn.

The night air felt cool to her cheeks. Without looking back, she melted into the shrubbery, keeping close to the wall until she reached that gate so overgrown no one remembered its existence bar her. She slipped through, closed it carefully and began walking down the lane.

At Half Moon Cove, Jac kept watch, poised to pick up any

53

small disturbance, any unfamiliar presence. From his vantage point on horseback, he could see every one of his uncle's men, each of them personally known to him. People living in the vicinity knew to stay indoors on nights when the cove played host to a harvest you couldn't trawl for with fishing nets.

Men heaved. Shoved. Lifted and rolled. Older ones stopped now and then to get their breath back or rub their aching backs; sometimes shooting envious glances at the younger ones working tirelessly. Much of the booty was on the beach. The French boat, having sought an Irish haven en route to Wales, rested at anchor in the bay.

Also on the beach was Morwenna. Jac could see her hooded figure, yards away from him. None of the men questioned her presence. They knew he had her in his sights and that was good enough for them.

He hoped Rebecca was on her way. If someone had heard her leaving the manor and followed her, there'd be hell to pay. He wouldn't put it past Geraint to position a man in the manor grounds with his prize so near. One of the obnoxious lord's men would be no match for Jac. Rebecca, though spirited, couldn't be expected to fight off an assailant pouncing from behind. He cursed himself for not thinking of this before and tried to reassure himself Morwenna's ruse must have worked and a welcome party was gathered at Firefly Cove, now cut off from Half Moon by deep, treacherous water.

His eye snagged a movement. His heart seemed to miss a beat. As he'd glanced back at the beach, Rebecca must have rounded the curve. Her feet would touch the sand before he knew it. In the shadow of overhanging rock clusters and beneath the sheltering cliff face, Morwenna would transform Rebecca. Within the hour, the woman he couldn't stop dreaming about would be out of his life and on a voyage to the continent. Every part of him yearned to go with her.

He watched Morwenna come forward to claim Rebecca. Their dark shapes disappeared behind a towering rock. His vigilance hardly seemed necessary but as he wondered whether to go and help unload the remaining goods, an influx of men spilled like a swarm of bees down the lower reaches of the grassy slopes and towards the beach.

'Curse Will Bevan for this!' Jac was always prepared for trouble but tonight was different. The raiders weaved their way among his uncle's men, making it clear they weren't only interested in contraband goods. He smelt jealousy. He smelt violence. He should be at Dermot's side, helping him see off these unwelcome visitors. A nip with a sword tip, a swift sharp slice of a dagger could sometimes work miracles as a man thought better of what had seemed an exciting escapade with the chance of coins jingling in his pocket.

But abandon Rebecca and Morwenna? He couldn't carry both of them on his horse at once. The only solution was to get them on Sofia's back and guide his precious cargo to the waiting boat, still discharging spoils. Would there be time? He needed to move quickly if this was his plan. But Dermot would wonder what the devil his nephew played at.

Torn between heart and head, Jac hesitated. The struggle on the sand intensified each moment he remained an onlooker. Bevan wouldn't expect to smell a female's scent tonight. But if the women stayed where they were, they might be fair game for a gang master hungry for power. Especially if Jac lost the fight. The decision was made.

Beyond a headland up to its waist in water, Lord Geraint sweated and fretted at Firefly Cove. He and his small party of men stood on the shingle with their horses; scanning the sea for a vessel Geraint suspected was never destined to arrive. Further infuriating him were the sounds of unrest drifting on the night breeze from Half Moon.

He swung round to address Tom. 'The witch made mincemeat of you, didn't you? Wound her legs round you and made you forget you had a mind of your own, let alone a tongue in your head? Didn't she?'

'I told you what she said to tell you, my lord.'

'Of course you did. I should have known better than trust you with such an errand. More fool me.' He flipped his gloved hand against Tom's cheek. 'No time to punish you now. We need to ride along the track to Half Moon.'

One of his men touched his shoulder. 'Shall I try and get round the headland, my lord?'

'Yes, numbskull. If you want to feed the fishes. I need every one of you. Not only have I been duped but I'll have to show my face. Will Bevan needs help. And I want that girl. If the witch or a Maddocks gets in our way, you know what to do. Come on!

Chapter Six
David and Jac

'HURRY,' COMMANDED MORWENNA'S SMOKY voice. Already halfway out of her day dress, Rebecca took her new clothes from the witch's outstretched arms and Morwenna helped her into them.

'My hair?' Rebecca held her hands to her head.

'I'll cut through the plait so you can pull your cap on. Bend your head and be thankful you're tall for a woman. You'll make a fine boy.'

Rebecca closed her eyes as Morwenna sliced through the thick auburn braid. Saying goodbye to a coil of hair and dressing up as a boy was nothing compared to what she felt about leaving Jac. As she wondered whether he was still close by, she realised the rumble and thump of cargoes being manhandled on to carts was now replaced by yells, curses and the neighing of startled horses.

'What's going on?' She jammed a woollen cap on her head.

'Trouble for sure. Here, take these boots.'

Rebecca used the rock to lean against. 'My father? How could he possibly have found out?'

'My guess is, either Will Bevan wants in on the action or my lord Geraint's discovered I bamboozled his spy. Either way, it's not good. If the crew take fright and haul anchor before we're on board … you stay here while I find Jac.'

Morwenna was wearing Rebecca's discarded green cloak. She'd covered her dark hair with the hood. The bright plait lopped from Rebecca's head was pinned so it rested on one shoulder.

Rebecca knew better than to protest. Morwenna was risking

her life for her but this was no time for questions. She ached to follow but finished doing up her laces. She wriggled her toes into emptiness and prayed the knots would keep the boots on if she had to run. Already her heart pounded as though it would burst. She touched the place where her plait had hung and felt rough-cut ends pushing below her cap. Everything was changing. Everything and nothing. Her fate still lay in the hands of men, whether noble lords puffed up with power or scavenging ruffians. It seemed she must cower behind this towering rock and see what Morwenna had to say on her return.

The only man Rebecca trusted was out there, somewhere amid the ruckus happening only yards from her hiding place. Would Morwenna be able to attract his attention? Rebecca, desperate to see what was going on, pressed herself against the rocky surface and dared to peer out.

Not far along the beach she saw Jac fighting off two men. One shrieked, dropping to the sand while the other turned and ran, heading for inland and the cart track which looped around the coastline above the coves. Jac didn't pursue him. She saw him scanning the sands. A man on horseback also surveyed the scene from his position a little away up the beach – a bulky man, too big to be Lord Geraint. Rebecca sighed with relief.

The man on the horse turned, gathered his reins and began to canter towards the headland. Something or someone in the tangle of men must have caught his attention because he didn't notice Jac hurtling across the crescent of sand. Half Moon Bay always retained that half circle. It made running easier. Or galloping. But the big man wasn't galloping. Rebecca watched Jac launch himself on the horse and clutch at the rider. The animal reared, its front hoofs pawing at the moon. Its rider lunged at Jac then slid boneless to the ground. Jac slithered after him and stood, hands on hips, looking down at the still figure.

Another shape loomed. How she'd done it, Rebecca didn't know, but Morwenna's arrival caused Jac to sprint towards her. He grabbed the witch's arm, almost shaking her. She appeared to be trying to calm him. He let go of her as she pointed to something going on behind him, something beyond Rebecca's view.

Out of the corner of her eye, she saw Jac's mare, instead of waiting where he'd left her, begin trotting across the sand towards him. With disbelief, Rebecca watched Jac grab the reins and help Morwenna leap into the saddle. The coppery coil of hair gleamed in the moonlight as the mare took off, heading up and across the beach towards the cliff path. Rebecca knew it would take more than the witch's homespun magic to tackle that slope. Was she supposed to follow and climb the cliff too? All hope of escape crumbling, Rebecca saw a small group of men running towards Jac. Instinct drove her into the open and she ran towards him, propelled by fear and fury.

Jac barred her way before she could hurl herself, big boots and all, into the knot of men.

'Hold on, David. No fists, boy,' he said, grabbing her roughly by the arm. 'I fancy my lord Geraint wishes to speak with me.' He made a mock bow. Rebecca, numb with fear, followed suit.

'Two questions, Maddocks,' said Geraint. 'I want the truth as much as you want your uncle to wake up in one piece tomorrow morning. Yes?'

Jac shrugged. 'All right.' He released his grip on the lad standing next to him.

'Where is Rebecca Beaumont? And where's Will Bevan?'

Jac didn't hesitate. He waved an arm in a vague gesture embracing the whole of the beach. 'If you mean the red-haired gypsy girl who stole my favourite mare, I'd be grateful if you catch her for me. As for Bevan, I've seen him in the cove – where he has no business to be.'

Rebecca gulped. Looked down and kicked at a pebble.

Geraint turned towards his men. 'You two – follow the coastal path and cut her off when she gets up the cliff. Bring her to me, with or without the horse. Tom, you stay with me.'

'I'm surprised your lordship's interested in Half Moon's grubby goings-on,' said Jac. 'I notice most of your henchmen have turned tail. Though, aren't you in the export business – not the import?'

The sound of Geraint's voice kept Rebecca's head down. She reached her arm up to wipe her nose on her sleeve with a loud sniff. His lordship shot the lad in the cap a disgusted look. 'Don't play games with me, Maddocks. I don't trust you and if I find you've had a hand in my business – I might just cut it off for you.' He turned and set off towards the headland, where one or two men were gathered.

Jac grabbed Rebecca's arm. 'Run towards the boat. Fast as you can.'

Her feet pounded over the sand, borrowed boots chafing her heels. Soon she and Jac were splashing through the shallows. How could she travel alone?

They were forced to wade. 'What's happening?' She gasped.

'Mary and Elizabeth couldn't make it. David and Jac sail tonight in their place.'

She stumbled on, shoulder-deep in freezing water. His grip tightened. 'I hope you can swim the last few yards, my lad.'

If there was anyone living in the vicinity of Half Moon Cove who knew its secrets better than Rebecca Beaumont, it was Morwenna. High above the beach and astride Jac's mare, she trotted under cover of woodland, back-tracking towards the headland. She bent her head towards Sofia's, saying, 'Not long now, little one. You'll get a good welcome from Dermot. I'm not so sure about mine.'

Horse and rider proceeded without pursuit. Morwenna wondered if Geraint, in his fury, would have her cabin ransacked once Rebecca's father raised the alarm. She'd amassed a treasure chest of trinkets and coins she'd hate to lose but something told her he'd be anxious not to infuriate a woman whose skills and knowledge allowed her access to people he never met even with his status.

Sofia plodded on. Soon, Dermot's sprawling old house loomed before them. The gate stood open, allowing for Jac's return. As the mare trotted into the yard, Morwenna saw a man standing in the shadows. Sofia stopped, whickering softly in recognition.

'Good evening, Dermot.'

'Dear God, I thought at first you were Hugh Beaumont's girl. What's going on?' The moonlight heightened the planes of his face, concern creasing his brow.

'Jac's alive. It might be better if you let me indoors where I can speak to you in private.'

Dermot helped her dismount, 'I didn't think to be welcoming you to my house tonight,' he said, leading the mare towards the stables.

'It's been a long time.' Morwenna waited while he woke up one of his lads.

'I could never tame you like I could tame a horse,' he said.

'You were still in love with Marion.' She followed him in through a door leading into a dimly-lit passage.

'You always could read my mind,' he said. 'Let's go in here.'

'This room looks no different from the last time I visited you,' said Morwenna, looking round.

'It still lacks a woman's touch. Now, where's my nephew got to?'

Morwenna watched the only man she'd ever contemplated settling down with approach the table and pick up a flask of wine.

She unfastened her hood and reached round to unpin the plait. 'Plans sometimes go awry,' she said as he handed her a filled glass.

'Don't tell me he's been captured?'

'Not unless you're talking about his heart.' She sat down.

Dermot took his place in the big chair opposite. 'It's the girl, isn't it? It's Rebecca.' He pointed to the lustrous plait lying in Morwenna's lap. 'You'd better explain everything. I'll not get a minute's sleep tonight if you don't.'

'And after I've told my tale, will you let me help you get a good night's rest?'

She sipped her wine, watched him catch his breath. Knew neither of them would sleep much that night. As she'd hoped, the old attraction already smouldered. The wine tasted sweet on her lips as she licked them. Gazed into his eyes. The nephew had been but an interlude. Jac had made his choice. Now she knew where she wanted to be. She began her explanation. Dermot listened in silence.

At last, he sighed. 'I might have known he wouldn't listen to me. But I can't help admiring the pair of them. She's too beautiful to waste on Geraint. And what could be sweeter than passion reciprocated?'

'Shall we find out?' Morwenna got up and stood before him.

He smiled up at her. 'You've sampled youth. Why would you want me?'

She coiled herself into his lap. 'I always wanted you. But you'd put your emotions in a box. I've been seeking ever since. Sampling, yes but finding … no.'

Their mouths met. Morwenna felt a surge of love for this handsome, distant man. This was now or never. She was tired of woodland living. But she was surprised by the desire his kiss invoked.

'Have you cast one of your love spells on me, Madam?' His hands caressed her breasts.

'Should I have?' Her fingers stroked his groin.

He groaned. 'I'm not sure I can wait to get you upstairs.'

'What's wrong with that fur rug?'

'The times I've dreamed of taking you in front of the fire. Feeling those long legs of yours coiled round me ...'

She was unbuttoning his breeches. 'Then stop dreaming and fuck me.' She broke free from him. Stood up and unpinned her dark hair so it tumbled round her high-cheek-boned face. She swayed before him. Ripe. Beautiful. Awaiting him. Dermot joined her. They pulled at each other's clothes like eager 18-year-olds. Half-naked, they stopped to kiss. She sucked on his tongue. He squeezed her breasts together, thumbs thrumming her nipples until she broke away, gasping. Tore off her skirt and drawers. He pulled off his breeches.

They sank on to the rug. Fell into a favourite position. As Morwenna took his cock inside her mouth, she felt his tongue flick inside her witchy frills. In unison, like old friends singing together, each brought the other to ecstasy.

*   *   *

Biddy knocked and knocked on the bedroom door. Still her charge didn't respond. Inside, she bent to shake Rebecca's shoulder, only to recoil in disbelief.

'Becca!' Her yell echoed round the room. 'Is this one of your tricks?'

Deep down Biddy knew this was no girlish prank. She would check the rest of the house; trail around the grounds, calling, all the time knowing by the time Hugh Beaumont returned from his morning walk, she'd be forced to give him unwelcome news. Rebecca had disobeyed him. Run away rather than wed a man she didn't love. Deep inside her, Biddy not only respected the girl, but envied her.

Catrin appeared in the doorway. 'What's the matter?' She stood there in her white nightgown, still befuddled by sleep. With Rebecca's nuptials so near, her cousin was staying in the manor house again.

'She's gone,' said Biddy.

'Gone where?'

'You tell me.'

Catrin rounded on her. 'Why should I know anything?'

'Her father will be furious.' Biddy walked towards the window.

'You sound very calm. Aren't you frightened?'

'Why should I be?'

'Becca was in your charge.'

'We all know she ran rings round us all.'

Catrin shook her head. 'It was only a bit of fun – keeping out of your way. I didn't think she really meant to leave home.'

'You know where she's gone, don't you? They'll question you, Catrin. What will you say?'

The girl squared her shoulders. 'I'll tell the truth. I have no idea where she is.'

'I have,' said Biddy. 'She was desperate to get to the beach the other day. So I followed her. Oh, not down that steep path. But there's nothing wrong with my eyesight. And I can count to two. She's been meeting that young smuggler.'

Catrin's jaw dropped. 'And you haven't told Uncle Hugh?'

63

'I've spent years wishing. How then could I spoil things for her? Nor could I encourage her.'

'You really think she's with Jac Maddocks? What will you say to my uncle and the toad?'

Biddy smiled. 'I'll suggest she might have decided to join a nunnery. That should keep them off her trail.'

Catrin gazed at the older woman in admiration. 'I've been so selfish. I'm marrying someone I care for. I should have listened better to her. She'd be so pleased to hear you talk like this.'

'You won't betray my confidence?'

Catrin put her arms around Biddy. 'I swear on my mother's life, I won't say a word.'

Chapter Seven
Tumult

LORD GERAINT RODE INTO the courtyard with the dawn chorus. Dermot, lying beside Morwenna, regretted leaving her perfumed warmth. Slipped from beneath the covers and pulled on an old pair of breeches. He closed the door quietly and padded downstairs.

'You're up and about early, my lord,' he called from the back door. What can I do for you?'

Geraint, prowling the stables, turned to face him. 'I've come for my property,' he snarled.

'I wasn't aware we were stabling one of your horses.'

'Where's Rebecca?'

Dermot raised his eyebrows. 'Rebecca who?'

Geraint moved a step closer. Dermot stood his ground. He was bulkier than the other man. From what he'd heard, the girl had good cause to escape. He only hoped she and Jac were safe.

'Your nephew has a hand in this,' said Geraint. 'And the witch. You used to sniff round her skirts, didn't you? She's led me a fine dance. Should I pay her a visit? Or do you prefer to give me the whereabouts of my bride and your murdering scumbag kin?'

Dermot's energy level should have been vastly depleted. The night before, he'd spent hours at the cove, supervising the unloading of sensitive cargo then helping his men eject usurpers from down the coast. His most trusted servant wasted no time in telling him how his nephew had narrowly missed being killed by Bevan. Jac was able to wrest the dagger from the big man's hand and in the ensuing scuffle, he'd stabbed his adversary in self defence.

Expecting Jac's return last night, Dermot had been stunned to find his own past turning up on his doorstep. He'd been astonished to hear of Rebecca's presence at the cove and of the plot to get her away from Wales. Even after passionate hours with Morwenna, he still felt like a young lover. Now, this odious fellow, noble only by title, stood before him, bad-mouthing the young man who meant as much to Dermot as any son. What's more, my lord was threatening to harass the woman still slumbering between Dermot's sheets.

He lunged at Geraint and grabbed him by the throat, almost gagging at the smell of stale, brandy-soaked breath. But he didn't lessen his hold.

'Listen to what I say. You and your nasty ways are not wanted round here. You get off my premises and you don't set foot here again. Understand?'

Geraint's eyes bulged but he said nothing.

'Oh dear. Maybe you'll understand this, then … my lord.'

Dermot's well-aimed kick despatched his visitor to the ground, where he lay writhing, moaning and clutching his groin in agony.

'And if you dare interfere with Morwenna's cabin, I have certain men around me – fathers who'd like nothing better than to send you swiftly to hell where you'll no doubt end up anyway, one day.'

Dermot stood glowering at the man he'd despised for a very long time. It had taken a momentous event to stir him to action but he believed he'd acted with justification. As soon as he tidied himself up, he'd visit another old friend. This time, to tell a few truths to Hugh Beaumont.

'You'd best be off,' he told Geraint. 'Before I let my dogs out.'

Rebecca dreamed she was on a boat. The sensation was real enough for her to feel the hammock beneath her. When her fingers found prickly fabric in place of fine cotton, she opened her eyes to a symphony of damp clothing, stale tobacco and fresh human sweat. Not to mention the all-pervading odour of fish.

A man slept beside her on the floor of a cramped cabin, one arm flung across his makeshift pillow. Rebecca froze under her thick blanket. Was it Jac? Last night's events flashed before her eyes, a kaleidoscope of excitement, fear and unreality. She'd launched herself on top of the water and swum the few strokes necessary to reach the waiting boat. Remembering Jac's hands under her behind, shoving her upwards and into the calloused hands of a fisherman pulling her aboard, her cheeks grew hot. She'd swigged down a tot of brandy, the hot spirit making her splutter and cough. Jac had done the talking, explaining in a language she recognised as a sort of French.

Rebecca had wondered how she'd survive even a short sea voyage, the only woman on board. But Jac introduced her as his younger brother and pushed her in front of him when the sailor led them below.

'Get your clothes off,' he ordered once they were alone.

She'd stood there, teeth chattering.

'I'm trying to keep you alive, sweetheart,' he'd whispered.

Her numb fingers couldn't achieve much but he helped rip off her clothes, turning his back as she stripped naked. When she wrapped her bare body in a thick grey blanket he'd stood behind her, massaging her back and her limbs through the material, making her tingle as blood rushed to her extremities.

He'd taken her hands in his. Held them to his lips and blown on them. Taken each finger in turn and pushed it inside his mouth, warming and revitalising her. The sensation disarmed her. Her nipples pushing against the coarse blanket spoke her arousal. At one point, the blanket fell away, revealing two fully-awoken breasts.

She'd heard the gasp interrupt Jac's breathing. 'I need to remember you're a lad,' he'd said. His voice sounded hoarse from swallowing sea water. Or so he told her as he wrapped her up like a package. She'd brushed her lips against his cheek.

He'd groaned. Shaken his head. Moved away from her as though she scalded him.

When a cabin boy arrived, bringing bread, cheese and cider, she'd stayed, hunched against the wall, head turned away.

'Mal de mer,' Jac said.

Rebecca had smiled to herself. If she was suffering from any form of sickness it wasn't caused by ocean rhythms. When she'd devoured her share of the supper, Jac helped her into her sleeping place. Exhaustion and the drink she'd consumed provided oblivion.

Now she pushed herself cautiously upwards but, unused to a hammock, she misjudged and toppled out, landing half-splayed across Jac's blanketed body.

He opened one eye and smiled lazily, sending more tingles through her. 'Good morning,' he said. Then he groaned. 'Even after a midnight swim, even wearing a sack, you're still beautiful. To be sure, one of us needs to move quickly.'

'Don't I get even one kiss?'

He scrambled up before she could nestle closer. She saw him straighten the baggy drawers he'd borrowed.

'You're a boy, David. A boy in big trouble. If anyone suspects you're a girl, you'll be in even bigger trouble. It's as well the sea water washed away your perfume but you'd best stay here while I go up on deck. I need to talk to the captain. Don't leave the cabin while I'm gone. If anyone knocks on the door, don't answer. Lie on the floor and pretend you're asleep.'

On her own she thought how grim he sounded. How different from the tender man kissing her in the cave. This whole escapade had turned into a nightmare. There'd been no time for reasoning last night. Too much was happening. Now she recognised her vulnerability. She'd lost her travelling companion. She'd lost the bag containing the wherewithal to exist. She'd no idea where Morwenna's relations lived. She'd thrown away her old life by stepping into her disguise. Jac probably hated her for upsetting his own plans. Maybe even now, he was regretting ever becoming involved with such a troublesome baggage. She lay down, unable to prevent hot tears from trickling down her cheeks.

While Rebecca headed for her new life, her father sat in his study, digesting the news of her disappearance.

Biddy watched as he shook his head slowly, eyes focused

on a portrait of Rebecca with her mother and brother, painted before Rhys died. It was obvious what was in Hugh's mind. Every person he'd loved was lost.

'Try as I might I cannot imagine Rebecca living in a nunnery,' he said. 'Are you certain she hasn't been concealing some other plan?'

Biddy spread her hands. 'I don't know, my lord. I can't think where else she would go.'

Hugh Beaumont's voice showed his despair. 'How do you control a girl like her, Biddy? I know you've tried your best. Maybe I should have locked her up. I've tried to give her some freedom and look how she's repaid me.'

'You mustn't think like that!' Biddy's cheeks pinked as he looked at her. 'You've been a good father but none of us knew how much she dreaded marrying my lord Geraint.'

Hugh drummed the fingers of one hand on the carved arm of his chair. 'I thought it was the best solution. When he came to me first, yes of course I wondered about the age difference. But there seemed sense in combining the two estates. With no one left to run this one …'

His words were interrupted by a servant. 'Dermot Maddocks is asking to speak with you, my lord.'

Hugh shot to his feet. 'What the devil! All right, then show him in.' He looked at Biddy. 'We haven't spoken in years. I wonder why he should turn up now.'

Biddy stood up too. 'I'll leave you to talk alone. But I'll be close at hand in case you need me.'

She left the room as Dermot was about to enter. They acknowledged one another with a brief nod then the old friends stood face to face for the first time in years. The servant closed the door.

'Why are you here? Do you have news of Rebecca?'

'I'm here as a friend, Hugh, even if you don't acknowledge me as one. As for Rebecca, I think your daughter's a courageous young woman and you should be proud of her.'

Hugh grunted. 'Courageous or foolhardy?'

'Has the unlucky bridegroom called upon you yet?'

'No. Not that it's your business.'

'He thinks it is. I booted him out of my yard not two hours ago.'

Hugh frowned. 'You'd best sit down. Take a drop of ale with me now you're here.'

'I'll do my best to explain. Try not to interrupt and please trust my judgement.'

Hugh heard Dermot out in silence. Now and then he gnawed on his thumbnail. Only at the end did he get up and walk to the window where his dogs snoozed in the sunshine.

'Jac will look after her, Hugh. If he didn't care about her welfare, he wouldn't have got on that boat.'

'You expect me to believe a man like that won't force himself upon my daughter?'

'I expect you to accept my word,' said Dermot, eyes flashing. 'My nephew has his own code. I'm not denying he's good with women and horses. But I'd stake my life he won't steal Rebecca's virtue. Had she stayed here and married Geraint the Grim, she'd have lost her soul and her mind and the will to live. Can't you accept that?'

Hugh put his head in his hands. Dermot waited.

'I never knew all that about Geraint,' said Hugh. 'That filth – why didn't you come to me before?'

'Would you have even let me through your front door, leave alone listen?'

The two men stared at each other.

'I've been so wrapped up in my own affairs, so eager to assure the future of my estate, I didn't take enough notice of people. I didn't see through Geraint's fine clothes and smooth talking.'

'Rebecca's like her mother,' said Dermot. 'She doesn't settle for something or someone she's not sure of. That's why Marion chose you, over me. She didn't want a black sheep.'

Hugh smiled. 'And Jac's not a black sheep?'

Dermot shrugged. 'What you see is what you get. He wears his heart on his sleeve. He gives more than he takes. He passionately defends those he cares about. I know who I'd rather see my daughter marry.'

'You're saying Rebecca wants to marry Jac?'

70

'I have no idea. But I've a feeling that if she wants to, he won't keep her away from her father. Unless of course her father happens to be too proud to allow her home again. And isn't it time that father thought about his own situation? Come on Hugh, you've known joy and plenty of it. Don't you think it's time to forget the sadness of the past and find contentment with a woman who obviously adores you?'

Hugh began to weep. Soundlessly.

Dermot walked to the door and opened it. He entered the hallway and called Biddy's name.

She appeared, eyes questioning.

'He needs you,' said Dermot. 'Go to him.'

Chapter Eight
Half Moon Cove

THE BOAT HAD TIED up at a fishing village on the south coast of Ireland.

'It's fate,' Jac said when they disembarked. 'We're only an hour's ride from my father's farm.'

Rebecca preferred to forget the end of the voyage. Howling wind and lashing rain had sent the boat bucking and dipping through terrifying walls of water.

'You've earned your sea legs and that's a fact,' Jac had told her.

They threw themselves on the hospitality of his sister. Yesterday Jac had borrowed a horse from his brother-in-law and set off to see his father. They hadn't seen anything of him since. Rebecca, wearing a gown too big in the body but too short in length, was making herself useful, as well as trying to hide her uncertainty over her future. Jac's brother-in-law was also a farmer. She was well aware it was a struggle to feed guests.

She held her breath when Jac rode into the yard late morning and found her sitting outside, shelling peas.

He tied the horse to a post and walked up to her.

'What happened?' She bit her lip.

'We've made peace.'

She smiled up at him. 'I'm glad.'

'He wants me to go back – help build the farm up.'

She didn't trust herself to speak, knowing tears weren't far away. She'd known this might happen. Who wouldn't want Jac around?

'I've told him my heart's not in farming. I'll help as much

as I can while I'm here but what I really want is to go back and breed horses in Wales.'

'With Dermot.' Her voice was quiet.

'If he'll have me back.'

'Of course he'll have you back. I ... I'll need to look for work of some sort.'

He knelt on the grass in front of her. She caught her breath as she read the expression in his eyes.

'We need to wait till everything calms down,' he said. 'Just now your father will be wishing he could shoot me. Unless Sir Geraint can beat him to it and slit my throat.'

'But that's not fair. I was the one who went to you for help. If everything had gone according to plan, I'd be in France with Morwenna now.'

'Is that where you'd like to go?' His voice was gentle.

'Of course not. I don't know anyone there. Morwenna's idea suited me because I was desperate. I was relieved when the captain decided to rest up here but I know it's impossible for me to stay. I'm imposing on your family's hospitality.' She was dropping peas into the shell pile and placing empty pods in the bowl.

He took her hands and trapped them in his. 'Rebecca, where do you really want to be?'

She wanted to say, "with you", but couldn't form the words.

'Will you marry me?'

She stared at him as if he'd grown two heads.

'Now, didn't that go well?' His eyes sparkled with mirth.

Jac's face swam before her eyes. Maybe she'd misheard. 'You don't need a wife,' she said.

'Ah, but the Jac who thought that wasn't thinking right. He almost let something very precious slip through his fingers. But fate took a hand. Like my uncle says it often does. You can't fight it.'

'Is that right?'

He laughed. 'You're already picking up the Irish lilt. Before I ask you again, I'd better tell you I've bedded more than one woman on the peninsula.'

'That's why you wouldn't go back to the cave with me?'

'That's the reason. I couldn't trust myself. Knew I was falling in love with you. All I think of is being with you. For ever.'

Her throat was dry. 'I couldn't believe it when I realised you were prepared to end up in France, rather than let me go alone. Then I thought you'd begun hating me once we got on that boat.'

He touched her cheek, so gently she knew how foolish she'd been to doubt him.

'Being cooped up in that cabin with you could have been heaven on earth. Having to treat you like a fellow was hell. How else was I to cope with it, David my lad? It was vital we kept up the charade. If they'd caught Morwenna ... who knows?'

'Promise me,' she said, 'promise not to call our first son David.'

Joy shone in his eyes. 'First things first, you hussy. I'm asking you again. Rebecca, will you marry me?'

'You want to wed a penniless runaway with no pretty gowns and hardly a lock of hair left on her head?'

He raised his hand. Wound a curl around one finger. 'I do.'

She looked into his eyes. Joy still shone there. So much so, she felt it wriggle itself round her heart, making her want to coil her body around him.

'And so do I want to marry you, Jac without a K.'

He stood up and took the bowl from her lap. Empty pea pods scattering, he pulled her up, taking her in his arms. They clung together till he tilted her chin and moved his lips to within a hair's breadth of hers. 'I'm going to kiss you. Then I need to prepare to return to Wales and face my demons. We'll move you into my da's place. He's got a nice old housekeeper. She'll spoil you as much as she does me!'

She clung to him, tasting him, breathing him in, feeling his warmth, telling him with every fibre of her body how much she loved him. Wanted him.

They broke apart and he hugged her to him again, whispering, 'if anyone's watching, I don't care. But next time I kiss you like this, I want it to go on all night.'

Rebecca's legs almost didn't support her. It was as if a pink cloud enveloped her, disturbing her vision and breathing. She wanted Jac so much. How could she wait weeks, or months, for their situation to be resolved? But she recognised the firmness in his voice. Loved him for it as much as she yearned for him.

Two months later, Rebecca and Jac were married in the little chapel near her father's manor house. Wanting no dark reminders, she wore a simple gown of white lace. Biddy, who'd wept tears of joy when Rebecca returned, fashioned a snood from pale blue velvet so the bright hair appeared to be mostly hidden beneath. She'd no idea what changed her father's mind but hoped, if she waited long enough, he'd tell her. The sad, questing look in his eyes was gone. There was a new tenderness in the way he spoke to Biddy.

Tongues wagged about Morwenna's presence at Dermot's house. But nobody dared question him. She was beside him to see Jac and Rebecca wed. She and Jac seemed to have an easy camaraderie. More than that Rebecca didn't want to conjecture.

Lord Geraint had rented his house to a wealthy merchant from London and was rumoured to be travelling on the continent. He'd left an estate manager in charge.

Jac and Rebecca were to live in Beaumont Manor, in a suite of rooms first used by her parents when they were newly-weds. Jac, pledged to forego his smuggling ways, was to breed horses, advised by his uncle. He'd also learn to run the estate.

After the ceremony, guests walked the short distance to the manor. Suddenly Rebecca took Jac's hand. Drew him aside and whispered to him.

'On our wedding day?' His eyes sparkled with humour.

'Especially on our wedding day.' She saw Catrin smiling at her and placed one finger on her lips.

Rebecca ran. He pelted after her. They hurried. Scrambled. Screeched with laughter when they swayed and staggered like drunkards on the shifting dunes. Jac slipped and sat down, cursing, on a thistle. She stopped to catch her breath, giggling at his frustration. Rebecca knew if she wanted, he'd take her there in the sandy hollow. Still she made him follow her. She knew this would be no polite deflowering. She'd asked Morwenna about love. The witch had told her to learn for herself, but not to hold back when she truly wanted a man.

'Low tide,' said Jac, pulling her close on arrival at the beach.

'Of course,' she said, lifting her face to his.

They kissed greedily as if they wanted to burrow inside each other's body. He scooped her up in his arms and set off purposefully towards the headland.

'You'll have no strength left,' she warned.

'You think so?'

This was a momentous journey for Rebecca. No crashing seas and curious sailors. Every step Jac took nudged her closer to womanhood. At the cave, her eyes widened at sight of the blanket on the shingle. Gently he set her back on her own two feet.

'Jac ...?'

'The water never comes up this far.'

'You knew what I wanted?'

'I wanted it too. So much. That time you asked me if we'd be safer going to the cave ... I thought I'd burst my breeches.'

She reached inside his waistcoat. 'I'm glad you made me wait.'

His mouth sought her lips. His tongue touched hers. Ripples of desire flickered. Nothing could stop their hunger for one another.

His hands cupped her breasts. Her breathing was ragged. His fingers found the buttons at the back of her gown. 'You smell like a rose garden,' he said as she stepped from the lacy folds.

She placed her hands on his chest. Smoothed them over his nipples. Let her fingers walk his ribs then reach lower. With one finger she followed the tapering arrow of dark hair disappearing beneath his breeches. Unfastened one button. Then another. With wonderment she found how real and warm that intriguing bulge felt in her hand. Breasts spilling above her bodice she stooped to caress him. Hearing his groan of pleasure, Rebecca felt triumphant. Now she knew how wise the witch's words were.

'It's a good job I've nerves of steel,' said Jac, reaching to unfasten her stays.

She removed her hand to help him. When she stood naked before him, she laced her fingers round his stiff cock again. 'I hope you won't be disappointed,' she whispered.

'Impossible,' he said, pushing her twin globes together so he could flick his tongue from one pink nipple to the other. He licked then sucked on each firm nub in turn, making her gasp. Increasing her arousal.

Rebecca was drowning in a sensuous sea of pleasure. Jac's mouth moved down her body. Lazily. Finding each curve. Each dip and hollow. Tasting, titillating, teasing till she whimpered in his arms. She knew he was ready to take her on the sands where they'd first met. Still he didn't rush her.

Once they lay down, her voice became urgent. 'Please,' she said.

He bent his head over the soft coppery mound hiding her sex. 'I need you nice and wet, sweetheart. I don't want to hurt you.' Gently he parted her folds and she felt a new sensation as his tongue began its cunning work. Before long, she was writhing. Crooning little animal sounds. Jerking her head from side to side as she rode the spasms.

'What's happening to me?' She gasped.

Jac didn't answer. She curled her fingers in his hair, allowing his rhythmic rocking tongue to take her to the edge of reason. When she thought she could stand no more, he licked his thumb and pressed it to her little toy soldier. He needed only three strokes.

Lying there, eyes closed, hearing his ragged breath, she reached for him, longing for the end of girlhood.

'Now, Jac.'

Gently he pushed his forefinger inside her. She felt the taut resistance. He straddled her, fingers still parting her inner lips. She felt his cock's velvety head. Almost there.

Jac pressed harder. 'I can't stop,' he gasped. 'I have to …'

She opened her legs wide. Arched her back. Meeting him,

welcoming him deep inside, helping him stretch that tight, wet slit. He pushed harder and harder. And then that solid, beautiful thing she'd longed for without knowing what it would feel like, filled her.

A moan of sheer delight escaped Jac's lips. His eyes were shut, telling her he was in a world of his own. Rebecca knew she would join him there. She coiled her legs round him. He groaned again, pumping her gently but steadily, rhythm building as he slid in and out ... in and out. It was as if he couldn't get enough of her. He was thrusting with all his strength. Pushing his hands under her rump. Tilting her hips forward so her petals opened for him.

'Yes,' she said. 'Yes, Jac, yes ...'

They lay together, waiting for their breathing to steady. Her head was cradled against his chest.

'Was I wet enough?'

'You're a wanton woman. Shush ... I could fuck you all over again but we'd better get back, sweetheart.'

She pouted. 'One more kiss?'

'Not till tonight.'

'Tonight I shall ride you.' She kissed him.

He sat up. Grabbed a bunch of seaweed. Pulled her across his lap. 'Naughty girls need a spanking.' His voice was husky.

She felt him harden. Wriggled the cheeks of her bottom higher. 'Do it if you dare!'

The rubbery fronds whistled through the air. She felt the sharp sting. Gasped with surprise. He smacked her again. And again. Warmth spread through her.

'Enough?' He turned her round so she gazed up at him.

'Enough of what?' She ran her fingers along his erection.

Jac groaned. 'We can't go home yet. Climb on, sweetheart. You have me at your mercy.'

Rebecca took him at his word.

When they were dressed again, he pulled her close.

'Remember what I said about kissing you … wanting it to go on all night?'

'I remember.'

'I've changed my mind. I want it to go on for the rest of our lives.'

Cooking Up Trouble
by Elizabeth Coldwell

Chapter One

THE PHONE RANG JUST as Morgan was taking a tray of brownies from the oven. Whenever she was nervous, she took her mind off the situation by cooking, and a situation like this demanded a special recipe. If the rich, squidgy brownies, studded with dried cranberries and chopped macadamia nuts, were as delicious as she hoped, she'd feature them in her next collection of recipes. With her editor expecting her to deliver the completed manuscript at the end of the month, the bulk of the book was already written. This latest recipe was simply the icing on the cake.

Smiling at her little pun, looking forward to taking her first bite of her latest creation, Morgan almost dropped the cast iron baking tray, startled by the sound of her phone bursting into the opening bars of *Food Glorious Food*. Carefully setting down the brownies and peeling off her oven gloves, she answered the call.

'Morgan, it's Lucinda here,' said a perky voice on the other end of the line. 'How are you?'

Lucinda Leeson was the producer of *Cook's Treats*, the successful Saturday morning cookery show currently on its summer break. The programme's long-standing presenter, Graham O'Neill, had announced he wouldn't be returning when the new series started in the autumn, prompting an immediate avalanche of speculation in the press and on social networks about who'd be taking his place. Morgan had applied to attend the auditions to find O'Neill's replacement. Her own show, *Blissful Baking*, which had originally started as a segment on the local TV news programme in her native Cardiff, earned decent ratings for the small cable channel that broadcast it. Fronting *Cook's Treats* would bring her to the attention of a mainstream audience. She couldn't pass up such a chance – but nor, it seemed, could the dozens of others who'd also made it through to the final stage of the audition process.

Morgan walked away from the studio where the audition had taken place believing she'd done a good job and the production team had liked her. It was foolish to think she was the only one who'd had that feeling. Lucinda had promised to get in touch with her within the week to let her know the team's decision. Now, after four long, nail-biting days when she'd considered all the ways they could politely reject her, Morgan almost didn't want to hear what the producer had to say.

'Hi, Lucinda. I'm fine,' she replied, as breezily as she could under the circumstances. 'I've just been making some cranberry and nut brownies.'

'Mmm, they sound wonderful.' Lucinda paused for just long enough to let the sick feeling in Morgan's stomach intensify. 'And I hope you'll be showing the viewers of *Cook's Treats* how to make them when the new series starts. Congratulations, Morgan, you got the job.'

'That's wonderful,' Morgan managed to stammer out, hardly able to believe she'd beaten all the other highly talented candidates she'd mingled with at the audition. 'Thank you so much.'

'Well, it was an easy decision for us to make. You've got a natural warmth and a way of explaining your recipes in simple terms that are just perfect for the show. And we think you'll make the perfect foil for Scott Harley.'

At first, Morgan thought she'd misheard Lucinda. Had she really mentioned Scott Harley, the man she despised more than just about anyone else in the world? 'I'm sorry?'

'Oh, yes. We didn't mention it at the audition for fear of it leaking out before we were ready to make the announcement.

We're changing the format of the show. Graham's departure has provided us with the perfect opportunity to freshen a few things up, and we've decided to have two presenters working alongside each other. You and Scott are going to make a great team, I just know it.'

Something gnawed at Morgan. 'I don't remember seeing him at the audition.'

'Oh, darling.' Lucinda laughed, the sound high and tinkling. 'Scott Harley's the hottest chef in London right now. He doesn't *need* to audition.'

In that moment, Morgan came very close to telling Lucinda she was awfully sorry but she simply wasn't able to take the job if Harley was involved. But opportunities like this came round so rarely, she'd be committing career suicide if she passed it up. Still, as she thanked Lucinda once again and took down the details of the production meeting where she'd be meeting Scott for the first time, she couldn't help wishing her new co-star was anyone but him.

'So it's really going to be that much of a problem?' Carrie asked, as Morgan poured her a second cup of French Vanilla coffee.

The first thing Morgan had done once she'd ended her call with Lucinda was ring Carrie Gray and ask her to come over. Her best friend since she'd interviewed Morgan for a short-lived cookery magazine she'd worked on, Carrie was the one woman Morgan knew who could be relied on to drop everything when she needed to talk something over. It helped that Carrie's job as a freelance journalist meant she could be flexible with her time, and that she would do almost anything if it meant sampling one of Morgan's delicious tray bakes.

'You can't have forgotten what Scott Harley said about me?' Morgan replied, watching Carrie lick chocolaty crumbs from her fingers. She always found it hard to believe quite how much cake her friend could eat and still retain her petite, slender figure.

'Of course not. And those brownies are the business, by the way. But that was nearly two years ago.'

The length of time didn't make any difference. Harley's words were etched on Morgan's soul, impossible to forget. He'd been promoting both the restaurant he'd just opened in the City of London, The Ludgate Chop House, and his stint as one of the judges on *Britain's Next Top Chef*. He'd been asked his opinions on some of the other cooks with their own TV show, and, for whatever reason, Morgan's name had come up. Harley had dismissed her in a couple of sentences, making disparaging comments about her physical appearance as well as her cooking speciality. 'Never mind muffins,' he'd sneered, 'she ought to do something about that muffin top of hers.'

Accompanying the article had been a photo of the man stark naked, holding a shiny copper saucepan in front of him to preserve his modesty. To contrast with the long, lean lines of his admittedly spectacular body, they'd printed a blurry snap of Morgan in unflattering sports gear, revealing the soft expanse of her lower back and hips. The caption beneath it read "Mumsy Morgan Jones", completing her humiliation. Those words had stung then, and they still stung now.

'OK, so I'm never going to be a size ten,' Morgan said, 'but you know how hard I work to keep in shape.' Almost fanatical about her exercise regime, she jogged along the pavements close to her Clapham home every day, and when the weather was bad, she put in the miles on the stationary bike in her bedroom. Even if she still carried a few more pounds than she'd like despite all her efforts, that extra weight had settled on her breasts and hips, giving her body a voluptuous softness her last boyfriend, Mike, had enjoyed very much.

'I don't know why you worry about it. My mother always used to say she never trusted a skinny cook.' Carrie took a reflective sip of her coffee, twirling a lock of her blonde hair between her fingers before continuing. 'I mean, look at you. You've got your own TV show, a best-selling cookery book and curves most of the women I know would die for. And anyway, Harley was only being controversial to create some publicity for himself.'

'Whatever, he had no right to say those things,' Morgan insisted, even though, deep down, she knew Carrie was right.

'The arrogant bastard doesn't even know me.'

'Well, he'll find out all about you soon enough.' Carrie's eyes brightened. 'Tell you what, Morgan, why don't we go shopping? You're going to need a killer outfit for your first big TV appearance, and we'll find something that'll show Scott Harley just how wrong he was.'

Carrie was right. Nothing lifted the spirits like a spot of retail therapy, particularly when it could be justified as a way of celebrating Morgan's good fortune in landing her new job. They spent a couple of happy hours shopping in the West End for a simple teal blue wrap dress that complimented Morgan's long, dark brown curls and hazel eyes and would look good under the studio lights. But when she walked into the *Cook's Treats* production office the following Monday morning, she wore a black scoop-necked jersey top over faded jeans, her lucky peridot choker round her neck. Hardly the sex siren image Carrie had wanted her to portray when she finally encountered Scott Harley in the flesh, but in her casual outfit she felt comfortable and confident.

That confidence evaporated a little as she walked into a scene of utter mayhem. Lucinda barely acknowledged her as she found a seat at the large round table in the centre of the room, and it was a good five minutes before the show's runner, the junior member of staff charged with fetching and carrying, came up and asked whether he could get her a coffee. People were shouting into mobile phones, each one's conversation seemingly more important and more vital to the smooth running of the show than the next. For the first time, Morgan realised the difference between working for a small TV company and one of the major players. Before, there'd never been more than three egos competing for attention in a room at any one time. Here, she counted four times that.

Scott Harley striding in brought the figure up to a baker's dozen. Morgan had never met a man whose entrance could silence a room, until now. If he'd looked good in his magazine feature, he was something else again in the flesh. A good head taller than Morgan's own five foot ten, he had the wide-shouldered build of a professional athlete and a taut, enticing arse outlined by tight-fitting black trousers. Pushing his thick mane of dirty-blond hair out of his face, he fixed Morgan with his piercing green eyes. Despite herself, she felt a sudden rush of lust, settling low in her belly and sending a faint, guilty flush to her cheeks. Of all the reactions she'd expected to have, she'd never thought she would find him as compellingly attractive as she did.

'Scott,' Lucinda chirped. 'How lovely to see you, darling. Looks like you're the last one here. Take a seat. Jamie's just about to go on a coffee run if you'd like anything.'

'Double espresso, thanks,' he replied, pulling up the only vacant chair in the room which, as luck would have it, was next to Morgan's.

She'd once read the man's need for caffeine bordered on addiction. It probably went a long way to explaining his legendary bad temper, showcased on *Britain's Next Top Chef* whenever he chewed out a hapless contestant for burning a hole in a saucepan or dishing up a steak so chewy it was practically inedible. Sitting beside her he was calm enough, though she sensed an unspoken tension beneath the surface, like a coiled spring waiting to be unwound. As she knew only too well, when that tension broke, Scott was likely to let out a vicious verbal volley, just like the one he'd launched in her direction in that bloody article.

'Scott, may I introduce you to your co-star, Morgan Jones?' Lucinda continued. 'I'm sure the two of you are about to embark on a very productive working relationship.'

'Nice to meet you, Morgan,' he murmured.

He acts like he doesn't even know who I am, she thought incredulously. He ridicules me in public, then sits here and smiles at me like butter wouldn't melt. But he probably spent so much money on that nice, white smile of his, he just wants to show it off at every opportunity.

To her surprise, he reached out and took her hand. At that simple contact, electricity shot through her, bringing her body to life. Her nipples made their traitorous presence felt, crinkling against the cups of her bra. Scott seemed to feel a similar reaction, too, if the way he reluctantly broke the connection was anything to go by. Fortunately, no one else in the room seemed to notice a thing.

This can't be happening, Morgan told herself. Of all the people to find herself so instantly, powerfully attracted to, why did it have to be him? Biting hard on the end of her ballpoint pen, she fought to keep the feeling buried. But as Lucinda began to outline the innovations she intended to bring to the *Cook's Treats* format, hoping to gain an even bigger share of the Saturday morning audience than the show already attracted, Morgan found her thoughts wandering.

She pictured again the image of Scott naked but for the concealing saucepan, his magnificent body revealed for everyone to see. In her mind's eye, he stood in exactly that same pose. Only this time, he moved the pan away from his groin, exposing a long, hard cock that almost invited her to touch it. She pictured herself unfastening the wrap dress she'd bought for the show. Her fantasy self wore no underwear, and, beneath the dress, Morgan's body was a symphony of soft curves. Scott's lips curved in a lustful smile at the sight of her full breasts, their nipples suckable peaks, and the fluff of dark hair on her mound, pussy peeking out between her rounded thighs.

Time seemed to stand still as they each eyed the other's glorious nakedness, waiting to see who would make the next move. Then Scott took a pace forward, hand moving along his cock, pushing its velvety foreskin back so the head popped out from beneath it.

Morgan saw herself sinking to her knees before him, reaching out to take his thick shaft in her hand so she could feed the tip between her lips. His breath hissed out at the sensation of being enveloped in Morgan's warm, wet mouth. Clutching him at the base, bobbing her head up and down so he almost, but not quite, fell from her lips with every pass, she licked and sucked till he couldn't take any more. His warning cry gave her the opportunity to pull her mouth away. Instead, she held steady, gulping down every drop of his hot, salty …

'So what do you think, Morgan?'

Swept away by her fantasy, it took Morgan a moment to realise the question was being addressed to her. Looking at the pad before her, on which she'd failed to scribble a single note while the producer was talking, wondering how she was going to cover up her complete lack of attention, she stammered, 'Well, it's an interesting idea, but –'

'I think what Morgan is trying to say,' Scott cut in, 'is that the idea of everything needing to have a competitive element is getting a little old. If there are good amateur cooks who'd like to take part in the show, why don't you simply make the feature a showcase of their abilities, rather than pitting them against each other?'

Grateful to Scott for having dug her out of a hole, she flashed him a smile before continuing, 'That's exactly how I feel. People want something more relaxed on a Saturday morning, and there are plenty of good cooks who might not put themselves forward to appear if they're expected to take part in a competition, simply because they don't like the idea of their efforts being criticised in public.'

'OK, well, that gives me plenty to think about.' Lucinda broke off as the runner appeared in the room, carrying the lid of a box of printer paper which he used as a makeshift tray for the coffee order. 'And here's Jamie with the drinks, which I think marks the perfect time for us to take a break.'

As Jamie handed Morgan the gingerbread latte she'd asked for, Scott muttered, 'Don't expect me to cover your arse in public all the time, sweetheart.'

'I beg your pardon?' Morgan's eyes flashed with barely concealed anger at Scott's patronising tone.

'Sit there daydreaming all you want, but don't think it'll get you very far. You're not broadcasting to six people on No-mark TV now, you know. I expect certain standards of professionalism from the people I work with, and so far you haven't come anywhere near those standards, not by a long way.' He took the lid off his espresso cup, stirring a couple of sachets of sugar into the dark, potent brew before continuing. 'I have an awful lot of artistic input into this show, and if you don't pull your weight, I only have to say the word and you're out. Understand?'

Oh, she understood only too well. He might be the most handsome man she'd met in a long time, with a strong, raw sexuality she found almost impossible to ignore. But like she'd told Carrie, Scott Harley was an arrogant bastard who believed his own publicity. Working with him would either make her or break her.

Chapter Two

MORGAN WAS STILL MULLING over Scott's behaviour on the tube home. She'd always thought his appearances on *Britain's Next Top Chef* had been selectively edited, building an almost caricatured persona of a fiery-tempered perfectionist who didn't suffer fools. A couple of hours in his company and she knew that portrait to be devastatingly close to the truth. One thing was certain, if she was going to succeed as the co-host of *Cook's Treats*, she'd have to be at the very top of her game, both as a cook and a presenter. She wasn't going to give him the satisfaction of kicking her off the show.

Anxious to discuss her opinion of the man with Carrie, she fired off a quick text. 'Free for a drink tonight?'

The answer came back, lightning quick. 'Sorry, Morgan. At a press launch. Let's talk tomorrow.'

Deprived of her usual sounding board, Morgan settled for the next best option. When Carrie's reasoned arguments couldn't calm her mind, a long, foamy bath and a glass of white wine would always do the trick. Letting herself into her basement flat, she headed for the bathroom, turning the taps on full and adding a generous amount of ylang ylang and jasmine bath soak. While the tub filled, Morgan poured a glass of Chenin Blanc, savouring its crisp, honeyed bouquet. She undressed in her bedroom before wrapping her Chinese silk robe around herself and returning to the bathroom.

A cloud of sensually scented steam enveloped her as she stepped into the tub. Morgan couldn't prevent a satisfied sigh escaping her lips. The bathroom was her haven, her escape from whatever life chose to throw at her. Here she could dream and scheme, with no one around to judge her, or pour cold water on her suggestions. Where Carrie kept a notepad by her bed, to record the ideas for articles and short stories that always seemed to come to her as she was on the verge of dozing off, Morgan thought up all her best ideas in the tub.

But even though she let her mind drift, drinking her wine and enjoying the feel of being enveloped in jasmine-scented water, she received no inspiration for new recipes. Instead, she saw herself twined naked in bed with Scott Harley, his full lips placing a wet trail of kisses down her throat and the deep cleavage between her breasts. He would know how to kiss, she was sure of it, driving her to a helpless mess of wanting with his mouth and tongue before he even thought about pleasuring her with his cock. In her experience, a love for food always equated to a love for sex, and despite Harley's posturing and showmanship in his TV appearances, reviews of his restaurant never failed to praise the quality of his food and his instinctive knowledge of how flavours complemented each other.

Almost unaware of what she was doing, Morgan let a hand slip down between her legs, to caress herself under the water. In her fantasy, it was Scott's hand playing over her body, touching her in all the places that couldn't fail to excite her, pinching and teasing her nipples until she was almost crying out for him to turn his attentions to her pussy. Seeing how he was driving her crazy with need, he would smile that lazy, megawatt smile of his, and bend his head to nuzzle first at the sensitive buds, then gradually work his way down toward her liquid cleft. He would take his time, lapping up her juices where they coated the insides of her thighs, ignoring all her pleas to use his tongue on her clit. Only when he decided he'd made her beg for long enough would he press his mouth to her cunt.

Morgan's fingers worked feverishly on her clit as she pictured Scott kissing and sucking the soft folds of her sex. She was oblivious to everything but the pleasure she was giving herself as she imagined how he would bring her to a gasping, body-shaking climax. This being fantasy, she didn't have to tell him what do to turn her on; he instinctively knew. The insistent pressure of his muscular tongue, coupled with two long, thick fingers slipping up inside her pussy, would bring her to the verge of climax.

Lost in a world of her own creation, Morgan stroked and teased till delicious spasms rippled through her body, leaving her flushed and breathless. If only, she thought, taking a sip from her wine glass where it stood neglected on the edge of the tub, the real Scott Harley was more like her fantasy lover, sensitive to her needs and ready to do whatever it took to satisfy her, rather than the self-centred control freak he'd shown himself to be earlier in the day.

Scott looked at the line of stationary cars snaking all the way down Old Street and almost banged his hand on the steering wheel of his Alfa Romeo Spider in frustration. The traffic was usually bad at this time of day, but tonight it was an absolute nightmare. There was nothing for it; he'd have to call Chris and let him know he was going to be late.

In the two years he'd been running The Ludgate Chop House, Chris Baxter had become an invaluable part of Scott's business empire. With his commitments on *Britain's Next Top Chef*, and now the presenting job on *Cook's Treats*, it simply wasn't possible for Scott to work in the restaurant every day of the week. He'd needed someone to run the kitchen on the days he was absent, and Chris fitted the bill perfectly. One of the best chefs in London, Scott had been lucky to recruit him. He had ambitions to acquire a restaurant of his own, and Scott knew if he was to retain Chris's services, he needed to keep him sweet.

That meant doing something he hated – apologising for running late. His ex-wife, Sasha, was among any number of people who'd willingly stand up in court and testify how impossible he found it to accept events that were outside his control, never mind those he'd been responsible for. Anyone else would regard a traffic jam as one of life's minor inconveniences. Tonight, Scott took it as a personal insult.

'Hey, Scott, how's it going?' Chris sounded remarkably laid back for a man who should have left for the day after the lunchtime sitting had finished.

'Not great,' Scott snarled into his Bluetooth headset. 'I'm about a mile away from you, but the speed this traffic's moving, it'd be quicker to get out and walk.'

'Look, don't worry about it, mate. We've only got half-a-dozen covers to cater for at the moment. We'll cope till you get here.'

Scott finished the call. Ahead of him, the traffic lights had changed from red to green, but still the traffic refused to budge an inch. Sighing, he thought back to the morning's production meeting, and his introduction to Morgan Jones.

When he'd discovered she was going to be his co-presenter, he'd been less than thrilled. He'd been hoping to appear beside someone with a higher profile, more authority, not some cable TV nobody who'd made her name teaching viewers how to ice cupcakes. But Lucinda Leeson had been insistent. Scott had gained a reputation for being impatient and abrasive, his personality repelling as many viewers as it attracted. It was important, she said, to have someone warmer, more down-to-earth alongside him to provide a balance, and Morgan fitted that role perfectly. It also helped that Morgan was tall enough not to be dwarfed by Scott when she stood alongside him.

He still wasn't convinced she was the right person for the show, not after he'd caught her daydreaming when she should have been giving her full attention in the production meeting. But he couldn't deny she was nothing like he'd been expecting. If he'd ever watched her show, her lilting Welsh accent might not have come as such a surprise to him, but even TV couldn't have prepared him for the reality of her voluptuous body, all tits and hips. She was the polar opposite of Sasha, whose whip-thin but perfectly proportioned frame had earned her any number of modelling contracts during the course of their marriage. Given the acrimony with which his relationship with Sasha had ended, maybe those differences were all part of the attraction.

And that hair! Though Morgan had styled it into a neat chignon, dark strands had come loose during the course of the morning to frame her face. Scott knew if he'd pulled it free of the pins holding it in place, it would have tumbled down beyond her shoulders. He pictured himself burying his face in those glorious tresses, breathing in the scent of her shampoo as his hands cupped her luscious breasts.

To his surprise, thinking about Morgan was starting to get him hard. He shifted in his seat, moving his erection into a more comfortable position. Forgetting his irritation at being caught up in this infernal jam, he found his imaginings taking on an increasingly erotic tone.

He pictured himself in the kitchen at the Chop House, Morgan working alongside him as the restaurant's pastry chef. Just as in the meeting this morning, she'd been daydreaming instead of keeping an eye on the tartlet cases she'd set to bake. When she pulled open the oven door, black smoke poured out, and the pastry was burned beyond recognition. Something very similar had happened on *Britain's Next Top Chef*, and the hapless contestant had received her marching orders at the end of the episode, but not before Scott had treated her to an expletive-ridden assessment of her culinary abilities – or lack of them. If one of his kitchen staff did the same thing, he'd more than likely sack them on the spot. Morgan was to receive very different treatment.

'You need to be taught a lesson, girl,' he told her, as Morgan stood before him, eyes downcast, waiting for him to do his worst. 'Something that'll make sure you never forget to pay attention to what you're supposed to be doing.' He pulled one of the chairs from the chef's table, where guests were able to sample his special tasting menu in the heart of the kitchen, and sat down on it.

'Over my knee, Morgan,' he ordered her.

Eyes wide, she began to protest, telling him she was sorry and she'd never do such a thing again.

'Saying sorry isn't good enough, Morgan. At least, not right now. Let's wait till you really know what sorry is, shall we?'

With that, he patted his lap, urging her to climb on to it. Meekly, she did as he asked, lying face down over his widely spread thighs. Though he was sure she'd feel foolish in that position, waiting to receive her spanking like a naughty schoolgirl, he thought she looked magnificent. Even more so when he eased down her blue and white checked chef's trousers to reveal her plump bottom, only partially covered by her plain white cotton panties. Morgan's protests as he stripped her were half-hearted, and he knew she wanted this.

He let her wait for a long moment, allowing the nervous anticipation to build, before he brought his hand down on her backside. Slowly, methodically, he slapped every inch of her soft, round cheeks, making her give out a series of cute, throaty little yelps. She wriggled on his lap, her movements stimulating his cock to full hardness where it lay trapped between her half-naked body and his thigh. And just when she thought her punishment was over and he'd let her go back about her kitchen duties, he reached for the waistband of her panties, pulling them down to bare the cheeks of her arse and the wet pouch of her pussy, ready to begin her spanking all over again ...

Behind him, a car horn hooted and he realised the traffic was finally on the move. Pulling his thoughts back to his surroundings, Scott tried to ignore the swelling at his groin. He'd no idea where the idea of spanking Morgan had come from; his sex life usually ran along a much more vanilla track. But something about the feisty Welsh cook intrigued him, her demeanour making him think she wouldn't object if he ever chose to act on his kinky fantasy. But there was no likelihood of that. He got the feeling she didn't like him very much, and their relationship would never be anything but strictly professional. Though it was a reaction he was used to from the people he worked with, he couldn't help wondering why it was so important the two of them clicked on a more personal level.

Putting his foot down on the accelerator, he took a right turn into Goswell Road, bypassing the emergency gas main repairs that must have caused the tailback. Taking the back street route which was the quickest way to reach the Chop House, Scott pushed thoughts of Morgan to the back of his mind, the better to concentrate on whatever lay in store for him in the restaurant's bustling kitchen.

Chapter Three

'SO, TELL ME ALL about Scott,' Carrie said, watching the world go by from the battered but comfortable leather sofa in the coffee shop window. 'I mean, I can tell you like him, it's written all over your face, but spill the juicy details.'

'Carrie, don't be so ridiculous,' Morgan said, breaking her almond biscotti in half and dunking it into her coffee cup. 'Scott Harley is the most arrogant, infuriating man I think I've ever met. He acts as though he's doing me a huge favour by allowing me to appear alongside him on the show, and, if he wants to, he can get rid of me at any time.'

'But that doesn't explain why you keep dropping his name into the conversation at every possible opportunity, or why you blush and keep fiddling with your hair when you talk about him. I've known you long enough to know that's what you do when you've got the hots for someone.'

'I don't have the hots for Scott,' Morgan protested, her voice so loud the woman on the neighbouring table leaned a little closer, hoping to hear more. Noticing her less-than-subtle attempts to eavesdrop, Morgan reined herself in. It didn't help that Carrie was dangerously close to the truth. Much as the man's presence rubbed her up the wrong way, Morgan knew she was displaying all the signs of being head over heels in lust.

'So you say.' Carrie sipped her hot chocolate. 'But one thing I do want to know – is he as good-looking as he is on TV?'

'Oh, yes,' Morgan replied without hesitation. 'He's got to be six foot three if he's an inch, and he's got the most incredible green eyes, studded with these little gold flecks ...'

Aware she sounded like she was gushing over Scott, she hastily changed the conversation. 'Anyway, you said you were at a press launch last night. Anything interesting?'

'Oh, one of the supermarkets was unveiling its Christmas range.' Even though Christmas was still three months away, the lead times on the magazines Carrie wrote for meant that if manufacturers wanted publicity for their products, they had to present them to the media well in advance of the actual occasion. 'And there's another showcase tomorrow lunchtime, and one next Tuesday evening. I tell you, give it another week and I won't ever want to see a mince pie again ...'

Morgan glanced at her watch, remembering the reason she'd arranged to meet Carrie in Islington. 'Sorry, but I'm going to have to dash. I've got to be at the photographer's in ten minutes and I really can't afford to be late. If I keep Scott waiting, I'll never hear the end of it.'

'Well, have fun – and don't do anything I wouldn't.' Carrie laughed, leaning back against the sofa to enjoy the rest of her drink.

Leaving the coffee shop, Morgan consulted the directions to the photographer's studio on her phone. A map popped up, telling her to cut through Camden Passage, with its world-renowned selection of antique shops, then weave her way through the back streets, surprisingly quiet after the lunchtime traffic and shopping crowds on Upper Street.

Martin Bayford lived and worked in one of the neat Georgian terraced houses within sight of the Regent's Canal. Morgan rang the doorbell and waited for an answer.

Bayford was a broad, florid man in his 50s, with a shock of white hair and a neat moustache. He greeted Morgan as though he'd known her all his life, ushering her inside.

'You have a really beautiful house,' Morgan told him, stepping into a hallway decorated in a rich shade of plum.

'Thanks,' he replied. 'I bought this place the best part of 30 years ago, when the area wasn't half as sought after as it is now.' He took her through into the living room, which looked out on to a small, neat square of garden. 'Can I get you a drink?'

Morgan shook her head. 'Thanks, but I've just come from having coffee with a friend. Is Scott here yet?'

'No, you're the first, but I had a call from him a moment ago to tell me he'll be here once he's found himself a parking space. And that might take a while.'

'In which case, I will have that drink you mentioned. But could I just have a glass of water, please?'

'Of course.'

In Bayford's absence, Morgan took the opportunity to study the photographs on his wall. Many of them were moody, black-and-white shots of canal side views, from the modern apartment blocks in the City Road Basin, a few minutes' walk from Bayford's house, to the brooding gasometer that dominated the stretch close to Cambridge Heath. The landscape of urban London varied greatly, even within the space of a couple of miles, and these photos captured those variations superbly. Morgan, however, was more interested in the small number of portraits on the wall. She recognised an actor here, a footballer there, all captured in candid poses. It seemed Bayford had a knack for making his subjects relax and forget the camera was there; something she'd need if she was coping with the distractions of being up close and personal with Scott once more.

As Bayford returned from the kitchen carrying a glass of iced water, the doorbell rang. He handed Morgan her drink, then went to answer it.

If Scott had found it difficult to snag a parking space, he didn't show it, looking cool and unruffled in a tight, light blue T-shirt that emphasised the toned muscles of his chest and upper arms.

'Morgan, nice to see you again.' Scott's smile contained more warmth than she might have expected. Perhaps he'd mellowed since their last meeting.

He waved away Bayford's offer of coffee. 'Let's just get the whole painful process out of the way, shall we?' Scott made it sound as though he was about to undergo root canal work, rather than have his photograph taken.

Unless he's referring to spending time with me. Morgan

quickly dismissed the thought, determined nothing Scott Harley did or said would dent her confidence. But why did it matter so much what he thought of her? Television was full of people who were prepared to trample over each other in the fight to become stars, and she'd never let any of them affect her, until now.

'OK, then, if you'd both like to follow me ...' Bayford led them upstairs to his airy photographic studio. Spotlights were already set up, awaiting their arrival, and Bayford switched them on while Morgan and Scott slipped into the outfits they'd been requested to bring.

The TV channel's publicity department had asked them both to provide what they called a "professional look". This translated to chef's whites and a large metal balloon whisk for Scott and a striped apron and wooden spoon for Morgan. Cheesy, but perfect for the TV listings pages in the daily papers.

Bayford reached for his digital SLR camera, having been briefed as to what was needed. 'Right. Let's have the two of you back to back to start off with. Scott, I want you to hold that whisk to your chest. Morgan, you do the same with the spoon. Now, big smiles ...'

This was going to be more difficult than she'd expected. Morgan looked towards the photographer, head half-turned over her shoulder, just as he'd requested, but she was all too aware of the contact where her back pressed against Scott's. A pulse beat hard between her legs, her pussy beginning to bloom against the crotch of her panties, and she wondered whether Scott felt the same excitement. If he did, he said nothing.

Bayford clearly sensed the chemistry between them. He took a few head shots, first of Scott, still clutching his whisk, then of Morgan, including a couple where she pressed the tip of the wooden spoon to her lips as though licking something from its surface.

'Good ... Great ... We're working really well here,' Bayford murmured. 'So now let's go on to the casual shots, shall we?'

Scott removed his loose-fitting white jacket without bothering to unfasten it, pulling it off over his head. As he did so, his T-shirt rode up beneath it, revealing a glimpse of his taut belly.

How had he acquired his light golden tan? Morgan wondered. She knew he owned a flat in Kensington with a spectacular roof garden; he and his ex-wife had let one of the celebrity magazines photograph them in every room of the place in happier times. Flipping through the feature as she sat in the hairdresser's chair, Morgan had admired the place, never believing she'd one day find herself working alongside the man who owned it.

Maybe he sunbathed on the roof, secluded from prying eyes. Her mind picked up the image and ran with it, so that now he lay naked, the sun beating down on the firm globes of his arse, turning him that same delicious honey shade all over. And when he turned over, his cock would be hard, so hard that he wouldn't be able to resist taking himself in hand. Secure in the knowledge he couldn't be seen by anyone as he pleasured himself so brazenly, he would stroke up and down his length, slowly at first, then with increasing intensity till he came, his come spurting out into the warm summer air.

Such a delicious image, and part of her couldn't help wishing she'd one day have the opportunity to see it in reality. Aware Bayford was waiting for her, she unfastened her apron, lifted the neck strap over her head and put the garment to one side. Beneath it, she wore a pretty floral dress with a V neck, revealing just a hint of cleavage. Not so sexy that it would be off-putting to a Saturday morning audience expecting good family viewing, but enough to remind them that she was as feminine as Scott was masculine.

'Right, we'll try something a little different this time,' Bayford said. 'Scott, could you stand behind Morgan and put your arms round her, then both turn your faces to me like you did before?'

Morgan half expected Scott to make some objection to this more intimate pose, but he didn't say a word, simply wrapped his arms around her waist. Was it her imagination, or could she feel his erection, harder than it ought to be for a man who swore to have no interest in her, pressing against her bottom?

When Bayford asked her to move her position slightly, leaning into her co-presenter just a little more, she felt Scott's cock twitch and knew he was turned on.

Whatever else she'd expected from taking part in this photo-shoot, it hadn't been such solid evidence that Scott found her so desirable, despite his very public comments to the contrary. Part of her wanted to share the details with Carrie, but she knew better. Given their earlier conversation, and her equally vehement insistence that she wasn't in the least interested in Scott Harley, she knew the kind of teasing she'd receive. And she couldn't deny that she'd deserve every last scrap of it.

Damn Martin Bayford! The man was clearly one of the most professional photographers Scott had ever posed for, but from the moment they'd stepped into his studio, he'd seemed intent on tormenting Scott by guiding him into poses that couldn't fail to make him conscious of Morgan Jones' bewitching loveliness. His whole body seemed to fizz with erotic energy every time they touched, and now here he was, holding her in his arms, his cock a solid bar, trapped in the confines of his underwear. All he could think of was what it would feel like to push up the hem of Morgan's dress, pull down her panties and slide his erection between her pussy lips. Fuck it, if she was willing, he'd screw her right here on the studio floor, dress up round her waist and her plump, bare arse on display, and let Bayford photograph every last second of that.

What made it all the more frustrating was that she seemed totally oblivious to his need for her. He longed to move his hands a fraction higher, so he could cup those gorgeous tits of hers, and discover whether her nipples were hard, but behaviour like that would probably just earn him a slap round the face. Instead, he simply clung to her, breathing in the scent of her freshly washed hair as Bayford continued to snap away.

At last, the photographer announced, 'OK, I think that's about everything I need. I'll be uploading the shots and sending them over to your publicity department this evening, so you'll be able to choose the ones you like.'

'Oh, they'll make that decision, surely?' Morgan said.

'Well, I know Scott had mentioned something about wanting final approval, so ...'

The look Morgan shot Scott at that moment made his erection wilt. In her eyes, asking for approval over which publicity photos went out appeared to mark you as some kind of prima donna. Obviously, she'd never been burned by the press the way he had over the years ...

The thought died almost before it formed. At last, Scott remembered the nagging sense of familiarity he'd had since the moment they'd met, the feeling their paths had somehow crossed, even though they'd never been in the same room before to the best of his knowledge. The interview with *Personal* magazine, and his assertion that Morgan Jones was giving TV chefs a bad name, with her gooey, ridiculously calorific recipes and the extra weight she – and no doubt those who baked and ate her cakes – carried. No wonder she looked at him as though he was something she'd scraped off the sole of her shoe. Well, maybe he regretted coming out with those words, now he'd held her in his arms and sensed an obvious chemistry between them, but she needed to toughen up. If his were the only harsh comments she heard during the course of her career, she'd be a very lucky woman. Fronting such a popular show, she'd soon find people queuing up to knock her down and pass judgement on everything from her presenting style to her choice of jewellery.

Maybe he was trying to justify himself, just a little, but he didn't care. Lucinda Leeson might call him abrasive, but his straight-talking, no-nonsense persona had made him a success, both in the kitchen and on TV. He wasn't about to change, simply because Morgan didn't appear to like him the way he was.

Scott gathered up his discarded chef's jacket and checked his phone for messages. No one had been trying to get hold of him, which was a blessing, though he needed to leave in the next few minutes. He had a meeting scheduled with a potential new supplier of game birds for the Chop House, and he couldn't afford to be late.

Saying his goodbyes on the doorstep, he was struck with a sudden desire to be courteous to Morgan. 'I don't know which way you're heading, but I could give you a lift as far as Farringdon station, if that helps?'

Morgan shook her head. 'Thanks, Scott, but I need the Northern Line, and it's as easy for me to walk back to the Angel, if it's all the same.'

'Sure.' Scott nodded. 'Well, don't forget we've got another production meeting scheduled for Friday morning. I'll see you then.'

Walking back to where he'd left his car, Scott tried not to wonder why he felt so disappointed at being unable to spend a few more minutes with Morgan. Maybe it just irked him that she'd seemed so keen to get out of his company, even though she'd phrased her refusal with perfect politeness. He'd become used to women falling over themselves to spend time with him, seduced by his aura of fame and success, particularly after his divorce from Sasha had become public knowledge. Morgan appeared utterly indifferent to all that and, try as he might, he couldn't see her attitude changing any time soon.

Chapter Four

MORGAN DIDN'T THINK SHE'D ever been as nervous as she was in the moments before she introduced *Cook's Treats* for the first time. Though she'd appeared on live television any number of times before – most recently as part of the extensive publicity tour she and Scott had taken part in over the last week, promoting the series on TV and radio stations throughout the country – she'd never been conscious of the fact such a large audience was tuning in.

The show's jazzy theme tune floated through the studio speakers, and Dan, the floor manager, gave Morgan and Scott their cue, silently counting down from three to zero with his fingers.

'Good morning and welcome, food lovers.' Scott sounded confident and relaxed as he parroted his lines from the autocue. 'I'm Scott Harley ...'

'And I'm Morgan Jones.' The dizzy thumping of Morgan's heart slowed as she concentrated on the words scrolling up on the monitor. 'And we're your Saturday morning brunch bunch, here to spice up the all-new *Cook's Treats*.'

The title sequence played out, visible for the benefit of the two presenters on small TV sets placed to the right and left of the set. When it came to an end, Scott continued, 'This morning, I'll be demonstrating a new twist on an old classic, smoked trout kedgeree, while for those of you with a sweet tooth, Morgan will be baking cranberry and macadamia brownies.'

The focus came back to Morgan. 'Soap star turned West End musical performer, Natalie Shakes, is popping in to tell us all about playing Roxie Hart in *Chicago* and the healthy recipes that give her the energy she needs for such a turbo-charged role. And we'll be launching our search for the best breakfast spots in Britain, and letting you know how you can nominate your favourite.'

Moving from where he leaned against the kitchen counter that was at the heart of the programme's set, Scott walked over to the gas-powered hob, ready to begin his first cookery segment. 'Now, kedgeree is one of my favourite dishes for a lazy weekend brunch ...'

Morgan took a seat on the sea-green sofa where Natalie, their studio guest, would be joining them later in the show. She caught the eye of Dan, who gave her a discreet thumbs-up, letting her know the production team, upstairs in the studio gallery, were happy with her performance so far. Reading a few lines was the simple part. The real test would come when she had to demonstrate her culinary skills to the viewers, as Scott was doing now. The show's running order was precisely timed, and both of them would very quickly have the director barking into their concealed earpieces if any item was taking longer than it should to complete. That added pressure made what should be simple tasks like chopping and whisking seem fraught with complications.

Though Scott was acquitting himself admirably under studio conditions, it had to be said. She watched him slicing leeks for the kedgeree with lightning speed, all the while keeping up a monologue to camera about the history of the dish and the various stages in its cooking process. Already, her mouth watered at the thought of tasting his creation when it was finished.

In the week they'd been promoting the show, Morgan had come to know the story of his career almost as well as her own. He'd started working in kitchens as a way of earning money to pay his way through university. At first, he'd washed pots and carried out the most menial tasks, chopping vegetables and preparing salads, but all the time he watched the chefs around him, recreating the dishes he'd seen them make in the cramped kitchen in his student digs. On graduating, he'd found a job as a commis chef in a London hotel kitchen, assisting the more experienced chefs and learning all the skills he needed to one day do their job. Eventually, he'd become head chef at Le Cartouche in Mayfair, where his innovative and superbly executed menu had helped the restaurant gain its third Michelin star. His unique blend of culinary expertise, good looks and fiery temper had come to the attention of the producer of *Britain's Next Top Chef*, and now, a couple of years later, here he was, looking thoroughly at home in the cosy setting of Saturday morning TV.

'And there you have it,' Morgan heard him say as he topped the kedgeree with quarters of egg, boiled till the yolk was only just set, and chopped parsley. He presented the plate to the camera. 'Morgan, would you like to come and take a bite?'

'I'd love to,' she replied, joining him by the counter. Taking a generous forkful of the finished dish, she savoured the spiciness of the rice, mixed with the flaked, gently smoked trout and the creaminess of the egg yolk. 'Mmm, that's delicious, it really is.' If she'd had the opportunity, she would have helped herself to more, having been too nervous to eat breakfast, but she had the job of introducing the next item, in which the show's resident wine expert, David Delaney, scoured the high street for the best in New World whites.

The pre-recorded piece gave the studio crew and the show's two home economists time to clear away everything Scott had used in the making of his dish and replace it with the ingredients for Morgan's. A tray of brownies was already baking in the oven, one of the tricks of the trade that enabled her to spend five minutes demonstrating a recipe that took over half an hour to prepare and cook, yet still have a completed version to show the audience.

She took her place at the counter, noticing how the crew were attacking the remains of Scott's kedgeree like vultures, devouring every last scrap. One of the perks of the job, she supposed. Natalie Shakes had been brought out from the green room, ready to be interviewed by Scott once Morgan's cookery segment was over. Scott was leaning over the couch, chatting to Natalie. Though flirting might be a better choice of word for the way he bent close to her ear, murmuring something that couldn't be picked up by the studio mikes. It wasn't surprising; Natalie, with her long, sleek blonde hair and endless legs, honed by weeks of rehearsal for her three-month run as Roxie in *Chicago*, was just Scott's type, if the pictures Morgan had seen of his ex-wife were anything to go by.

But why should she care if he decided to flirt with the guests? From her reaction, anyone would think she was jealous, and that was ridiculous. Yet, if you'd asked her to name her emotions as Scott bent a little closer to Natalie, treating Morgan to a beautiful view of his backside, round and firm in his faded blue jeans, jealousy would have been close to the top of the list, right behind pure, unadulterated lust.

Lucinda Leeson's voice in her ear warned her there was 20 seconds till David's wine round-up finished. Morgan plastered on a smile and waited for the cameras to turn to her. 'And David will be back next week with more top wine choices. Coming up, Natalie Shakes will be on the sofa with Scott. But first, here's something for all those of you wondering what to bake for a teatime treat this weekend ...'

Talking her unseen audience through the list of ingredients they'd need to make her brownies, Morgan felt herself relax mentally. For all her anxiety, she'd worked on the recipe so many times in rehearsal she felt as though she could complete it in her sleep.

But as she stirred cocoa powder into butter she'd melted on the hob, before adding the resulting mixture to eggs beaten with sugar, then sifting in flour and baking powder, she found her thoughts taking an increasingly erotic turn. If she'd been making the brownies at home, she wouldn't have been able to resist scooping the last of the batter from the sides of the mixing bowl and licking it up. Her fantasies strayed to a scene where, instead, she was eating the gooey mixture from Scott's fingers, the relish with which she sucked him making it very clear there were other parts of him she'd enjoy sucking just as much.

Or maybe she'd have him naked, splayed out on her scrubbed pine kitchen table. If she tied his wrists to the table legs with a couple of tea towels, she'd have him helpless. It was a nice thought – Scott, with his compulsive need to be in charge of everything, completely in her power and waiting for her to do whatever she chose to him. She'd daub his body with the brownie batter, painting it over his chest, belly and thighs, finishing off with a generous dollop crowning his cock. Then she'd take her time licking it all up, making sure she cleaned everywhere before turning her attention to the place he needed to feel her mouth the most. The taste as she swallowed him down would be like nothing she'd known before, salt and chocolate combining to tantalise her taste buds and set her juices flowing. Scott would be so close to coming, he'd beg her to take him over the edge, but she'd resist, determined to make this an experience they would both enjoy to the fullest.

Once his cock was completely clean, she'd take off her panties and hitch her skirt up to her waist. Climbing on to the table, she'd crawl up his body till her pussy was poised over his straining erection. Scott would glance up at her, imploring her with those incredible green eyes of his to take him into her tight, wet channel. All in good time. Teasing him further, she'd wriggle so that her sex lips just brushed the head of his cock, making him groan in frustration. Of course, she'd be frustrating herself too, and it wouldn't be long before she simply had to have him properly inside her. With a sigh, she'd sink down on to that thick shaft, feeling him stretch her pussy walls wide. Buried in her to the root, Scott would beg her to ride him till they both came, in an explosion of passion that was sweet and sticky and oh so good ...

Scott Harley, naked, tied and begging her to fuck him. The image was so powerful, so tempting, Morgan almost missed Lucinda telling her to wrap up the segment so they could move on to the interview with Natalie. Fetching the cooked brownies from the oven, she turned them out on to a rack, cutting a slice to enable the viewers to see how moist they were inside.

'Of course, if you leave them to cool for a while, they'll firm up and be easier to cut,' she explained. 'But I'm sure our guest won't be able to resist sampling them just as they are ...'

Placing the brownie on a plate, she carried it over to the couch. 'That looks incredible,' Natalie Shakes said as Morgan approached, with all the enthusiasm of a woman who'd been on a strict diet in her quest to get into shape for her stage role and couldn't wait to get her hands on something rich and sugary.

'Well, while Natalie tucks in to her brownie,' Scott said, 'we'll take a look at her in action. Here she is, giving it the old razzle dazzle as Roxie Hart ...'

The remainder of the show passed in a blur. When the closing credits rolled and Morgan was finally told she could clear the set, she almost screamed aloud with elation and relief. She'd managed to get through a whole 90 minutes of live television without fluffing her lines once.

'Well done,' came Lucinda's voice through her earpiece. 'You were excellent, both of you. And I do believe there's a glass of fizz or two waiting for you in the green room when you come through.'

As they walked away from the fake kitchen, Scott wrapped his arm round Morgan's shoulder, giving it a squeeze. Her nerves seemed to sing with delight at the contact, even as she wondered why he was being no nice to her.

'Looks like you've proved me wrong,' he said. 'I thought the old nerves might get the better of you, but you did a great job.' He broke away. 'And I'd love to stay and celebrate with you all, but Natalie's agreed to join me for a drink at this nice little place I know down on the riverside at Hammersmith. See you Tuesday for the production meeting, Morgan.'

With a little wink, he was gone, leaving Morgan fuming at his cheek. He clearly expected her to let the others know about his lack of interest in attending the after-show drink. Carrie's housemate, Josh, worked on one of the newspaper gossip columns. She was almost driven to ring him and let him know where the paper's photographers might find Scott. They'd love a photo of the famously temperamental chef in a cosy rendezvous with Natalie Shakes. Knowing Scott's reputation, he'd be so enraged at the arrival of the paparazzi that he'd probably try to punch someone, or at the very least damage a camera. And how would that sit with Lucinda and the rest of the *Cook's Treats* production crew?

Morgan shook her head. Much as she'd love to see the man squirm, she'd never been the vindictive type. And she couldn't help thinking her motives were fuelled as much by the fact he'd chosen Natalie over her. Wondering for the hundredth time why she was letting Scott Harley get so deeply under her skin, she went to grab a glass of Champagne before the studio crew guzzled it all.

Chapter Five

THE RINGING PHONE DISTURBED Morgan from a dream where she was standing in the *Cook's Treats* studio, about to introduce the morning's big-name guest. Only the name of that guest had completely slipped from her mind, and the autocue had ground to a halt, offering her no help. With millions of people watching, she fought in vain to salvage the situation, and just in her eye line she could see Scott looking on, his mocking smile indicating how much he was enjoying her obvious discomfort.

It was nothing more than a simple anxiety dream, Morgan thought as she groped for the phone, just like all the ones she'd had where she'd been sitting in an examination, only to find herself staring at a maths paper instead of the expected questions on geography. Though what she had to be anxious about, she didn't know.

A familiar laugh greeted her mumbled, 'Hello?'

'Hey, sleepyhead,' Carrie replied, 'sorry if I woke you, but it is nearly midday.'

Really? A glance at her alarm clock confirmed the truth of Carrie's words. Morgan didn't usually sleep so late on a Sunday, but then she had been up till two, working her way through a box set of episodes of her favourite crime drama.

'Hi, Carrie.' Why was her friend ringing? Had she forgotten something important? 'Er – I wasn't supposed to be meeting you for lunch or anything, was I?'

'No, nothing like that. I was going to ask you if you'd seen the *Sunday Clarion* this morning, but obviously not. In which case, let me read you a little extract from Will Harding's TV review.'

111

'OK, just give me a moment.' Morgan hauled herself out of bed and headed in the direction of the kitchen, needing a strong cup of coffee to help her cope with whatever might be coming next.

Carrie cleared her throat. 'You ready for this? Right, here we go. *The relaunched* Cook's Treats *is hosted by an eye-catching team in seasoned veteran Scott Harley and feisty newcomer Morgan Jones. As well as whipping up the kind of good old-fashioned comfort food viewers might actually want to make for themselves, Harley and voluptuous Valleys vixen Jones seem to be cooking up some definite sexual tension. Tune in next week for more significant glances over the stove and a welcome dash of Saturday morning sauce ...*'

'Wow! I wasn't expecting that.' Morgan spooned freshly ground coffee into her cafetière before putting the kettle on to boil.

'Do you seriously think I'd have rung you if it'd been a bad review?'

'Of course not,' Morgan replied, remembering how supportive Carrie had been when Scott Harley's hurtful comments appeared in *Personal* magazine. 'But it makes us sound like we were presenting some kind of burlesque show, rather than a cookery programme. And what did they call Scott? Oh yes, a seasoned veteran.' She repeated the phrase with relish. 'It makes him sound about a thousand years old. I'm not sure about being referred to as a "Valleys vixen", though.'

'Well, what can you expect when you posed for that photo licking that wooden spoon like you're about to give it a blowjob? And you can't deny that you and Scott look good together.' Carrie ignored Morgan's objections to her last comment, continuing, 'You're going to have to get used to a lot of speculation, Morgan. I think you're going to be trending all over the social networks by the end of today, and it won't be because they're anxious to get their hands on your recipe for red velvet cupcakes.'

Scott didn't see the *Sunday Clarion* review of his *Cook's*

Treats till more than a month later. The only parts of the Sunday papers he ever bothered with were the news, sport and financial sections; the rest were useful for wrapping fish and chips, nothing more, as far as he was concerned. So he never knew what compelled him to smooth out the crumpled sheet of newsprint with his and Morgan's faces on it as he sorted out items for the regular recycled waste collection.

Quickly scanning the review, he grew more incredulous by the moment, making a mental note to treat Will Harding to the full force of his wrath should they ever run into one another. The write-up had barely covered the cookery segments of the show. Instead, it discussed him and Morgan as though they were appearing in one of those comedy dramas featuring a couple who claimed not to be able to stand each other but were destined to end up in bed together in the final episode.

Or was that just his own take on the situation? He'd been thinking about Morgan more than he cared to admit over the last couple of weeks, and he'd be damned if he knew why. After all, the booking policy for the show seemed to involve a succession of glamorous female guests who couldn't have been closer to his idea of perfect eye candy. Natalie had only been the first. After her had come newsreader Paula Langdon, world champion hurdler Kym Sadler and pop star twins, Jade and Jennifer Blue. Pert, identical blondes, for God's sake! Wasn't that every man's fantasy?

There'd been a time, not too long ago, when he'd have been all over those girls like a rash, inviting them for cocktails, an intimate dinner cooked by his own fair hands and whatever came after. But now, he just couldn't see the appeal.

It had started with Natalie Shakes. She'd accepted his invitation to join him for a drink at the Schooner. In the shadow of Hammersmith Bridge, it was one of his favourite London pubs, with a cosy, wood-panelled interior and a beautiful view out on to the Thames. If Morgan had been there with him, he'd have enjoyed pointing out all the yachting memorabilia on the walls while drinking a fine pint of locally brewed stout. Instead, he'd found himself listening to Natalie complaining about the bitchiness of her fellow cast members, and how much her feet ached at the end of every performance. The actress was pretty but shallow; he'd known that from the brief conversation he'd had with her while Morgan demonstrated her cranberry brownie recipe. Not too long ago, that wouldn't have been a problem. He'd have hung on her every word, made her feel like she was the only woman in the world, then taken her back to his flat where they'd have fucked for hours, those spectacular legs of hers locked round the back of his neck as he ploughed into her pussy. He'd cook her breakfast the following morning, and afterwards they'd go their separate ways with no regrets.

Now, though, the prospect of such a meaningless encounter didn't thrill him the way it used to. When he'd divorced Sasha, he'd vowed never to get involved with another woman on a long-term basis. He'd grown to like having his own space too much. For the first time in longer than he could remember, he had the freedom to do what he wanted when he wanted. Yet he found himself imagining what it would be like to wake up every morning with Morgan's glorious hair spread out on the next pillow, rousing her with a long, sensuous kiss before crawling down under the covers to lick her clit till she cried out his name.

It was such an enticing image, and more than once it had come to his mind while he'd been lying on his bed, fist enclosing his thick, hard cock. He saw himself licking a slow, wet trail over the sumptuous peaks and valleys of Morgan's body, losing himself in the taste and feel of her soft, yielding flesh. He ached to take her nipples between his lips, sucking till they peaked, before moving down towards her wet, waiting pussy. By the time he reached it she'd be desperate to feel his tongue there, begging in those throaty, lilting tones of hers for him to make her come. Using the fantasy to spur him on, he would wank harder and faster, until his come jetted out to land in pearly strings on his taut, heaving belly.

He had to get this obsession with her out of his system; the tension between them might be great for the show, but it wasn't doing the rest of his life any good at all. If only he could find some way of making that happen.

*   *   *

'Oh, just one last thing before you all leave ...'

The production meeting was breaking up, people making plans for lunch or heading out to work on filmed segments for next Saturday's programme, but Lucinda's voice cut through the babble of voices. She was clutching her BlackBerry with a wide smile on her face.

'I've just had an email with the latest viewing figures. We're up almost four hundred thousand a week since the first show in the series, and last week we peaked at just over three million viewers. Isn't that fantastic?'

'It's wonderful news,' Carl, the assistant producer, commented, 'and given how the ratings were slumping towards the end of Graham O'Neill's time on the show, it completely justifies the decision to bring in Scott and Morgan.'

'Oh, there's been a lot of hard work all round,' Lucinda replied, 'and I'm sure the figures will be even better this coming Saturday, seeing as we've got Zachary Klein on the show.' Hollywood heart-throb Klein, currently appearing as the villain in the latest of the *Captain Fearless* blockbusters, was in the UK on a promotional tour, and the booker for *Cook's Treats* had managed to secure him as a guest. Quite a few of the female members of the production team were already giddy at the prospect of the man parking his much-photographed bottom on the studio couch.

'How many more times is she going to mention the fact they've booked that bouffanted airhead?' Scott grumbled to Morgan.

She smiled, amused to see his nose clearly out of joint for once. 'Oh, he's not so bad,' she replied, even though the last film of Zachary Klein's she'd seen – some romantic comedy Carrie had dragged her along to, where he played a laid back boat captain who found himself stranded at sea with a spoiled, uptight heiress, a role that required him to spend most of his time shirtless – was so bad she'd struggled not to walk out before the end. 'I can't wait to see you being nice to him over a plate of eggs Benedict.'

'You haven't been paying attention, sweetheart. We

115

dropped that recipe. It doesn't fit in with his macrobiotic lifestyle, and his publicist is very anxious that we don't prepare him anything involving meat, dairy or processed foods. So I'm making buckwheat noodles with tofu.' Scott's lip curled in distaste. 'Just the thing the average viewer needs after a Friday night out on the lash.'

Morgan dragged her attention back to Lucinda, who was still talking. 'Anyway, people, I think we should celebrate. If you've got plans for Saturday night, cancel them. Everyone's invited to a party at mine.'

With a glance over at Scott, Morgan wondered whether he'd try to find some excuse for not attending. If he was working in his restaurant, fair enough, though she suspected he delegated the chef's duties to someone else at weekends. And she had to admit he'd been behaving himself over the last couple of weeks; no more sneaking off with the show's female guests or giving self-aggrandising interviews to the press where he tore into the reputation of his fellow chefs. As long as he wasn't too put out at having to accommodate the needs of Zachary Klein, a situation that for once would place Scott in the unusual position of not possessing the largest ego in the room, she suspected he might actually show up at Lucinda's.

'Oh, Morgan, a quick word ...' Lucinda beckoned to Morgan as she shovelled her notepad into her handbag and prepared to leave. 'I've been asking everyone else to bring a bottle on Saturday, but I wondered if you could whip up a few dozen of those delicious Parmesan and chilli biscuits you did on the show last week?'

'No problem,' Morgan replied, glad she hadn't made plans for Saturday afternoon either, 'and I'll do you some of my famous red onion and sheep's cheese tartlets, too, if you'd like?'

'Fabulous, darling. You're a real life-saver.'

It never failed to amaze Morgan that, despite being in charge of what was now officially the country's highest-rated cookery programme, Lucinda could barely boil an egg. But the party would be a good excuse for the crew to get to know each other a little better; the high-pressure schedule involved in preparing the show meant there wasn't usually much time for socialising once the cameras stopped rolling. Though Morgan thought it might be safer if she avoided Scott as much as she could; somehow, they always seemed to rub each other up the wrong way when they spent any time in each other's company. She'd been working so hard it wouldn't hurt to let her hair down for once, and she didn't want him ruining her enjoyment of the evening.

Lucinda lived in a beautiful four-bedroomed terraced house in Clerkenwell, close to City University and within walking distance of Scott's restaurant. Her husband worked for an investment bank, which was how they were able to afford to live in such a desirable part of London. Casting an appreciative glance at the house's ochre brick façade and high, white-framed windows, Morgan rapped the wrought iron knocker against the door and waited for an answer.

She'd spent most of the afternoon in her own kitchen, preparing the nibbles Lucinda had asked her to bring. The results of her baking were contained in a couple of plastic containers, the crumbly biscuits and delicate tartlets separated by layers of greaseproof paper. After the manic scenes in the studio that morning, there'd been something deliciously soothing about rubbing butter into flour to make the pastry for the tartlets, and slicing jalapeño peppers to place on top of the biscuits.

Never having had to deal with anyone, either on a professional or personal level, as high maintenance as Zachary Klein, she'd been astounded by the demands his publicity assistant had made. Even before Zachary would agree to appear on the show, a list of questions had to be emailed over for her approval. Anything that didn't relate to his new film was removed, apart from a couple of fairly bland questions relating to his diet.

It didn't get any easier once he arrived at the studio complex. A specific brand of bottled water had to be waiting for him in the green room, chilled but not cold, along with a bowl of organic dried apricots for him to munch on. 'Zachary has issues with low blood sugar,' the publicist explained.

'Hardly surprising, when he's living on tofu and fresh air,' Scott commented. Though he was cooking for Zachary during the show, he'd delegated the task of interviewing the actor to Morgan. No one on the production team had a problem with this; Morgan was sure they were hoping for some flirtatious banter. But though the actor was probably the most handsome man she'd ever seen, with glossy black hair that simply demanded to be ruffled by female fingers, and cheekbones so sharp they could be classified as lethal weapons, he had almost nothing in the way of personality. Every question she asked was answered with a reply that sounded like it had been given in a hundred interviews before, and would be given in another hundred after. He praised the buckwheat noodle dish – which, for all Scott's complaining about having to cater to such a restrictive diet, was packed with perfectly cooked, crisp vegetables and gave off a mouth-watering aroma of ginger and garlic – but Morgan noticed he didn't let more than a forkful pass his sculpted lips. She was glad when Lucinda told her to wrap up the segment. Zachary gave her a polite peck on the cheek before scooting off to his hired limo, ready for the next engagement on his publicity tour. The girls in the gallery squealed with envy into her earpiece, but as she told them after the show, they really hadn't missed out. Indeed, when she spoke to Carrie later, who'd rung demanding every last detail of her meeting with a genuine superstar, she compared it to being kissed by her grandmother,

'Morgan, darling, do come in!' Lucinda let Morgan into her home, giving her a welcoming hug in the hallway.

'Careful,' Morgan warned her. 'I've managed to get the nibbles all the way over from Clapham in one piece. I'd hate them to break now.'

'Well, bring them through into the kitchen, and we'll get them plated up. Gerry will get you a drink. Gerry?'

A man who had to be Lucinda's husband popped his head out of the living room doorway. With his close-cropped silver hair and the tracery of lines round his blue eyes, he had to be a good 20 years older than his wife; not quite what Morgan had been expecting. But his affection for his wife was strong, patting her on the bottom as she passed, and the smile he turned on Morgan was warmer and more genuine than any of those she'd received from Zachary Klein.

'Morgan, nice to meet you. What can I get you?'

'I'd love a glass of red wine.'

'Of course. We've got a rather nice bottle of Merlot open, if that's OK?'

'Lovely, thank you.'

Gerry poured her a glass of wine, which Lucinda carried for her, leading the way down the hall. The kitchen was better appointed than the one she had in her own flat, Morgan couldn't help but notice. She wondered whether Gerry cooked, or if the shiny copper pans, wooden block containing half-a-dozen cook's knives and string of garlic bulbs hanging from a hook on the wall were simply for show. Platters containing an assortment of cheese, pieces of fruit and seed-topped flatbreads stood ready to be taken through to the living room. Morgan put the containers she'd brought down on the scrubbed pine table and set about decanting their contents on to plates, pausing every now and again to take a sip of her wine.

When she'd finished, she took a better look round the kitchen, admiring the big, American-style fridge and the top-of-the range stove. French windows stood open, leading out on to a small walled garden. Glass lanterns hung from the branches of a cherry tree, the softly flickering tea lights within them creating an almost magical atmosphere. Though it was early October, there was just enough warmth left in the air to make it comfortable for those partygoers who chose to go outside to smoke or chat.

Lucinda scooped one of the Parmesan biscuits from a plate, popping it into her mouth. 'These are delicious, Morgan. I did think about putting in an order with that nice little delicatessen on Farringdon Road, but your biscuits are better than anything they have. Have you never thought of selling them?'

'Oh, I used to, a long time ago ...' It had long been a dream of Morgan's, back home in Cardiff, to open a little bakery, but she'd never been able to pull together the finances she needed to open premises of her own. Instead, she'd persuaded a local café cum delicatessen to take some of her biscuits to sell along with their range of speciality teas and home-made preserves. One of the regulars in that café turned out to work for a TV company based in the city and had loved Morgan's baked goods so much he'd tracked her down and persuaded her to demonstrate the recipes on the local news show. The rest was history.

'Well, I'll just have one more before the gluttons get their hands on them, then we'll take everything through, if you don't mind helping me?'

'Not at all,' Morgan assured Lucinda.

Having carried the food into the living room, Morgan felt she'd discharged her duties for the night and went to join the party. Quite a few of the production team had arrived by now, and most had brought their spouses or partners with them. She spotted Dan, the floor manager, with an arm draped round his visibly pregnant wife, and Carl, the assistant producer, feeding his boyfriend a sliver of Brie. Rumour had it they were planning to tie the knot in a civil partnership ceremony at Christmas, but they wanted to keep it a secret from Carl's mother, who was in denial about her son's true sexuality, even though he and David had been openly living together as a couple for three years.

And no doubt Scott would have found himself a date for tonight; she couldn't see him arriving at Lucinda's without some prime piece of arm candy to show off. Though, as she looked round the room, he didn't appear to have arrived yet.

'Been here long?' a familiar voice murmured in her ear.

She turned to see Scott, a bottle of Italian lager in his hand. He wore a battered leather jacket over a tight white T-shirt, and his hair appeared more windblown than usual. Morgan thought she'd never seen him looking quite so handsome. 'Yes, I've been helping Lucinda in the kitchen.' She glanced over at the table, where Donny, one of the cameramen, was piling his plate high with chunks of cheese, celery sticks and slices of French bread. 'I was going to suggest she might have over-catered, but you know how much the studio crew eats.'

'So that's what that little confab you were having at the end of the production meeting was about.'

'Why, did you think I might have been negotiating a pay rise behind your back?' Morgan replied, with the sweetest of smiles.

He shook his head. 'You're far too straightforward for that. And no, I wouldn't do something like that to you, before you say anything.' Scott took a swig of his lager. 'That's my agent's job.'

'Touché.' Morgan was surprised to find herself relaxing into this easy banter between herself and Scott. Still she couldn't resist asking the question that nagged at her. 'So, are you here on your own tonight?'

He nodded. 'I thought it probably wasn't a good idea to bring anyone, just in case there's an emergency at the restaurant that needs my attention. I don't normally go anywhere near the place on a Saturday, but seeing as it's five minutes down the road it would be hard to refuse ...'

To Morgan's ears, that sounded like a flimsy excuse. Maybe Scott was trying to disguise the fact he'd asked someone to come with him and been turned down. And wouldn't that be a turn-up for the books?

'Have you met Lucinda's husband?' Morgan asked, quickly changing the conversation.

'Gerry? Yeah, he's a nice guy. We've been having a chat, and it turns out he used to eat at Le Cartouche when I was head chef there. It's always nice to meet a fan of my roast saddle of rabbit ... Look out, Janice is on the prowl.' He waved his bottle in the direction of a grey-haired woman walking towards them with a determined expression on her face. The show's chief home economist, Janice was the person least likely to switch off from work mode in a social setting.

'What do you think she wants?'

'I don't know, but I don't fancy sticking around to find out. Come on, unless you want to find yourself pinned in a corner discussing the best way to julienne vegetables all evening.' Scott grabbed Morgan's hand, guiding her through the little knots of party guests and out of the living room. By the time

Janice made her way out into the hall, Scott and Morgan were already standing on the first-floor landing.

'D'you think she'll follow us?' Morgan asked in hushed tones.

'Maybe, but just to make sure …' Scott opened the door of the first room they came to, and hurried Morgan inside.

They found themselves standing in a bedroom that must double as a study, judging by the shiny new iMac sitting on a sturdy oak desk in the corner and the bookshelves that filled all the available wall space, crammed with everything from old university textbooks to dog-eared Agatha Christie paperbacks. Giggling, Morgan plonked herself down on the sofa. Scott sat down beside her, so close she could smell his signature cologne, something subtle and woody.

He smiled at her, his features softening. 'Phew, that was a close shave, but I think we've given her the slip.'

'How long do you think we should give it before we make our way back down there?' Morgan's heart pounded in her chest. Try as she might, she couldn't put the reaction down purely to having raced up a flight of stairs.

'That depends on whether you need that wine glass refilling, or whether you can cope with one of these …' He produced two more bottles of lager from his jacket pockets. Whether he'd brought them with him or liberated them from the supply on the dining table she didn't ask.

'That will be perfect,' she said, watching Scott prise off the bottle tops with a metal opener shaped like a shark's mouth that hung from his key ring. He passed one of the opened bottles to her, then chinked his own against hers in a toast.

'Here's to *Cook's Treats* blowing all the other cookery shows out of the water,' he said.

Morgan took a drink, relishing the crisp coldness of the lager. 'You sound awfully cheerful for a man who was absolutely convinced he'd been given the wrong co-presenter.'

'Hey, I don't think I ever said "wrong". Inexperienced and unprofessional, possibly, but you've proved I was wide off the mark on both counts. I mean, you dealt with Zachary Klein beautifully this morning. You completely avoided being sucked

122

into the vacuum that is his personality.'

'You're not still smarting about having to cook vegetables for him, are you?' Morgan grinned. 'Or is it the fact he was just so damn handsome? Handsome – and incredibly boring.' She wasn't sure how it had happened, but somehow they seemed to be sitting even closer together than before. Scott's muscular, denim-clad thigh pressed against hers; she swore she could feel the heat radiating from his skin, even through the layers of clothing. Trying to ignore the fact her pussy was coming alive even with this minimal bodily contact, she continued, 'You know, this reminds me of the last time I sneaked away in the middle of a party.'

'Really? So you make a habit out of this kind of anti-social behaviour, then?'

'Not exactly. I was 18, and my friend, Bronwen, threw a party to celebrate finishing our A-level exams. Well, you've never seen anything like a bunch of Cardiff girls when they let their hair down. It's a scary sight. People were getting absolutely wasted on cheap cider and Irish cream liqueur, and someone had brought along one of those portable karaoke machines, so we could murder our favourite Take That songs ...'

Scott regarded her, bottle halfway to his lips. 'So why did you flee this scene of wanton debauchery?'

'Because I'd finally got my hands on the guy I'd fancied all year. Rhodri Thomas. He was captain of the rugby team at our sixth form college and he was absolutely lush. Playing rugby gives you the best thigh muscles ever, you know?' Even as she said it, Morgan couldn't help thinking whatever Scott did to work out had much the same effect. Doing her best to fight her powerful physical reaction to the man, she continued, 'So we did one of the most clichéd things you can ever do at a mate's party. We crept up to the room where everyone had piled their coats on the bed so we could share our first kiss.'

'Ah, how innocent that sounds.' From the faraway look on his face, Scott appeared to be reliving some similar incident from his own past. 'And how was that kiss?'

'Well worth waiting for,' Morgan admitted. 'It would really

have put me off if he'd been a bad kisser, but he knew how to use just the right amount of tongue, and when to spice it up by breaking off so we could look into each other's eyes ...'

'Why is it you have the uncanny knack of making everything in life sound like a recipe?' Scott asked, but he was clearly hanging on her every word. More than that, he'd put his bottle down, and his face was only inches away from Morgan's, so when she looked directly at him their eyes met, just as hers had with Rhodri's more than a decade ago. And, just as on that night, she saw pure, undisguised desire reflected back at her.

She didn't answer his question, couldn't do anything but act on the overwhelming erotic impulse surging through her. For the briefest moment, Morgan wondered whether she was about to make the biggest mistake of her career, mixing business with pleasure – and there was another cooking metaphor for Scott to add to his list, she thought giddily – then his lips met hers.

All the kisses she'd experienced up to this point in her life paled in comparison to the feel of his mouth against her own, soft lips and clever tongue working to turn her to a helpless, melting puddle of need. Her fingers twined in Scott's thick, untidy hair as his fingers roamed over the nape of her neck and the soft skin exposed by her sparkly vest top.

She wasn't sure, but when they finally broke the kiss she thought she heard him murmur something like, 'Want you so badly.' Was the brash, self-centred Scott really expressing his desire in such heartfelt tones?

Her only response was to pluck at his T-shirt, working it free of his jeans so she could stroke the warm, flat expanse of his belly. He pulled away for long enough to peel the garment over his head, revealing firm pecs, lightly sprinkled with soft, sandy hair.

So this was how it was going to be, quick and urgent? That suited Morgan fine. She was all too conscious of the party taking place downstairs, and a small voice at the back of her mind warned her that if she and Scott were away from the gathering for too long, someone would surely notice and come looking for them.

His hands on her top, seeking to remove it, brought her back to the present. Letting Scott strip it from her, she didn't object when he quickly followed up by flicking open the catch of her bra. Teasing him, she held the cups tight to her chest with her hands as he pulled the straps down, so her breasts weren't revealed to him until the last possible moment.

He took a breast in each hand, cupping the soft flesh as though he held something more precious than diamonds. 'Oh, they feel even better than they look,' he exclaimed. Bending his head, he latched on to one nipple with his greedy, sucking mouth. Morgan's nipples stiffened to peaks in his mouth, and she felt the suckling sensation all the way down to her pussy, wanting his mouth there too.

Reaching for his belt, she made short work of undoing it, not wanting anything to impede their race to be naked. Her palm brushed over his cock, trapped behind his zip, and she felt it twitch in response, anxious to be free. In other circumstances, she might have delayed the pleasure of releasing him, but they didn't have the luxury of time. So she brought his zip down in a smooth movement, reaching in to discover that, unlike in her fantasies, he hadn't bothered with underwear tonight. Her fingers closed round the hot, solid length of him, and he sighed at her touch.

'Oh, Morgan ...' His words tailed off as he buried his face in her freshly washed locks. Fingers still toying with her hard nipples, he breathed in the scent of her hair.

Undoing her skirt, Morgan let it fall to the floor. The lacy boy shorts she wore beneath it were already soaking with her juices, and she rubbed herself through the wet material, feeling little sparks of pleasure shoot through her sex.

'How do you want me?' she asked Scott.

'The sooner the better,' he replied, guiding her up on to the couch so her curvy rump was facing him, high in the air. When he hooked his fingers into the waistband of her shorts and began to ease them down, she shivered in anticipation of the moment her pouting pussy would be revealed to him, peeping out from between her thighs.

Once he'd bared her completely, Scott stepped away.

Looking over her shoulder, Morgan watched as he hunted through his jeans pockets. Finding what he'd been looking for, he unwrapped the condom and rolled it over his shaft. Getting into place behind her, he smoothed his hands over her bottom before sliding his cock into her tight, velvet depths.

Having him inside her felt so good it was almost sinful. Big and deliciously thick, his cock stimulated her in all the right places. And unlike the other really well-endowed men she'd been with in her time, he seemed to know exactly how to use those extra inches, instead of believing that simply being big was enough.

'Fuck me, Scott,' she demanded, asking for her pleasure in a direct way that was usually alien to her. Scott responded with fast, urgent thrusts that made her breasts bounce and her knees slide along the cushions beneath her. She clung on tight to the back of the couch as he pulled out almost all the way before driving back into her, harder than before.

'Yes, yes, that's it!' she panted, even as she wondered quite how she'd reached a place where she was kneeling on a couch in her work colleague's house, naked but for her heels, while a man she'd barely been able to stand a matter of weeks ago ploughed into her with strong, confident strokes.

Scott reached underneath her to stimulate her clit with his fingers and she found herself shuddering with a tiny, unexpected orgasm, her inner muscles fluttering like a butterfly's wings around his cock. She cried out in pleasure, but Scott didn't even pause in his thrusts. She could feel his body banging against her buttocks as he neared his climax.

With Scott's hands caressing her breasts once more, Morgan felt the need to stroke her clit, the heel of her hand pressed against her mound, sandwiching the thin wall of flesh between it and Scott's cock. Again she came, her cry a pleasure-sated squeal this time. The sweetness of her orgasm seemed to have robbed her of her caution; she didn't care any more whether someone might pass by in search of the bathroom and hear the noise she made.

The rippling of Morgan's pussy around his shaft was too much for Scott, triggering his own climax. She felt every jerk as he filled the condom with his come, his hands snug around her waist.

'Thank you,' he whispered, dropping an affectionate kiss on her bare shoulder. For a moment, she felt closer to him than she ever had, then he pulled out of her with an abrupt motion. As though a spell had been broken, she remembered where they were, and where they really ought to be.

'Do you think anyone will have missed us?' she asked, scrambling back into her clothes. Her underwear had somehow been kicked under the couch in the throes of their passion, and she had to hunt to retrieve it.

Scott shook his head. 'If the booze keeps flowing, they won't have noticed a thing. You know,' he added, as he zipped his jeans up, 'as amazing a fuck as that was, I really think we should keep it as a one-off. I mean, the gossip columnists would have a field day if we started seeing each other on a regular basis, and it might not be the best publicity for the show.'

If he expected her to object to his proposal, hankering after a more meaningful relationship, he was disappointed. His words seemed to echo her thoughts about the danger of getting their personal and professional lives mixed up. Morgan ignored the small, traitorous part of her that thought how nice it would be to have that gorgeous cock filling her on a regular basis, to fall asleep in his arms and wake to find him hard and ready for her again. 'You're right. It's never a good idea to get involved with someone you work with, in my experience. There's too much at stake.'

When they left the study, they went in separate directions, Scott back down to the living room and Morgan in search of the bathroom, which she found at the far end of the landing. By the time she returned to the party, Scott was deep in conversation with a couple of the cameramen, laughing louder than anyone at the punchline to a joke. No one who saw him would ever believe that less than five minutes earlier, he'd been buried to the hilt in her pussy, calling out her name as he came deep inside her.

Helping herself to another drink and one of the last

remaining onion and cheese tartlets, she was cornered by Janice.

'Ah, there you are, Morgan. I've been looking for you everywhere ...'

Still buzzing from her unexpected fuck, Morgan barely heard a word of Janice's complaint about the extra work she'd had to do in preparation for that morning's show, accommodating Zachary Klein's dietary demands. She could have thanked the woman for inadvertently pushing her and Scott into each other's arms. Now came the small matter of behaving as though the whole thing had never happened.

Chapter Six

'AND SO WE BOTH agreed it would be better if it didn't happen again.'

Morgan wasn't sure quite why she was confessing to Carrie all the details of what had taken place at the party. She only knew she had to talk to someone about it, and Carrie had always proved herself to be nothing less than discreet when it came to the subject of Morgan's love life. Having replayed the scene in Lucinda Leeson's study over and over in her mind for a good 24 hours after it happened, she finally rang Carrie telling her she needed to see her, and was she free for afternoon tea? Now she sat in Carrie's small, welcoming living room, revealing how it felt to be naked and in Scott's arms, flushed with the heat of sudden, urgent sex.

Whatever the response she'd been expecting when she came to the end of her story, it wasn't the look of disbelief that crossed her best friend's face.

'Are you completely mad? If what you told me isn't an exaggeration, you've just had some of the best sex of your life and yet you've got no intention of going back for more.'

'Don't forget, this is Scott Harley we're talking about. The man who gets a kick out of bawling out his kitchen assistants in front of everyone. The man who sulks if he isn't the constant centre of attention. Why would I want to get involved with someone like that?'

In the kitchen, the kettle whistled as it came to the boil. Carrie rose from the couch, stretching the legs she'd had curled beneath her as she sat, and went to make a fresh pot of coffee. As she left, she shot a parting statement over her shoulder. 'You know, for someone who still claims to hate Scott Harley with a passion, your eyes light up every time you talk about him, like you can't wait to see him again.'

Morgan digested those words while she waited for Carrie to return with the coffee. If this was anyone but herself they were talking about, she'd be priding Carrie on her judgement. Her friend was one of the most perceptive people she knew. But she'd never met Scott, and until she saw what he was really like, she couldn't really grasp the truth of the situation. Not that there was any likelihood of that happening in the near future.

Carrie's voice cut into her reverie. 'Actually, it's funny we should be discussing Scott Harley *again*.' Her emphasis on the word was subtle but pointed. 'Because I have a surprise for you.'

'Really?' Morgan's interest was piqued.

Carrie refilled their coffee cups, and cut herself a second slice of the lemon drizzle cake Morgan had baked in advance of their impromptu afternoon tea, before continuing. 'You remember I told you Claire won one of the sealed bids at that charity dinner she went to a couple of weeks ago?' Claire was the editor of the magazine Carrie worked for. Morgan had never met her, but Carrie always spoke highly of the woman. 'Well, she can't use the prize now because her husband's whisked her away on a second honeymoon, so she passed it on to me because she knows it's my birthday next week. And you're never going to believe what it is. Dinner for two at the chef's table in The Ludgate Chop House. It's going to be a real treat. The man himself will be cooking for us.'

'Well, I've tasted Scott's food on the show enough times to know you're really going to enjoy –' Morgan broke off as she realised what Carrie had said. 'What do you mean, cooking for *us*?'

'I did think about asking Josh to come with me, but it's a tradition for the two of us to go out on my birthday. What was it last year, cocktails at the Llama Lounge? And the year before that, gourmet burgers at that place in Seven Dials?' Carrie's grin was undiluted wickedness. 'To be honest, I just want to see the look on Scott Harley's face when you walk into his kitchen. And I know you're not going to turn me down,

130

because there's nothing sexier than being fed by a man you really have the hots for, is there?'

Morgan very nearly backed out of dinner at the Chop House, her hand reaching for the phone to dial Carrie and tell her she was terribly sorry, but she'd come down with a 48-hour bug and why didn't Josh take her place instead? But she couldn't let her best friend down on her birthday, and anyway, she'd always been a terrible liar.

Looking in the mirror, fixing her peridot choker around her neck even though she couldn't have said why she needed the boost that came from wearing her lucky piece of jewellery, Morgan felt butterflies fluttering anxiously in her belly.

What do you have to be nervous about? she chided herself. It's only Scott. It's not like you don't see him almost every day of the week. And yes, you might be on his turf for once, rather than the neutral setting of the *Cook's Treats* production office, but you're a big girl. You can take care of yourself.

She wouldn't have needed the pep talk if it hadn't been for the fact the last week had been one of the most difficult of her life. Nothing had prepared her for the moment when she'd walked into the office and seen Scott for the first time since the night of the party. Even though they'd both made it clear there'd be no acknowledgement of what had happened between them, she couldn't stop herself hoping for some word, some little gesture that would let her know their lovemaking had meant something to him. Instead, he treated her the same way he always had in the office, with friendliness and professional courtesy. It was exactly what she'd wanted from him, so why did it leave her feeling so hollow inside?

To make things worse, the tension between them, which she'd hoped would dissipate after Scott fucked her, was stronger than ever. It might have made for good television, but she knew she needed a proper resolution to the situation. She'd thought sleeping with Scott once would be enough to get him out of her system, but she'd been wrong.

Spritzing herself with perfume before checking her reflection one last time, Morgan went to wait for the taxi she'd ordered to take her to the restaurant, determined not to let thoughts of what might have been spoil her evening with Carrie.

When the waiter brought the Gray party through to the chef's table, Scott's heart missed a beat. He didn't recognise the petite blonde with the long, luscious legs emerging from the hem of a daringly short blue crushed velvet dress, but her dining companion was all too familiar. Morgan Jones, looking as alluring as he'd ever seen her. Her hair tumbled down over her creamy shoulders, left almost bare by the thin straps of her floor-length black dress. Strong boning in the bodice supported her amazing breasts, pushing them together and forming a cleavage he could happily lose himself in, and a slit almost all the way to her thigh offered glimpses of her bare legs, glistening with some silky body oil, as she walked. Classy, sophisticated and unbelievably fuckable, she was a million miles from the frumpy girl in ill-fitting jogging gear he'd publicly criticised so long ago, and his cock stirred in his checked chef's trousers at the sight of her.

His first instinct was to sweep the place settings from the table, lay Morgan down on the crisp white cloth and bury his face between her beautiful tits. He didn't care that her friend would be watching on in astonishment, as well as the entire kitchen staff. Fucking her in the heart of his restaurant would be the most outrageous thing he'd ever done, but right now, he wanted her more than he ever had.

Was she wearing anything beneath that carefully engineered dress, or would he pull the zip down to discover she was braless beneath it? He pictured her in nothing but damp lace panties that he would simply tear from her body, not wanting any impediment to the moment when he buried his mouth between her legs. He hadn't tasted her pussy the night he'd fucked her at the party; there hadn't been time. But he knew when he did, it would be as sweet and juicy as the ripest peach he'd ever served up to diners, so delicious he wouldn't be able to stop himself lapping up every drop of her juice.

And when he'd driven her to the brink of orgasm with his

tongue, he'd spread her thighs and drive his cock into her wet, clutching channel, fucking her till her heels drummed against the table and she cried out in ecstasy, while all around them his staff looked on, so turned on they were stroking themselves through their chef's whites ...

With an effort, he forced himself to focus on the reality of the scene in front of him, rather than the reality. As waiters rushed in and out to pick up orders or return empty plates and various chefs shouted orders to their assistants or called for meals to be plated up, Morgan sat in the still eye of this culinary hurricane, awaiting his attention.

Scott hesitated for a long moment before going over and talked the two women through the menu for the evening. He hadn't been able to tell anyone what happened at Lucinda's party, much as he'd wanted to. Usually, he'd have bragged about his latest conquest to Chris, who'd been happily married for the last six years and never showed the slightest trace of envy when Scott talked about the actresses and lingerie models he'd slept with. But talking about Morgan meant dragging up emotions he didn't feel comfortable discussing. So used to women he could fuck and forget about, he'd woken the morning after the party and caught himself reaching out to feel Morgan's soft, voluptuous body in bed beside him, before remembering she hadn't even made it as far as his home.

What stopped him from admitting that, for the first time since he'd split from Sasha, he wanted more than just a one-night stand? Pride? Fear of losing his independence – or, worse, that Morgan would reject him? She'd been ice-cool to him in rehearsals all week, so maybe he didn't mean anything to her after all. Though there was something about the way she kept her head turned as he approached the table, not wanting to meet his gaze, that made him wonder whether she too was struggling to conceal her real feelings.

Get over yourself, Harley, he told himself. Or just admit you fucked up.

He did neither. Instead, he greeted Morgan and her companion with a broad smile. 'Good evening, ladies. Welcome to the Chop House. Let me explain how the tasting menu works …'

In the short interval between seeing Morgan walk into his kitchen and launching into his usual spiel about his special tasting menu, he'd already decided what he'd be cooking for her, even though he never revealed his choices until they arrived at the table, to offer his diners the element of surprise. He'd start with roasted red pepper and tomato soup, topped with a wild mushroom foam. In turn, that would be followed by ravioli of lobster and scallop, served with a delicate fennel-infused sauce, tender Welsh lamb with a leek and potato puree and seasonal vegetables and, for dessert, gingerbread soufflé, served with malted milk ice cream. Each course, should the women wish it, would be perfectly matched by the restaurant's sommelier to a wine that would compliment it in terms of richness and flavour.

The waiter arrived with glasses of prosecco for Morgan and her friend, who she'd introduced as Carrie. He waited till Scott finished his speech before setting them down.

'Well, I'm really looking forward to what you're going to cook for us,' Carrie said. 'What do you think, Morgan?'

Morgan sipped her drink before replying. Scott couldn't help wondering why he found it so important that she be impressed by the sight of him working in his natural environment, given that she was hardly a stranger to his style of cooking.

'I'm sure Scott's going to astonish me,' she said, her eyes meeting Scott's for the briefest moment before looking away, giving him no time to decipher the emotions they conveyed. 'He always does.'

Stepping on to the pavement outside the Chop House, Morgan found the coolness of the autumn evening a sharp contrast to the steamy warmth of the restaurant's kitchen. Pulling her black velvet wrap a little tighter around her shoulders, she hoped she and Carrie wouldn't have to wait too long for a taxi. At that moment, a sleek black cab turned the corner, its yellow "FOR HIRE" light blazing. Carrie stuck out a hand to flag it down.

It hadn't taken much for Carrie to persuade Morgan to go back to her house for a nightcap. Taxi drivers were notoriously reluctant to ferry late-night passengers south of the River Thames for fear of not picking up a return fare to make the journey worthwhile. Morgan knew she ran the risk of falling asleep on Carrie's sofa in all her finery, but at this moment that was not an unwelcome prospect.

The two women climbed into the back of the taxi. Carrie gave her address to the driver and he set off in the direction of West Hampstead, the streets quiet at this late hour.

Seat belt safely buckled, Carrie relaxed back against the padded leather seat with a sigh. 'I think that was probably the best meal I've eaten in my entire life. Oh, that ice cream – and those little truffles that came with coffee ...'

'You and your sweet tooth. 'Morgan grinned. 'But I'm glad you enjoyed yourself.'

'Meaning you didn't?' Carrie sat up sharply.

'I didn't say that.' Morgan shifted in her seat. 'You're right, the food was delicious. But Scott's such a fantastic cook, I always knew it was going to be. And he runs his kitchen much more professionally than you'd expect from some of his TV appearances.'

'Which you must know are edited to make him look like a complete tyrant,' Carrie pointed out. 'So what's the problem?'

'I don't know. I – I just felt a bit awkward around Scott, that's all. Did he seem distant to you?'

'Well, why would you be asking me a question like that, if you really didn't care about the man? And for what it's worth, no, I don't think he was being distant at all. He was cooking for sixty covers in one of the busiest kitchens in London, so of course that was going to be his top priority. But he gave us as much attention as he could and he talked us through all the dishes when they arrived – which I suspect is something the waiter would normally do, so I think we were getting special treatment there.'

Morgan stared out of the window as the taxi sped past the vast Gothic façade of St Pancras station. This should have been Carrie's evening, yet she'd somehow managed to turn the focus back to her growing obsession with Scott, and she couldn't help feeling guilty. 'I'm sorry, Carrie,' she blurted out, 'I'll shut up about him now, I promise.'

'I'll believe that when it happens,' Carrie retorted, not unkindly. 'But if you want my opinion, I watched Scott Harley all evening and the man is crazy about you.'

'Are you serious?'

'The way he looks at you, the softness in his tone when he speaks to you, even when he's barking out instructions to everyone else in the room … And he can't stop finding excuses to touch your hand or brush your hair away from your face. If you ask me, he wants to be with you every bit as much as you want to be with him. But the problem is you're both so damn stubborn, neither one of you is going to do anything about it. You've made this ridiculous pact that you're not going to mix business with pleasure, but trust me, becoming a couple doesn't have to change anything about the way you work together.'

The way Carrie outlined the situation, it all sounded so simple. All she had to do was tell Scott how she really felt about him, and hope he reciprocated her feelings, just as Carrie claimed he would. But she suspected it might prove a heck of a lot more difficult than it sounded.

Chapter Seven

IT WAS RONNI WHO came up with the idea of filming *Cook's Treats* in Scott's home. Spending three weeks with the show as an intern, Ronni was studying for a post-graduate qualification in television journalism, and struck Morgan as fiercely ambitious. She arrived at every production meeting with a long list of suggestions, and was determined to get at least one of them on air before she had to return to her course.

Plans were already being drawn up for the shows to be broadcast over the Christmas period. These would be pre-recorded a couple of weeks in advance, meaning the crew could have some well deserved time off to spend with their families, and in previous years they'd been filmed on the usual set. Ronni, inevitably, had thought of a change to the format.

'Why don't you produce them on location?' she asked.

'Did you have anywhere in mind?' Lucinda replied.

'Well, I did have a couple of ideas ...' Ronni consulted her extensive sheaf of notes. 'You could maybe go down to The Ludgate Chop House, let the cameras take a behind-the-scenes look at what Scott does when he's in the kitchen.'

Scott vetoed that idea with a curt shake of the head. 'Sorry, sweetheart. You've no idea of the mayhem it would cause, trying to fit a film crew in the kitchen when we're working.'

'And it could be viewed as a breach of the rules on product placement,' Lucinda added. 'Some people might see it as a plug for the restaurant. Any other suggestions?'

Ronni glanced back at her notepad. 'In that case, how about filming in the presenters' actual kitchen?'

'Now that I like,' Lucinda said, before either Morgan or Scott had the chance to interject. 'And I think the viewers would love it, too. Seeing Scott preparing one of his gourmet meals at home, it'll make them realise how easy it would be for them to do the same thing. We can do one show from Scott's place and the other from Morgan's. Smart thinking, Ronni.'

Lucinda moved on smoothly to the subject of whether they should book guests for those shows or simply repeat a couple of the best interviews from the series so far, leaving Morgan to wonder just what she'd been let in for.

The quiet Regency building that housed Scott's flat was easy to spot. The battered white van bearing the production company's logo parked before it let Morgan know she was in the right place. Pressing the buzzer, she heard Scott's voice snap, 'Yes?' into the entry phone. From his abrupt tone of voice, she knew it was far from the first time he'd had to answer the door this morning.

'Hi, Scott, it's Morgan.' She shook her umbrella before furling it. A heavy rain had been falling all morning, showing no signs of letting up. When they'd first discussed shooting in Scott's home they'd looked into the possibility of filming on the roof terrace, but today's weather made that an impossibility.

'Oh, hey, Morgan. Come on up. I'm on the top floor.'

The door buzzed open and Morgan climbed the four flights of stairs to where Scott stood waiting for her.

'Remind me who thought this was a good idea,' he muttered, letting her into the flat.

When she'd seen the magazine photos of his home, it had been immaculate, with not so much as a stray newspaper cluttering up the place. Now, there was chaos everywhere. Cables snaked through the flat, and free-standing lights had been set up in the living room. A Christmas tree stood in one corner of the room, giving off an appealing scent of fresh pine. The strings of tinsel and coloured baubles hanging from its branches didn't strike Morgan as suiting Scott's tastes, and when she picked up one of the gaudily-wrapped presents sitting beneath it and gave it an experimental shake, it sounded suspiciously like an empty box. She wouldn't be at all surprised if that same tree found its way to her flat for the filming of the next show.

Walking through to the kitchen, she found the duo of home economists, Janice and Nina, busy chopping and peeling vegetables in preparation for Scott's cookery segment. Once they'd finished those, they'd be moving on to weighing out the ingredients for her own contribution to the show, cute little cupcakes decorated to resemble Christmas puddings.

'Can I get you a coffee?' Scott asked, and when she nodded gratefully, he poured her a cup from a shiny Italian coffee maker that stood on one of the work surfaces.

That was as close as they came to having any kind of conversation for the next couple of hours. Hardly had she taken a sip of the rich, aromatic brew than she was whisked into the bathroom to have her make-up touched up, before joining Scott on his butterscotch leather sofa to film the introduction and links to the various pre-recorded items that would be slotted in when the show was put together in post-production.

Cooking in Scott's lavishly appointed kitchen proved to be a pleasure, even with the camera's intrusive presence following her every step of the way. Unlike the appliances in Lucinda Leeson's home, his top-of-the-range stove with its gas hobs and convection oven was used on a regular basis, and his collection of knives was honed to razor sharpness.

As ever, she couldn't help but be struck by his air of calm self-assurance once the cameras rolled, and she wondered again how much of his barking, bullying chef persona was really an act. At one point, as the camera panned down to his finished plate of turkey pot pie, he slipped Morgan a little wink, unnoticed by everyone else. Carrie's words rung in her ears: 'He wants to be with you every bit as much as you want to be with him.' She had to discover the truth of those words, sooner rather than later.

As the crew packed up to leave, Morgan lingered in the kitchen, admiring the pots of herbs on his windowsill, the fruit bowl piled high with lemons and limes, ready to be sliced and squeezed into whatever recipe he was working on. 'I don't want to sound cheeky, but I'd love another cup of coffee if there is one. It's Blue Mountain, isn't it?'

Scott nodded. 'Just got a fresh supply last week, from the Algerian place in Soho. It's expensive, but it's so much nicer than some boring old French blend.'

'Well, I can't promise the same when you come over to mine for filming next week, but I do have some wonderful toffee vodka you might like.' Taking a deep breath, confident no one was left to overhear this turn in the conversation, she said, 'Scott, we really need to talk about what happened at Lucinda's party.'

He stiffened, pausing in the act of refilling the coffee machine. 'I thought we'd decided not to discuss it. It was a pleasant one-off. It didn't mean anything more.'

'But that's the point. It did – does mean more than that to me, and if you're honest, it does to you, too.' Growing bolder, Morgan continued, 'We were so worried about what might happen if the press got wind of the fact we were more than just colleagues on the show, but you know what? I really don't care what they think. Carrie said some things that made a lot of sense the night we had dinner at the Chop House, and she made me see that if I'm not careful, I'm in danger of missing out on something very special.'

'Morgan, you know I don't have time for a relationship ...'

'Says who? OK, so you work long hours in the restaurant, but not every night of the week. We could make this work, I know we could. And you can't deny there's a spark between us whenever we're together. If the viewers can see that, I'm damn sure you can.'

She reached out, linking her fingers in his loosely enough that he could pull them away if he wanted to. If he did, she'd take it as a sign she was wasting her time, and he really didn't want to be with her on anything but a professional level. Instead, he tightened the grip a little, pulling her to him.

For a moment, neither of them spoke. Morgan's eyes blazed, defying Scott to deny the electricity sizzling between them. A pulse beat steadily between her legs; she felt weak with need for him.

'Do you feel that?' she whispered.

By way of answer, he crushed his lips to hers, his kiss driving the breath from her. She cupped the point of his chin in her hands, returning the kiss with equal passion. His tongue traced along her lips before delving back into her mouth, probing and exploring. Their lower bodies ground together, the bulge in Scott's jeans leaving Morgan in no doubt as to how badly he wanted her.

Breaking the kiss, he murmured, 'Shall we take this to the bedroom?'

'Lead the way,' she replied.

'OK, though we'll need some supplies to take with us.'

Baffled as to what he meant, Morgan watched Scott take a pot of clear manuka honey from one of the cupboards and a pomegranate from the fruit bowl, before pulling a little paring knife from the wooden block. Satisfied with his choices, he turned and left the kitchen. Morgan followed him to the bedroom, with its white-painted walls and huge king-sized bed, topped and tailed with wrought iron rails.

Scott set the honey and the pomegranate down on the night stand. Sitting on the bed, he beckoned Morgan to join him. She kicked off her shoes, and did as he requested.

'Now, where were we …?' Scott murmured, before kissing her with even more passion than before. Rolling together on the bed, they fell into a caress, beginning to learn more about the other's body. Before, they'd been pressed by the constraints of their surroundings and the fear of a curious partygoer walking in on them. Now, they had all the time in the world to discover the sensitive places, the little touches that made them squirm with delight or sigh with the sweetest of pleasure.

Morgan nuzzled at Scott's neck, breathing in his familiar cologne, mixed with a richer, muskier scent all of his own. Crouching over him, she settled her crotch on to the solid contour of his cock, still trapped in his jeans. Humping herself gently against the hardness there sent little quivers of pleasure through her pussy.

In return, Scott's hands had worked their way up under her top, and were squeezing her breasts together. The catch at the front of her bra came undone as he fiddled with it, letting the soft mounds of flesh spill out into his welcoming grasp.

Two could play at that game. She pushed his T-shirt up, revealing the flat, golden expanse of his stomach. While Scott worked to strip her entirely of her top and bra, she peeled off the T-shirt so she could nip and lick at his flat, pink nipples.

Suddenly, a comment of Carrie's popped into her mind and she giggled.

'What's so funny?' Scott asked, breaking off from thumbing her nipples into tight, aching peaks.

'Oh, something Carrie said, when I first found out I was going to be working with you. She told me you should never trust a skinny cook. I just wondered what she'd say about one who was such a nicely put together arrangement of muscles and –' She reached lower, unzipping his fly and pushing her fingers inside to touch the hard length of his shaft. 'What would you call this? Just another muscle or …?'

'I'd call it a rock-hard cock that's just dying to sink itself in your tight pussy,' Scott replied, his voice a low, erotic growl that made Morgan's juices flow more strongly than ever. 'A cock that could never get tired of fucking you. Anywhere, any time, whenever you want me.' He tugged at the waistband of Morgan's black leggings, pulling them down, leaving her in nothing but her soaking wet panties. 'Because you're not so badly put together yourself, Morgan Jones, with your beautiful hair and your gorgeous breasts …'

His mouth closed around her nipple, the soft suction causing Morgan's pussy to clench with desire. Slipping a finger between her thighs, she teased her clit through the wet lace of her panties.

'In fact,' Scott continued, 'I'd say you looked good enough to eat.' He grinned, lust etched across his handsome features, and for a moment she thought he was about to rip off her panties and replace her busily circling finger with his tongue. Instead, he reached for the pot of honey.

'Lie back, Morgan,' he instructed her. 'I've had this recipe in mind for a while, but never had the right person to prepare it on.'

'Don't you mean prepare it *for*?' she asked, but the first

cool drops of honey landing on her naked, overheated skin let her know he'd chosen exactly the right word. Working quickly, Scott drizzled a trail over both breasts, down to the soft curve of her belly, stopping just short of her underwear.

Setting down the pot, he took the pomegranate, quickly cutting it open and squeezing one half over Morgan's torso, the seeds falling to land like scattered jewels on her flesh. Only then did he peel down her panties, tossing them aside before removing his jeans and boxer shorts. His cock reared up from its sandy nest of hair, bobbing with his movements as he crawled up the bed beside her.

'Mmm. Definitely the tastiest thing I've whipped up in a long time,' he told her, before bending his head to lick up the mixture of sticky honey and tart pomegranate seeds. He took his time, guided by Morgan's sighs and moans to spend a little longer sucking at the stiff points of her nipples. When he eventually moved low enough that he could run his tongue tip over the puffy outer lips of her pussy, Morgan was practically begging him to give her the satisfaction she needed. His erotic feasting on her body had taken her to a state where she knew it would only take the lightest of touches on her clit to have her dissolving in orgasm.

At last, he guided her thighs wide apart, gripping her bum cheeks and pulling her on to his waiting mouth. His tongue lashed over the molten folds of her sex, licking along the whole length of her cleft. Briefly, he brushed over her anal rosebud, and she shivered at the thought of him pressing his tongue deeper, maybe even teasing that tight, untried entrance with a finger.

Scott seemed to realise where she needed to be stimulated most urgently, for his tongue returned to her clit, flickering like a lizard's over the swollen bud until she cried out, gripping fistfuls of his hair and crushing his face against her as she wrung every drop of sensation from her orgasm.

Riding out the last shallow waves, she released her hold on him. He gazed up at her, chin and lips glazed with her juices. When they kissed, she tasted herself on him, a rich, complex bouquet that was uniquely hers.

143

'And now for the main course …' Now Scott reached for a condom, sheathing himself before laying back and inviting Morgan to mount him. With his cock primed and ready for her, and a look of undisguised lust in his stunning green eyes, it was an invitation she couldn't ignore. Gripping his shaft by the root, she held herself poised over him for a moment. He strained up towards her, his cock anxious to bury itself as deep in her body as it could go.

'Please, Morgan, don't tease me. You can't know how badly I need to fuck you.'

She'd never heard him beg before, never seen him at a point where all the control had been wrested from him. He was, literally, in her hands. She toyed with the idea of tying his wrists to the bedrail, rendering him completely at her mercy, but that was just too cruel. Maybe in the weeks to come … For now, she could only acquiesce to his urgent need to be inside her.

Inching herself down, she engulfed his cock in the velvet clasp of her pussy, watching the play of emotions on his face as he registered the feel of being lodged to the hilt inside her, just as he'd craved.

She rode him slowly, shifting up and down on his thick length, her eyes never leaving his. His hands clamped around her breasts, thumbs teasing her nipples, adding more strands to the web of sensation that seemed to wrap around her body from head to toe.

'Good?' she asked him.

'Better than good,' he assured her. 'Bloody marvellous, in fact.'

'Just what I wanted to hear.' She'd aimed to string the pleasure out for as long as she could, but her self-control was fracturing further with every passing second and she bucked and heaved, inner muscles catching and releasing his cock with ever-increasing speed. It seemed as though their whole world had been reduced to this one room, the once-crisp bedsheets crumpled beneath them, the insistent pattering of the rain against the window the only accompaniment to their lovemaking.

Senses swamped with the feel and taste and touch of Scott's body, Morgan surrendered to the overload of sensation. 'Oh, God, Scott, I'm coming!' she cried out, her last coherent words before her pleasure crested wildly and she threw her head back, almost sobbing with the force of the orgasm thundering through her.

Dimly, she registered the way Scott's cock jerked inside her as he reached his own peak, calling out her name over and over. He held her safe and secure in his arms, as though he couldn't bear to let her go.

At last, she eased herself off him, snuggling up against his bare, sweat-sheened back.

'So,' she asked, echoing her earlier question, 'do you feel what I feel?'

'And what's that, exactly?' Turning to face her, Scott brushed a stray lock of hair out of her eyes.

'Well …' She could hardly bring herself to say the words, afraid what his response might be. Then she steeled herself, driven by a need to spell her emotions out. They'd wasted so much time worrying about how other people would react, when all that mattered was their obvious need for each other. But Morgan had to know whether Scott felt the same all-consuming desire she did. 'I feel as though you're someone I could very easily fall in love with.'

He didn't laugh, didn't stiffen and turn away in a manner that would tell her he didn't feel the same. Instead, he hugged her tighter. 'Yes, I do feel it. And you don't know how hard it is for me to admit something like that. After Sasha and I split up, I didn't know whether I'd ever be able to open my heart to anyone again. But if we keep working on this recipe for passion we seem to be cooking up together, who knows what might happen?'

Those words were all she needed to hear. The man by her side wasn't the self-centred, career-obsessed Scott who, she now realised, was largely the media creation Carrie had always claimed. This was a man who was willing to put his heart on the line for her, no matter what anyone else might think, and she couldn't believe it had taken her so long to separate the two.

Now she had, she was determined to make up for lost time. Between soft, nibbly kisses, she reached for the pot of honey, struck with the urge to act on all her fantasies of anointing Scott's cock with some delicious foodstuff before licking it off. 'Sounds wonderful to me. So why don't you lie back, and this time I'll treat the cook?'

Migrations
by K D Grace

Chapter One

'IT'S THE ROAD TRIP from hell! I knew it would be. I just knew it!' Val didn't bother to speak quietly. After what she'd been through, no one could possibly blame her for losing it and talking to herself. And this was just the beginning! How the hell was she going to survive this little misadventure all the way to Oregon? She glanced quickly over her shoulder as she stepped behind the bathrooms at the rest area, trying desperately to block out the memory of Aunt Rose accusing the elderly gentleman at the vending machine of stealing her change.

She needed to vent or she'd explode. Once behind the building she turned her face to the wall and banged her head against it. 'Why me? I'm not a bad person. I never murdered anyone, I always recycle. I volunteer for the autumn fucking bird count. Why?' She banged her head for emphasis. '… the hell.' Bang bang bang. '… Me?' Bang, bang.

'Sounds like you could use a good wank.'

She couldn't have stopped the yelp that escaped her throat if she'd tried, but as she spun around to make a run for the car, what she saw stopped her in her tracks.

'Sh!' A man in a faded blue T-shirt and jeans that were even more faded raised a finger to his lips. It was impossible not to notice that the other hand was occupied, wrapped around the big stiffy that looked as though it had parted his fly like Moses parting the Red Sea, and my, what a staff!

When he was sure he had her full attention, as if there was any doubt of that, he spoke. 'Quiet.' He glanced around quickly. 'If word gets out,' he nodded to his stretching cock, 'everyone'll be back here getting a little relief from the road. Though, in your case ...' he leaned closer and she could see startling blue eyes peeking over the mirrored shades that slid down his sun-freckled nose, '... I reckon you need it more than most.'

She pressed her back against the wall and moaned, not taking her eyes off the fascinating handwork on his cock. 'You saw then.'

He nodded and gave a little grunt and a flutter of sun-bleached lashes as he lifted his balls free from the peek-a-boo squish of his fly. 'And heard. Hard not to really.'

'Fuck!' She cursed.

He chuckled. 'I never fuck on a first date, but I'm happy to choke the chicken in solidarity.'

She nodded to his efforts. 'It really helps?'

'Absolutely,' he grunted at a particularly rough tugging of his cock. 'Best kept secret in the world,' he said following her gaze, giving his balls a smile and a grope as though he'd just realised they were there. 'The world would be a much better place if everyone would just chill and treat themselves to a little self-love every now and again. Can you imagine the bliss? Go on, indulge yourself.' He nodded to her trousers. 'I'd say you could use the relief.'

She shook her head. 'I don't have time. Aunt Rose will be on me like a screaming banshee if she catches me.'

'Of course you've got time. If I'm not mistaken, she took her copy of *The National Enquirer* into the bathroom with her, didn't she? And your cousin, she is your cousin, isn't she? Well, she's on her cell phone with her kids, something about not pouring tomato soup in the toaster.'

'Jesus, you heard?'

'Sweet cheeks, everybody heard,' he said with a tug on his schlong for emphasis. Trust me; the misdeeds of your cousin's little angels and the condition of your auntie's bowels are now common knowledge at this rest stop.'

'Fuck,' she said again, running a hand through her hair, now beginning to curl around her temples from the unseasonably warm spring heat.

'Really, darlin',' he nodded again to her trousers. 'It'll make you feel better. I won't look if you don't want me to.'

Maybe it was just a testament to how desperate she was, or how loopy she had already become, but she opened her fly and stuck her hand down inside her panties. When she made contact, her breath caught and her body gave a little involuntary jerk.

Without missing a beat, he gave her an appreciative nod. 'There now. That's better, isn't it? You wet?'

She nodded. 'How'd you know?'

'No surprise really. Anger and frustration can often be a turn-on. Well not a turn-on per-se, but the body compensates for the stress in the best way it knows to make itself feel better.' He shrugged. 'Plus watching someone else handle their junk usually will do the trick too.'

'Sh!' she hissed. 'Don't talk, just touch it, and let me watch, and relieve my stress.'

He did as she asked, easing his jeans down enough that she could see the lovely straight lines of his hips perfectly balanced by the muscular swell of his ass-cheeks, which clenched and relaxed with each thrust. 'What else?' he grunted.

'Huh?'

'What else do you want to see? Not that I'm an exhibitionist or anything,' his breath accelerated noticeably, 'but I'm sympathetic to your circumstances, and right now this is so working for me.'

It wasn't doing too badly for her either, as she slipped two fingers in between her swell and began to scissor them while her thumb went to work on her clit. 'Turn around a little,' she breathed. 'I want to see your ass.'

He did as she asked, half bending over to give her an exquisite view, and she felt herself gush, as he spread his ass-cheeks. 'Oh my!' she gasped.

'You like that, do you? You wanna see my back hole?'

'Oh God, yes.'

'And you'd like me to finger it while I wank, wouldn't you?' He didn't wait for her answer. And he really didn't need to. Almost as though he knew what was going on in her panties, he stuck a thick middle finger into his mouth and sucked it until it was wet and shiny with his saliva. For a moment, she found what he was doing to his finger with his yummy mouth almost as hot as what he was doing to his cock. Through all of his efforts, his eyes, peeking over the mirrored sun shades, never left hers.

Watching her over his shoulder, making sure he was at just the right angle for her to see what was going on in front and behind, he bent over still further and spread his legs so that the twitch of his asshole was centre stage. With a tight breath released between his teeth, almost like he'd touched something hot, he eased his finger in to his back grip. 'Ah, that's nice,' he breathed. 'Such a tight fit, and my asshole's so sensitive.' Then he shoved it all the way in. His eyelids fluttered, his ass cheeks clenched and he positively growled and bucked against himself, tugging at his penis as though it were in serious need of subjugation.

Her panties were beyond wet, and she now gave herself the whole hand hump, four fingers shoving and wriggling inside her wet snatch while her palm exerted exquisite, almost painful pressure against her mons, which put the squeeze on her burgeoning clit. She shoved the other hand inside her blouse and manoeuvred her left breast free from her bra, at least free enough that she could knead it while pinching and stroking the nipple until it was tight and engorged and raw.

'What else,' he gasped.

'I want to see you come.' Her voice was a harsh whisper, and she felt the blush crawl up her face that she would even ask such a thing. And yet, her pussy clenched against her fingers at the thought, and her clit surged. 'I know you're close. You look like you're about to burst, so go ahead. I want to see you unload on the ground like the nasty man that you are. I want to watch you spurt.' Jesus, what was the matter with her, talking like some street whore, but even as she spoke, she felt wet slippery approval from her cunt.

'Your wish is my command,' he grunted. Three hard jerks balanced by the finger digging at his asshole, and he shot thick white streamers of semen across the well-manicured grass.

'Valareee! Valerie Louise, where are you?' The shrill voice of Aunt Rose broke the mood.

'Oh Jesus! Oh God!' Val jerked her wet hand from her panties and stared at it as though it were a total surprise to her while she shoved her tit back into her bra then tried to close her fly with one hand.

Wank Man handed her a pristine white hankie and she frantically wiped her fingers. Before she could wonder what to do with the hankie, he snatched it away.

'I'll take that,' he said, as Aunt Rose bellowed for her niece again, this time loud enough to wake the dead in the next county. 'I'm a frequent wanker,' he lifted the hankie to his nose and inhaled deeply before stuffing it back in his pocket. 'I'm always happy for some nice props.' Then the smile slipped from his face. 'But you didn't come.'

'Tell me about it,' she whispered between her teeth. 'So now I'm horny as hell as well as stressed out. And I have to somehow make it all the way to Oregon with at least a little sanity intact.'

Aunt Rose bellowed again.

'Two words,' he said, stuffing his still heavy cock nimbly back into his jeans and adjusting the tell-tale bulge to sit comfortably against his groin.

'Two words?' She breathed.

'Car engines.'

'What?'

'Car engines, sweet cheeks. Car engines are nothing more than built-in vibes. Just shift around on the seat.' He demonstrated with a slow undulation of his hips that did nothing to ease the road rage in her cunt. 'And then when you find the sweet spot, open your legs and let the car do the rest.' He spread his stance until he reminded her of a cowboy who'd been in the saddle too long. Then he offered her a wicked smile. 'Your aunt will never be the wiser.'

'Valerie, there you are!' Aunt Rose erupted from around the

153

corner. 'What in the world are you doing back here? I was beginning to worry that some pervert had abducted you.'

'Birds,' Valerie managed. 'Some meadow larks, and when I came around here, Mr –' She turned around to find Wank Man gone. The only trace of him was the white streaks of jizz on the grass, but Aunt Rose didn't notice that. She grabbed her niece with the hard grip that Val and her cousin, Sally, jokingly referred to as the claw, and tugged her back toward the parking lot.

'You and your silly birds. We'll never make it to Portland in time for my poor Harry's surgery with you stopping to look at everything that has feathers. Now come on. We've got a long way to go. You're walking funny, dear. Are you chafing?' Aunt Rose's voice wafted loud and clear across the rest area and the wheat field beyond. 'I certainly would be if I wore those scratchy denim jeans you young people all wear, and in this heat too. Anything that tight against your crotch can't be good. I have some talcum powder if you need it. A little bit of that between your thighs and some decent cotton panties, not those stringy little thongy things you girls wear now. One hundred per cent cotton, that's what you need. That and a little talc and you'll feel right as rain.'

The teenagers at the vending machine shot them a curious glance and sniggered. Two elderly women coming out of the rest room looked up, then quickly looked away, pretending not to have noticed Aunt Rose's personal comfort lecture. Just then Sally, still on her cell phone, fell into step next to them telling her husband not to feed the dog bacon because it gives him diarrhoea and the last time he'd pooped in the middle of the children's sand box.

Val mentally cringed, as they got into the car under the surreptitious stare of everyone at the rest area. As she belted herself in, her pussy twitched with nearly painful need, then her stomach clenched as Aunt Rose pulled a bottle of antihistamine spray out of her enormous bag, shoved it up each nostril and sniffed hard enough to inhale a fencepost. It was going to be a very long trip.

Chapter Two

'YOU SURE THIS IS the right road?' Aunt Rose asked.

'I'm sure.' Val white-knuckled the steering wheel, hoping bared teeth passed for a smile.

'If you say so. Doesn't look right to me.' Aunt Rose pressed her nose to the window. 'There's that Hell's Angel again. This is the third time we've passed him. I don't like it. See this article?' She shoved her copy of *The National Enquirer* at Val, who pushed it aside so she could see the road. 'They think bikers murdered that hot-shot businessman.'

'Tip Beranger?' Sally chimed in from the back seat.

Aunt Rose nodded. 'He was last seen going into a diner that's a known biker hang-out. They found his car but no sign of the body.'

'Excuse me if I'm not sympathetic,' Val said. 'He's responsible for some really nasty clear-cuts in Idaho and Wyoming. He's always in trouble with the EPA, but they just slap his wrist. His kind never get what they deserve.'

'I think he did this time,' Aunt Rose said. 'They suspect the bikers cut him into little pieces and scattered him over some bird reserve near Gruid. Not far from here. We're not going there are we?'

'Wish we were.' Val sighed. 'The sandhill cranes migrate through there. It's a little late in the migration, but if you know where to find them, there are probably still some hangers on who haven't flown north yet.'

'You should be giving your poor mother grandchildren instead of wasting your time off in some barbaric place every chance you get chasing down birds. Must cost you a fortune,' Aunt Rose said.

'It's a part of my studies,' Val replied.

'You're over 30. You're too old to be studying. You should start looking for a good husband to take care of you. God knows you'll need somebody to pay the bills.'

Val rolled her eyes. 'I pay my bills just fine, Aunt Rose.'

Sally looked over Aunt Rose's shoulder at the tabloid. 'I heard they suspect cannibalism with this Beranger guy.'

Aunt Rose wrinkled her nose. 'Wouldn't put it past them, eating the evidence. You're sure we're on the right road?'

Sally reached over the seat and cranked the volume of the country station Val had been out-voted on. 'That biker was at the rest area.' She squinted at the man on the Harley as they passed.

'Oh dear Lord!' Aunt Rose jerked away from the window and laid a hand against an abundantly lipsticked mouth. 'Did you see that? He waved. I think he's stalking us. We should take a different road.'

'We've passed each other half a dozen times,' Val spoke around the twitch at the corner of her mouth that had mysteriously developed after her first hour trapped in the car with her relatives. 'He's probably just being friendly.'

'Says here police are checking anyone on a motorcycle for information.' Aunt Rose glanced over her shoulder at the Harley now falling behind. 'I wonder if they've talked to him.' She shook her niece's arm. 'Can't you drive faster?'

Val ground her teeth and stepped on the gas. Since Aunt Rose didn't drive and refused to fly, Val got shanghaied into taking her to Oregon to be with her son for his surgery. It was just a nose job, but Aunt Rose wanted to see her angel one last time before she died. By Val's count, this was the fourth time Aunt Rose had drafted naïve relatives for her pre-demise pilgrimages to see her Harry. Sally volunteered for the ordeal – an expedition Lewis and Clark would have fled in terror. But Sally did have the kids from hell, so Val understood her willingness to make the journey. A two-week purgatory must be a welcome respite.

Aunt Rose thumbed through the paper. Sally dug through her condo-sized handbag. Something just short of suicidal droned on the radio. This was as good as it was likely to get. Before Val could actually enjoy the brief peace, she noticed the flashing lights in the rear-view mirror just as the cop gave a short, polite burst of his siren. Great! Just what she needed. Cursing to herself, she turned off the radio and pulled over.

The officer approached with a bit of a swagger. He squinted in the window. 'Speed limit's 65, Ma'am. I clocked you at 79. 'Fraid that's a 60 dollar fine round here. I'm gonna need your licence and registration.'

She handed over her documents. He took them and returned to his car.

'I knew you were driving too fast,' Aunt Rose hissed.

Sally snapped open a small compact and checked her makeup. 'I've never had a speeding ticket. With three kids, I have to be careful – precious cargo.'

Val resisted the urge to gag.

'Not even out five hours and you get us arrested,' Aunt Rose growled. 'We won't need a hotel. We'll be spending the night in jail with the whoors and felons.' Aunt Rose rubbed her chest between the stout summits of her brassiere-shaped breasts. 'After all this, you'll probably have to put me in the hospital next to poor Harry, if I make it that far.'

'It's just a traffic ticket!' Val's knuckles ached against the steering wheel.

'Look.' Sally pointed out the window. 'It's that Hell's Angel again. The cop's motioning him over too.' She practically bounced off the seat.

Aunt Rose glared over the top of clip-on sunglasses. 'You think he's the one who ate that poor businessman? Sure hope the officer's got enough sense to call in reinforcements.'

Sally whimpered.

'Did you notice what he was packing?' Aunt Rose craned her neck. 'Because he'll probably need some serious heat to overcome a cannibal biker.'

Val shot her aunt a raised eyebrow.

'Well, a man doesn't want a wimpy piece at a time like this. That cop's gun may be the only thing keeping that biker from eating us.'

Sally whimpered louder.

As the three watched, the biker dismounted and followed the cop around to the front of the patrol car.

Aunt Rose strained at the seatbelt. 'What's that cop think he's doing? Would you look at that! He needs to keep the cannibal in plain sight. Oh dear lord! If the cannibal takes out the cop, then we're next, and no doubt he'll have his way with us first, don't think he won't.' The seatbelt looked like it could snap with her forward press against it. 'Maybe he won't be interested in a cougar.' She honked into a delicate lace hankie and dabbed at her forehead.

'Aunt Rose, are you all right?' Sally hissed from the back seat.

'I'm having palpitations,' Aunt Rose wheezed. 'And I think my blood sugar's out of whack.' She grabbed an open packet of chocolate covered raisins she'd stuffed in the glove box and began shoving them into her mouth.

'Don't worry.' Sally squared her shoulders and patted Aunt Rose on the arm with a shaky hand. 'We're all in this together.' She reached into her bag and pulled out a can of pepper spray. 'We'll go down fighting if we have to.'

Val laid her head against the steering wheel and groaned. What the hell had she done in a past life to deserve this?

'Look. Look! The officer's coming back.' Aunt Rose spoke around a mouthful of raisins. 'What's he think he's doing? Would you look at that! The Cannibal's getting away.'

Sure enough, the biker mounted the hog, started his engine and drove off down the highway.

The patrolman leaned in the window and handed back Val's license. 'You can go now, ma'am, but try to slow down a little.'

'What about the fine?'

He jerked his head toward the biker rapidly shrinking in the distance. 'The Good Samaritan took care of it. You be careful now, hear?' He tipped his hat and walked back to his car.

Before Val could unravel what had just happened. Aunt Rose shoved her raisins back in the glove box and squirmed in the seat. 'Well now we're screwed, aren't we? The cannibal has us by the short hairs now, doesn't he? He's letting us go just for the sport of it, that's all, and us, three helpless women.'

Sally whimpered. 'We're gonna die! My children'll be orphans.'

'Can't think he'd have much taste for me,' Aunt Rose said between snorts of her nasal inhaler. 'My Ed used to deer hunt. He said the old ones weren't good eating. Too tough.'

'Will you two stop it? The man's not a murderer or a cannibal.'

'Then how do you explain him being so nice?' Sally breathed.

'Do people have to have a reason?'

'For 60 bucks, they have a reason.' Aunt Rose clutched her inhaler. 'And that'll no doubt involve having his way with us first.'

Chapter Three

ABOVE THE CONTINUOUS DRONE of the country station, Aunt Rose and Sally speculated over half a bag of Cheetos and a couple of Diet Cokes on what the biker would do when he finally finished toying with them. The car only lapsed into silence for a few minutes before Sally dug shoulder-deep into her bag and pulled out a CD.

'Auntie, I know how much you love your romance novels, so when we stopped at that last truck stop, I picked up an audio book for you. It might help us all take our minds off the cannibal. Look.' She handed Aunt Rose a CD in a case that had a bodice-ripping cover.

Val was manoeuvring through road works that had lanes narrowed to long, tight rows of orange PVC construction cones, but out of the corner of her eye, she did make out something about the Montana rancher's mail order bride. She supposed anything would be better than what was spewing from the radio.

Aunt Rose shoved the CD into the player and cranked the volume. Then she and Sally passed a package of Oreos back and forth as the saga began. Entertainment for at least the next few miles, Val thought. She'd be left alone with her own thoughts, those of them she could hear above the woman reader, who was attempting to read in both male and female voices, complete with a cowboy accent for the hardened rancher with the heart of gold.

There was the usual conflict of the poor innocent virgin bride from out east, who missed her family terribly and felt hard done by to have to give herself over to such a brute. And yet she was so terribly attracted to his manliness. Surely she couldn't be happy in such a barbaric place. Of course, the two of them didn't get on from the beginning, and that led to sleeping in separate rooms until the rancher could send the prissy city girl back to where she belonged. She would certainly never make a rancher's wife, but oh how he yearned to feel her curvy, nubile body next to his. Then an argument erupted, as they do. It was a terrible argument, and the lovely young thing stormed out of the house, but the rancher brute caught her behind the barn, spun her around and …

'His lips were bruising as he took her there, pushing her up against the rough wall of the barn, her fighting like a wild cat, which only made him want her more.'

Then the rancher ripped open the bodice of his virgin wife's dress and began to manhandle her full succulent breasts, which rose and fell in great heaving gasps. At last she gave up fighting and held him to her as he suckled a tender pink nipple until it was swollen and ached with need she had never felt before, need she felt down deep in her womanhood.

'Oh my,' Aunt Rose breathed.

Sally cleared her throat loudly. 'I'm sorry. I didn't know it was that kind of romance, Auntie. I'll take it out.'

As she reached for the CD player, Aunt Rose grabbed her with the claw. 'Leave it,' she grunted as the rancher's hand found its way up under his little woman's skirt to fondle the honeyed dew of her treasure box. 'You paid good money for it. Might as well hear it out.'

By the time the rancher guided his bride's delicate trembling hand to rest against his throbbing manhood, Val's unrequited pussy was throbbing in empathy, as memories of her encounter with Wank Man behind the toilets at the rest area came flooding back to her. She shifted restlessly against the seat, looking for the sweet spot that Wank Man had told her about. Her breasts felt heavy and her nipples felt like they'd drill slits through her blouse as she thought of the virgin bride's swollen, well-suckled mammaries.

Aunt Rose's lips were pursed tight and her hands crushed the handkerchief she held as the cowboy found the pearl hard seat of his wife's pleasure and she whimpered and squirmed in

161

wonder that anything could feel so good.

'Now how do you suppose some cowboy living out in the back of nowhere would know anything about the seat of a woman's pleasure,' Aunt Rose observed.

Both Val and Sally shushed her in unison just as the man dipped a calloused finger into his brides aching need.

Through the rear view mirror, Val caught a glimpse of Sally, hands clasped in her lap, head bowed as though she were praying.

Val was beginning to wonder if an erect clit could split the seam out of a pair of jeans as she wriggled against the seat trying to be subtle, but feeling like she would burst more than a seam if she didn't come and soon.

Just as the rancher lifted his bride into his arms and whisked her up the stairs to his bed, Val found the sweet spot and felt her pussy gush and swell even further against the delicious vibration of the engine. She swallowed back a little whimper, which neither Aunt Rose nor Sally seemed to notice, as clothing removal began in earnest in the master bedroom of the ranch house.

When the rancher released his turgid, pulsing pole, and his bride moaned her appreciation and opened her legs feeling so terribly naughty at giving in to such powerful lust, Val wriggled hard against the seat to get closer to the sweet spot, and the shoulder strap of the seat belt shifted and pressed in tight against her right nipple. She didn't adjust it, but let it rub, as they hit a stretch of rough road that suddenly seemed to translate every uneven spot, every imperfection in the asphalt straight to her cunt lips.

As the rancher lowered his face to taste his bride's creamy swollen womanhood, Aunt Rose spoke again. 'And that's another thing. I can't see a loan rancher who has only ever had cows for company taking the time to … to do that to his wife. I'd think he'd be all business. About to explode. All anxious to get the job done.' She nodded her conviction and stared straight ahead like a statue, all the while her hands worried the hankie in her lap. Sally nibbled her bottom lip, still holding her prayer posture. And Val wriggled again, feeling as though there was barely room for herself and her clit in the car seat, feeling wet and sticky and heavy all over.

The rancher positioned himself and softly reassured his trembling wife that he would be as gentle as he could for her first time, that if she relaxed the pain would pass quickly and the pleasure would be more than worth it. The lovely bride promised him that this was exactly what she wanted – him inside her. She told him that she wanted to give herself to him, that she wanted to be a wife in more than name only. Sally cleared her throat again, very softly, and Aunt Rose grabbed the hand rest on the door like she was expecting a rough ride.

As the rancher thrust home with his probing member and the virgin bride cried out in pain that quickly became pleasure, as she wrapped her legs around her husband's waist like he was her wild stallion, Val wriggled against the seat one last time and shifted against the sweet spot, driving her distended clit hard against the vibration of the motor. And as the virgin mail order bride orgasmed on her rancher's enormous manhood, Val practically shook the seat loose in her own release, the shoulder strap still raking deliciously against her nipple. Neither Aunt Rose nor Sally seemed to notice that she was shaking like a leaf. Neither Aunt Rose or Sally seemed to notice anything, not even the tide-pool scent of woman heat that was now so obvious to Val. They didn't even notice as Val accelerated to pass the Hell's Angel again. Nor did they notice his friendly wave.

Chapter Four

IT WAS BARELY MID-AFTERNOON when Aunt Rose decided she needed to eat or she'd die from hypoglycaemia. By the time Val found a truck stop, Sally was digging into her bag for the rest of the Cheetos to stave off Aunt Rose's demise. Val dropped them at the diner, and they hobbled inside with Aunt Rose leaning heavily on Sally. Then she went to fill the car – a job that was bliss after hours of listening to her relatives comparing illnesses over an endless soundtrack of country music's whiniest. That had been the entertainment after the rancher got his mail order bride properly knocked up.

While waiting to pay, she picked up earplugs and a bag of Snickers. Under the circumstances, she'd rather have Jack Daniels, but Snickers would have to do. As she waited in line, a super-sized woman perched on an overworked stool did slow-mo checkout. Val called Sally on her cell phone. 'I'm gonna be a while. Order me a burger and fries … I know it's bad for me … My heart and I'll take our chances.' She crammed the phone back in her bag with a stifled curse.

'Good for you! You should eat what you want.'

She turned to find herself face to face with Wank Man. Startled, she bumped into the man in front of her and dropped her stash.

As Wank Man bent to retrieve her goodies, his unshaven face broke into a smile and dark glasses slid down his sunburned nose once again revealing his lovely blue eyes. 'Forget chicken or fish,' he said as he handed her the Snickers. 'There's nothing like a good hunk of red meat. Now that's real comfort food.'

The cashier left her post for a price check. The man ahead

164

of Val grumbled about poor service.

'Tell me,' Wank Man said, moving closer and speaking barely above a whisper. 'Did you try my suggestion?'

'You mean about the sweet spot. I did, actually.'

He raised an eyebrow. 'And?'

'Worked like a charm. With a little help from the Montana rancher and his mail order bride.'

'Auntie still making you crazy?' He nodded to the earplugs.

'You have no idea.'

'Did you say you were taking her to Oregon? Quite a trip to volunteer for.'

'I was drafted.'

He leaned in close. 'I can help make it easier, if you'd like.'

Her insides jumped, and she bumped into the man ahead of her again, who shot her a caustic look.

Two more cashiers joined the fat lady, and Wank Man moved to a shorter line. 'Keep my offer in mind,' he said. 'It could come in handy.'

Clutching her goodies, she offered him a polite smile, with thoughts of just how he might go about making the trip easier shoving their way into her head, and her panties.

No food had been ordered for her when she slid into the booth at the diner where Sally was nibbling daintily at pasta primavera and Aunt Rose was just sending back her steak after berating the waitress for it being over cooked.

Sally watched as the poor waitress rushed off with Aunt Rose's unsatisfactory steak. 'Sorry, Val, but Aunt Rose said to wait to order for you till you got here 'cause she says cold French fries give you gas.'

The couple at the table next to them looked up and quickly turned their attention back to their meals pretending not to listen.

'It's true,' Aunt Rose said. 'Terrible gas. And that car of yours is awfully small, what with me having to sit next to you and all, better not take chances.'

Val slumped down into the seat and tried to hide behind her menu while Aunt Rose added another packet of sugar to her iced tea, and flipped through her ever present copy of *The National Enquirer*.

Aunt Rose and Sally had just begun the pregnancy war stories competition when Val noticed Wank Man standing by the hall that led to the restrooms. Once he had her attention, he motioned her toward the back.

With her heart summersaulting, Val excused herself to go wash up just as the confused waitress approached.

In the dark hallway between the restrooms, Wank Man stood with one well-muscled bicep draped over the cigarette machine, which caused the faded T-shirt to ride up just enough to give her a tantalizing view of his navel peeking out above the low ride of his jeans.

'What do you want?' she whispered, glancing back over her shoulder like a naughty child.

'I want to make it up to you,' he said. 'You know, I was a bit ... premature, at the rest area.' He shrugged. 'Though you did order me to let rip. But I certainly would have been more than happy to reciprocate if your aunt hadn't interrupted our rendezvous.'

Val moved closer to him to make room for the mother and her toddler who squeezed past them making pee-pee talk on their way to the ladies.

'We can't do it here, can we?' she hissed.

'Got a good place all picked out,' he said, raking her with his electric blue gaze.

'And what about them?' She jerked her head back to where she could hear Aunt Rose talking about the terrible acid reflux she had when she was pregnant with her Harry.

He stepped still closer. 'I'm wagering she'll send the steak back at least one more time. And didn't I see a copy of *People Magazine* on the table next to that *National Enquirer*?'

Just then Sally's phone rang and he offered a satisfied nod. 'That will be the frantic father of the little darlings in the middle of a crisis, and it's not likely to be a crisis that will be solved until at least dessert. Poor man. He's way out of his depth.' He crowded closer to her, closer than was actually necessary as a trucker pushed past them into the men's room.

'I'm guessing I can get you there very nicely and back in time for dessert if you'd like.'

He shifted so she could see the bulge in his jeans, then twirled a strand of her hair around a deliciously thick finger. 'Of course if you want to skip dessert, I can get you there even better.'

Her heart raced. 'I hardly know you and you want me to fuck you?'

He leaned in close and nibbled her earlobe, then the nape of her neck, causing a shudder to run down her spine right into her pussy.

'There are lots of delicious ways to get you there that don't involve fucking sweet cheeks. Yummy, juicy, sizzling ways.'

'And what will I tell them,' she asked when she could manage enough breath to speak.

He nipped her again. 'You'll think of something.'

Strangely enough neither Aunt Rose nor Sally seemed suspicious, or even over solicitous when she excused herself without eating. She said she had a headache and wanted to go back to the car and rest a bit. She insisted that they take their time and enjoy their meal, have dessert, have coffee, enjoy their magazines.

Wank Man was waiting just outside the door of the diner. Without a word, he grabbed her hand and pulled her away from the restaurant at a fast trot toward a bright red 18-wheeler that looked as though it had just been washed and waxed.

'Your truck?' Val asked.

'The company's truck. I get to use it.' He opened the door on the passenger side and placing his large hands on her hips, hoisted her in.

She barely had time to notice the spotless interior before he heaved himself into the seat next to her and shut the door behind him. 'This is the best bit.' He pushed aside the plush blue curtain to reveal the sleeping compartment.

The inside of the sleeper made her think of the tent of a rich Bedouin. It was all decked out with mountains of plush pillows and tapestries that perfectly covered each of the interior walls.

It smelled of sandalwood and maleness.

'And you want me to get in there with you?' Her voice sounded breathless, it sounded almost as nervous as she felt.

'That was my plan.' He sounded no less breathless.

'I don't even know your name.'

'Hawk.' His breath was hot against her neck. 'My name's Hawk.'

'Of course it is.' Her chuckle ended in a little yelp as he placed both hands on her bottom and boosted her up into the cloud of pillows. He was right behind her, crawling and shoving his way in so close to her that she got a good raking with the bulge in his trousers before he settled a steamy kiss onto her mouth, his tongue taking the opportunity to dart in between her lips, still parted in the gasp of surprise. And she gave as good as she got, grabbing him by his wind-blown hair and returning the favour with her own hungry tongue.

By the time they came up for air, he had pushed her legs apart and lay on top of her, his hips shifting and undulating so that his erection, pressing hard against his jeans, raked right where she needed it. She wrapped her legs around him and thrust up to meet him, tightening her grip, until he gasped. 'Oh you are a naughty, naughty girl, aren't you? I can feel your heat practically scorching my cock all the way through my jeans.'

'I'm having a bad day,' she said. 'I've earned the right to be naughty.'

'And so you have.' He caught his breath, just before she grabbed his hair and pulled him back into another bruising kiss. Then he pushed her away. 'Keep that up and you'll have me coming in my jeans, which is all right, but I don't think that's really what you want, is it?'

She pushed him away and scrambled into a sitting position against the tapestried wall on the driver's side. 'I'm sorry, I'm sorry!' She ran a hand through her hair and shot an anxious look around her. 'I'm not usually this poorly behaved and I never intended … I don't know you–'

'You don't know me well enough to fuck me, yes I know.' He pushed himself against the opposite wall and yanked the glasses off, which were sitting askew low on the bridge of his nose. Then he offered her an edible smile that was somehow reassuring. 'And I told you there are other things we could do besides fuck, in fact there are things we can do that don't even involve touching each other.' He slid his shirt off over his head and nodded to her. 'Your turn.'

She followed suit. 'Shall I take off my bra?' Her voice sounded thin, almost childlike.

'If you want to, that would be nice. I'd like to see your breasts.'

In the interest of time, she just slipped her arms free of the straps and shoved the bra down to where the cups rested on her belly. He nodded his approval.

'I'm a breast man myself, and yours are lovely. Would you play with them for me, make your nipples nice and big. Ah that's right. Maybe on our next date you'll know me well enough to let me nurse on them. I'd like that. Would you like that?'

She responded with an incoherent nod.

'And can I take out my cock now before I rip my jeans?'

'By all means,' she said. 'Give yourself some breathing room.'

He deftly opened his jeans and slid them down around the scuffed leather boots he still wore. She couldn't keep from noticing there were no underpants. His cock bounced to full attention and his balls lolled against the tight muscle of his right thigh. 'And you,' he wrapped his right hand loosely around himself and grunted his satisfaction. 'You must be sopping. You must really need to touch yourself down there.' He nodded to her crotch. 'You'll feel so much better if you release some of that pent-up stress.'

She didn't wait for him to ask twice. She slid her jeans and her wet panties down, slipped off her flip-flops and pulled her left leg free.

'That's a girl,' he sighed, his gaze locked on her crotch. 'Open wide and let your pussy breathe.' He let out a low whistle, and his hand began to move, with purpose, up and down the length of his erection. 'Goodness, you're swollen, and I can see from here how slippery you are.' He raised his eyes to hers, almost shyly. 'Touch her for me. I want to watch you play with your little pussy.'

She gave a little shiver as she slipped a finger in between her pouting lips and began to stroke, in and out, in and out, then up and over and around the swell of her clit.

His handwork picked up speed and he began to knead his balls. 'One finger isn't gonna be nearly enough for you,' he observed, just as she inserted a second finger into her slit. Then he shook his head. 'You'll need more than that.'

Just when she was about to protest that he'd said there'd be no fucking, and for him to stop hinting around, he reached behind him and pulled out a black leather case. He flipped it open to reveal a pool cue, and in spite of the nervous quiver in her belly, her pussy let down a fresh flood as he began to assemble the cue from large end to small. And the large end was … well tempting.

'I can't believe we're doing this,' she breathed, lifting her ass and bending her knees until her feet were flat on the bedding and her pussy pouted right at him.

'Do you want me to stop?' He screwed the two parts of the pool cue together, then extended it full length to graze each of her nipples in turn.

'No,' she said, thrusting her chest forward to meet the caress of the cue.

He chuckled. 'I didn't think so.' With his free hand he got seriously in touch with his schlong, and she didn't know where to look – at what he was doing to his cock, or what mischief he was up to with the pool cue, which was now migrating down to circle her belly button then dip in and out. She was riding three fingers by the time the tip of the cue brushed her tightly trimmed pubes, but as she shifted her hips to make ready for the descent, he shook his head and pulled it back.

'That end's not big enough to do you any good, is it? You need something more substantial, don't you?' He studied the juicy grasp and slide of her pussy for a moment, then studied the pool cue and blew out a sigh. 'Well, if you can't have my cock …'

Her heart nearly jumped out of her chest as she saw his gaze light on the thick end of the pool cue. Granted it wasn't as thick as his cock, but it was long, and he was in control. Or was he?

Before he had a chance to take action, she leaned forward and grabbed the thick end of the stick and began to run her tongue around the tip of it.

'Jesus,' he gasped, as she took as much of it into her mouth as she could get and began moving up and down the length of it, farther each time until she nearly gagged herself.

'Jesus,' he repeated, his eyes locked on the thick end of the cue and her mouth. He now had his hand on the thin end, but he let her control the rhythm and the depth, until at last she pulled it free, heart hammering, feeling like a wild animal in full rut. Then she lifted her butt off the cushions and shifted her hips forward, making sure her gaping hole was centre stage. Still holding his gaze, she pushed the pool cue into her cunt farther and farther until she could take no more. He allowed her to dictate the speed and the depth, then she took her hand away to tweak and stroke her clit while the other mauled her breasts. But she never took her eyes off him, thrusting into her with the pool cue and thrusting into his fist with his cock.

She might have been able to maintain control a little longer if he hadn't suddenly taken the other end of the cue into his mouth, none too neatly, dribbling saliva as he did so, tonguing it loosely and pulling his lips along it. Then, still tugging on his cock like nobody's business, his gaze still locked on hers, he removed the end of the cue from his mouth, and slumped against the wall of the truck, shifting his hips until his pucker hole peeked into view. She was certain she'd hyperventilate. Still stroking himself, he lifted his legs and opened them wide, giving her the best possible view. Then he inserted the end of the cue up into his back grip.

'Jesus!' she breathed. 'I've never seen anything like that.'

He grunted a laugh. 'I've never seen a chick fuck a pool cue before either, though I've always wanted to.'

Then neither of them spoke. She stroked her breasts and her clit, gyrating and thrusting against the thick end of the cue, which was now slick and juicy from her cunt, He jerked his cock until she feared he'd do serious damage. His balls bounced from his efforts, and his other hand controlled the thrust and retreat, thrust and retreat of the thinner end of the pool cue, up his asshole considerably farther than she would have thought comfortable. They came together, her trembling and convulsing until she thought she'd break something, and him spurting like Old Faithful just centimetres shy of the padded ceiling.

Amazingly, the pool cue was dislodged and they were both dressed and out the door just as Aunt Rose and Sally stepped from the diner. He pushed her up against the truck and gave her one last tongue lashing before he let her go with a wicked smile. 'It's a long way to Oregon,' he said. 'Make sure you take care of yourself.' His hand brushed up against her mound, then he turned and disappeared behind the truck. She managed to get into the driver's seat of her car and do a pretty good imitation of a wake-up stretch and moan just as Aunt Rose thrust a takeout box into her hand.

'You need to eat, hon. You need to keep up your strength. Sally can drive now while you rest.'

Val felt a little twinge of guilt as Aunt Rose lay a hand against her forehead. 'You feel a little hot. I hope you're not coming down with something. Go on now.' She shooed her into the back seat. 'Eat the fries before they get cold. We don't want to smell you.'

Val did as she was told, wolfing down a handful of fries as Sally buckled in and started the engine. 'Auntie ...' Sally nodded at the side of the diner to a lone motorcycle. 'I don't know much about bikes, but that Harley sure looks like the one the cannibal's been riding. Don't you think?'

Aunt Rose shivered and pulled her sweater tighter around her. 'Yep. That's the cannibal's bike all right. I'm sure of it. I was afraid of that. He's following us. I really didn't think he'd let us off the hook that easy. Not with us owing him and all.' She nodded toward the interstate. 'I don't see him around anywhere. Maybe if we sneak away we'll lose him. Val, honey, make sure you lock your door back there.'

Sally whimpered and spun gravel getting out of the parking lot.

Chapter Five

VAL WOLFED THE BURGER and fries like a starving woman listening to Aunt Rose give the latest on Tip Beranger and the Hell's Angels who had killed him and eaten him. Apparently Beranger and the cannibal bikers were all anyone in this part of Nebraska was talking about at the moment. And any motorcycle rider who looked a bit on the questionable side was fair game for gossip and speculation. No one seemed to have much more love for Beranger than Val did. Most just hoped the poor bikers didn't get heartburn from eating the bastard.

'I'm telling you I won't sleep a wink tonight,' Aunt Rose was saying.

Maybe Aunt Rose wouldn't sleep, but after hot quasi-sex with a hunky trucker, Val was good to go. Two Snickers bars and a Diet Coke later and she was drifting in quiet oblivion in the back seat with visions of Hawk, naked and erect, dancing through her head. In her lovely dream world, he was just about to do very nasty things to her equally naked body when suddenly the car pulled to the side of the road and stopped.

'What's going on?' She yanked out the earplugs and was blasted by Aunt Rose's ranting. 'You young people don't take care of anything these days.'

'The hot light's on,' Sally said.

'When I was your age, a car had to last us.' Aunt Rose ranted. 'Money didn't grow on trees. And there were no credit cards either.'

Val could see a cloud of steam rising from under the hood. 'Shit!'

'And that's another thing. In my day, a lady didn't cuss.'

Ignoring her aunt, she got out of the car. Sally pulled the

hood release then joined her.

'My poor Harry'll be dead in his grave by the time we get there,' Aunt Rose wailed.

'I don't think anyone ever died from a nose job, Auntie,' Sally called over her shoulder.

'What would you know about it? He has a deviated septum.'

Val fanned steam with Aunt Rose's copy of *The National Enquirer*. 'There's the problem. Broken radiator hose.'

"Isn't there duct tape in the tool box?' Sally asked.

'Aunt Rose took the tool box out to make room for her second bag.'

Their aunt stuck her head out the window. 'Do you have any idea how dangerous it is for three women stranded along the side of the road with all the rapists and perverts on the loose?'

'The nearest town's Gruid,' Val said.

'You mean with the bird reserve ... and the dead businessman.' Sally shot a wide-eyed glance up the road. 'What're we gonna do?'

Aunt Rose stabbed a red fingernail down the highway. 'There's a motorcycle coming. Oh dear lord! It looks like the cannibal.'

Sally grabbed Val's arm. 'I knew it! We're goners. We know too much.' She nodded to *The National Enquirer* still in Val's hand.

'It's the *Enquirer*, Sally, not secret documents from the CIA. Besides, for all we know, Beranger's vacationing in the Bahamas having a good laugh at the hoop-la in the newspapers.' She tried to sound convincing, but even she could only take so much talk of murderous cannibal bikers before she got spooked, and this guy had been passing them off and on all day. Not to mention his deal with the cop. Who didn't seem to be all that bothered about it, she reminded herself. Maybe the cop was in on the whole scheme. But the biker had got them out of a speeding ticket. Come to think of it. Aunt Rose was right. It did seem a bit strange.

Sally vice-gripped her arm, bringing her attention back to

174

their present circumstances, which were not shaping up well at all. 'Oh God, Val! He's stopping.'

Aunt Rose wheezed and clutched the sweater tight around her frontal geography. It's the cannibal all right. And he paid your fine. He owns us.'

Sure enough, the man on the Harley pulled up behind them and dismounted. And there was no denying, he looked badass in the leather jacket and black helmet with mirrored glasses hiding all emotion. But his scuffed boots looked familiar. And his large hands looked like they could easily grip a… pool cue?

'We have to stop meeting like this.' Sure enough it was Hawk who slipped off the helmet and ran a hand through dishevelled hair. 'Looks like you could use a little help.' He held her in his iced blue gaze over the top of his glasses, and for a second Val thought she would pass out. Sally whimpered and eased her way back into the car, abdicating the driver's seat for the safety of the back, but his attention was riveted on Val. 'It's gonna cost you.' He offered a crooked smile.

'You said you were a trucker,' she hissed at his broad back as he dug through his panniers for some duct tape.

'I never said I was a trucker. I said it was a company truck and they let me use it.' He shrugged making the leather jacket look like it was swallowing his neck. 'Well the driver let me use it. He's a neat nick, Bill, so don't worry, everything in there is sanitized within an inch of its life every morning. Had to do some serious negotiating to get him to let me use it.'

He turned to face her with a roll of duct tape in one hand and a very large pocket knife in the other. 'Now, let's get your chariot driveable again.' He held her gaze. 'I'd gladly give you a ride, but thhog's not big enough for all of us.'

'You're a biker, then?' she said, following him back to the car, and trying not to let the way his magnificent backside filled out the jeans distract her.

'Sometimes, when it suits me.'

She watched with growing unease as he deftly taped the hose and emptied his water supply into the radiator.

'There.' He wiped his hands on his jeans. 'That'll get you to Gruid. It's not much of a town, but there's a nice bird sanctuary

175

close by.' He nodded to the *Cornell Laboratory of Ornithology* sticker on her bumper. 'No doubt, you'd enjoy that.'

'I'd love to see the cranes, Val said. 'Though this late in the spring, most of them have probably already gone.' She mentally kicked herself for letting him distract her with birds. That was a cunning ploy. One that a cannibal biker just might use.

'Oh there are still cranes around. You just have to know where to look.'

'And you know?' She followed him back to the hog. Cannibal biker or not, if he knew where the cranes were, well he couldn't be all bad, could he?'

'Of course I know,' he said, stuffing the tape and the knife back into the pannier. 'The cranes are one of the best things about this place.'

He walked back to the car and turned his attention to Aunt Rose, who was now leaning cautiously out the window watching what had been going on. 'There's a garage in Gruid with a hotel across the street. I'll phone ahead. They may be able to fix the car before closing time. You can have a rest, then be on the road first thing in the morning.'

Aunt Rose snorted more nasal spray. 'Good. I'm exhausted, and the pollen count's making my sinuses ache.' She honked into her lace hankie.

The cannibal raised his voice above the honking. 'I'll follow you into town just in case.'

Fifteen minutes later, the bedraggled convoy limped into the parking lot at the Starlight Motel, Restaurant and Lounge.

'Look at all those bikes in front of the diner.' Sally pointed to three long rows of mean-looking Harleys gleaming in the low sun. She grabbed the *Enquirer* Val had thrown over the seat. 'I thought so. You see?' She nearly poked a hole through the article. 'This is the diner Beranger disappeared from. I bet those bikes belong to the guys who did it.'

Aunt Rose heaved herself out of the car. 'Well I don't care. I'm tired. Besides, I have a little surprise for anyone who tries to mess with me.'

'Oh God, Aunt Rose, please tell me you're not carrying a gun.'

'I'm not stupid, Valerie. It's illegal to carry concealed. The Peacemaker's at home under my pillow, where it always is.'

Val shuddered at the thought of the woman waking up some morning to find an ear blown off. As hard as her aunt's head was, she doubted the bullet would penetrate anything more vital.

Aunt Rose opened her handbag and peeked inside. 'I brought mace, and a stun-gun, and oops ...' She snapped the bag shut on her arsenal and smoothed her hair daintily. 'Well I'm pretty sure that law doesn't apply to the Walther. It's so small, and besides it's foreign. More like a piece of jewellery, really.'

Val desperately wished she'd bought the Jack Daniels instead of the Snickers.

Hawk, if that was his real name, was waiting for them beneath the green-striped awning above reception. 'Give me a second. I'll see the manager treats you right.' He disappeared into the office.

'Bet the manager's in cahoots,' Aunt Rose said.

'God,' Sally groaned. 'I won't sleep a wink.'

He returned promptly and handed Val the key. 'I got you the suite and a discount because you're with me.'

'I'm sleeping with the Walther,' Aunt Rose mumbled.

Once inside the suite the two women forgot their distress. 'Would you look at the size of that television?' Aunt Rose ran a covetous hand over the remote.

'Free movie channels, plus movies on demand.' Sally flipped through the directory. 'And look at what's on!'

Soon the smell of microwave popcorn wafted through the air. Aunt Rose and Sally were well into *Sleepless in Seattle* and hardly noticed when Val excused herself to take the car across the street to the garage.

The gossip at the garage was all about Beranger, with speculations on ever-more gruesome methods of demise. The mechanic said he couldn't get to her car before morning now. When she asked how much it would be, he said Hawk had already taken care of it. Her debt seemed to be mounting at a frightening rate.

Feeling more than a little sorry for herself, she pulled the pair of binoculars from the glove box and walked back across the street to the hotel, but instead of going in, she parked herself on the bench outside the door under the striped awning. She closed her eyes and leaned back against the wall. She couldn't bear the thought of an evening dominated by the television. Damn, she had hoped the car would be done tonight. She had wanted to sneak out to the bird reserve. No one would miss her, and besides, she had earned a little R&R. Well she wasn't going to get it now, was she?

Her silent pity party was interrupted by the roar of a motorcycle, and she opened her eyes to find Hawk in front of her, astride the hog.

'Figured I'd find you here. Auntie let you out on good behaviour?'

She offered him an anaemic laugh, hoping he wouldn't hear her heart jack-hammering. 'Movies on demand put her in a much better mood.'

Beneath the open bomber jacket, he wore a fresh T-shirt with Grateful Dead stretched 3-D across well-developed pecs. She wondered if the muscle came from eating all that red meat. The stubble was gone, and without the sunglasses she could see a slight bump far up the bridge of his nose – broken in a biker brawl, no doubt. At least she hoped it was nothing more sinister. She hadn't noticed it when they were in the truck, but then she had been somewhat distracted.

He smiled, revealing dimples the stubble had hid. 'Figured she'd like the television. Told you I could help make it easier for you.'

'Yes, you did. Thank you for that, and for everything else. I'll pay you for the car. I don't like being in debt. If you'll just tell me how much I owe you, I really have to go. Aunt Rose'll be worried about me.' The words tumbled out in a torrent of nerves. 'I told her I'd only be gone a little while. As I said, thanks so much, you've been very kind,' she glanced at her watch. 'But I really have to be going now.'

'With movies on demand, I'm betting your aunt won't even miss you.' He looked at his own watch. 'And the complimentary pizza should be delivered any minute now, so what's your hurry?' He offered her the extra helmet that was hanging over the handle bars. 'You afraid?'

She stuffed her hands in her pocket, so he wouldn't see them shaking and ignored the helmet. 'Should I be?' Her voice sounded breathless in the early evening stillness.

'Not of me, you shouldn't.' He offered her the helmet again. 'I can show you where the cranes are.' He nodded to the seat behind him and revved the engine.

Chapter Six

TWENTY MINUTES LATER, VAL and Hawk were sitting side by side in the grass. To their right was a cornfield that had been harvested last fall. On their left, the Platte River mirrored a rising gibbous moon that shone in the fading blue of the sky. The plaintive call of a whippoorwill broke the silence.

At last he spoke. 'I can understand you being nervous with Beranger's disappearance and all the rumours. No doubt you've heard. Everyone has.'

'I've heard, yes.'

'You an ornithologist?' He nodded to the binoculars she now wore around her neck.

'Studying to be one. My aunt thinks I've been studying too long, but there's so much to learn. You?'

'Me? No. I'm just a lover of nature. Since you're an expert, perhaps you can tell me something.' He scooted closer. 'Assuming the alleged murderers didn't eat this Beranger guy, you think the birds would?'

'What?' The knot in her stomach tightened.

'Would cranes eat Beranger?'

'Look, I've had to listen to this crap all day, then again at the garage. Just take me back, OK? This isn't funny.'

'Wait.' He took her hand. 'I'm sorry. My sense of humour can be a little off at times. I didn't mean to make you nervous.' He offered her a boyish grin. 'It's just, well, there are certainly worse things a man could do with his life than feed the birds. I figure feeding the birds might be the most noble thing that greedy-ass bastard ever accomplished. Assuming that's what happened, of course.'

'I read he was buying up adjacent land for an industrial

site,' she said. 'And that's just his latest atrocity.'

'I see you've done your homework. Sounds like maybe he deserved to be crane food.' He took off the bomber jacket and slipped it around her shoulders engulfing her in lingering body heat.

'You think his murder was eco-terrorism?'

'Possibly. Assuming he was murdered,' he said. 'Beranger was always unpredictable. Who knows what he might be up to.'

They sat quietly listening to the approaching night. The high grass in the nearby fields was motionless. The air smelled of moist loam and new growth. Everything seemed to be holding its breath.

He heard it first. She felt him tense. There was a shifting in the air, then the growing sound of distant cries and calls, accented by rattling woody trills. The calls of the sandhill cranes were nothing at all like the trumpeting sounds she had heard when she'd studied whooping cranes down in Port Aransas. It was like nothing she'd ever heard before, growing louder and more heavily syncopated, until she could feel it deep between her hip bones, down at the base of her spine. They were engulfed in a rolling sea of percussive trills and calls that sounded like endless, anxious questions waiting to be answered, and the moon disappeared in a sea of fluttering wings. 'Oh my God!' She rose to a half-crouch and squinted into the chaos. 'It's the cranes. It's the sandhills! You were right. They're here!'

'Looks like they've managed to slip in under curfew again.' He slid an arm around her and settled her back on the ground as the first birds landed and began feeding only yards from where they sat.

'They're huge!' she exclaimed. 'I mean I knew that, but actually seeing them, being this close to them, well, that's different, isn't it?' Then she added, not taking her eyes off the cranes. 'Did you know they're the oldest known bird species still surviving? They found a Miocene crane fossil right here in Nebraska, ten million years old. Can you imagine? And it was structurally identical to modern sandhill cranes. We're looking at the ancient past, Hawk.'

'They make me feel a bit like a time traveller,' he said.

She nodded agreement, as a large male close by raised his red head and rattled his questioning call. 'I think they could easily devour a greedy businessman – well chopped, of course.' In spite of her tasteless joke, such an end for Beranger did seem like poetic justice.

'They are the descendants of dinosaurs, after all, and a ravenous lot.' Hawk said, looking out over the sea of cranes.

'As far as some of them fly to reach their breeding grounds, a little extra protein certainly wouldn't hurt.' She pulled the jacket tight and let the feral aroma of leather and maleness caress her.

Another wave of cranes landed nearby. The air pulsated with warm bodies, the scent of distance and altitude still on their wings. As darkness settled, the fields around them seethed with need and urgency that brought the birds back to this same place year after year, generation after generation, millennia after millennia.

'My aunt thinks you killed Beranger.' Her boldness surprised her.

He laughed, cupping her jaw in a calloused hand and tracing her lower lip with his thumb. 'I had to. You said it yourself, the birds could use the extra protein.'

She nipped the tip of his thumb playfully and looked around at the feeding cranes. 'Bon appetit!' she called, uttering a startled gasp when he pulled her down onto the grass, his mouth covering hers as he engulfed her in his warmth and his scent.

'Is this payment for what I owe you?' she whispered when he pulled away.

'Only the first instalment.' He pushed the jacket off her shoulder along with the straps of her tank top and bra and bathed the sensitive hollow of her collar bone in warm kisses and nibbles, causing her to squirm against him.

'It's a big one then? The debt I mean.' She was finding it more and more difficult to think in coherent sentences as he cupped and caressed.

182

'You could be in the hotel room with your auntie and cousin watching movies on demand.'

'Enormous then,' she groaned, pressing up against him.

'Mmm. I doubt if you'll ever be able to fully repay it.' He insinuated one knee between her legs and wriggled and nestled until his groin pressed against hers, until she could feel the hardness of him through the rub of jeans against jeans. Then he went back to work on her mouth, his tongue dancing over hers and lapping at her hard pallet, as they rocked and shifted against each other, until the friction was exquisite.

He pulled away enough to shove her tank top up until her belly was bare, then he kissed her just below the waist band of her bra where her ribs came together, causing her to inhale in tight little gasps. He licked and nuzzled his way down to her navel, while he opened her zipper and slid a hand inside the low waist band of her panties, clearing the way for his hungry mouth. She arched up to meet his kisses, as he slid her clothing down over her hips.

It felt as though she'd been waiting forever for this moment, as he caressed and suckled the landscape of her, exploring with his fingers, with his mouth, with his eyes, like Lewis and Clark discovering a new land, like Darwin discovering a new species.

The little moan that escaped his throat against her clit might have been from the feel of her so engorged and open and receptive, or it might have been from the feel of his heavy penis pressing through his jeans. Whatever the cause, she returned the moan and curled her fingers in his hair holding him to her undulating groin. The cranes were all around them, so close she could almost touch a feathered neck or a slender leg. She felt their singleness of purpose as though it were her own, and Hawk felt it too, she was sure he did.

He nuzzled and nipped and licked at the split of her, burying his face in the warm wetness of her, caressing her fullness with deep, expressive lavings. And when she was practically in a frenzy with the want of him, he pulled away and looked up into her eyes, his face glistening with her juices. 'I don't want to play this time, Val. I want the real thing. I want all of you. I want to be inside you.'

'Me too,' she gasped. 'I want that too.'

And they were both on their knees fumbling with zippers and snaps, pushing and shoving at denim and cotton, all aflutter like the wings of the cranes around them. The need felt like a fast moving prairie fire, with too much heat to even notice the prickle of the grass and the scratch of last year's dead vegetation still not quite surrendered to new growth.

She heard the tear of the condom wrapper, and as she kicked free of jeans and panties he was already sheathed and ready for her, settling her bare bottom back onto his open bomber jacket and pushing into her with a grunt, which ended in an inhaled breath sucked between his teeth. 'Oh God,' he sighed. 'Oh God.'

She was slick and pouting, aching and heavy. She had been all day, ever since she first saw him stroking his cock behind the bathrooms at the rest area, and she took him with tight, yielding ease that rubbed and slid and gripped in all the right places.

She lifted her legs around his hips and he groped and kneaded her ass cheeks in an effort to pull her still further onto him. 'You're so deep and tight, and God, you feel better than anything,' he breathed.

She grabbed his clenching buttocks, running trembling desperate fingers down the crack between, parting them, fondling them, teasing, making him suck air as her fingers brushed his anus and lingered to explore timidly.

His thrusting had become tight, stiff, manic, and she was practically off the ground, wrapped around him so tightly, digging white knuckled fingers into the tense muscle beneath his shoulder blades. All breath was gone, all thought was gone. All that was left was instinct, hunger, need. It erupted in harsh cries that caused a startled rustling of wings and a few muffled squawks in the sea of feathers and sinew, but little more. It was as though the birds somehow knew they were no threat. They continued to feed and settle in to roost as though the earth hadn't moved, as though the fireworks of hormonal chemistry between two humans had nothing to do with them.

Chapter Seven

THE NEXT MORNING, VAL was sore from the thorough riding Hawk had given her. But she figured walking funny was a sure way to get another lecture on chafing and the health benefits of cotton panties, so she cranked the hot water and lingered in the steam of the shower a little longer.

There was something about wild animal sex with a mysterious biker in a field full of cranes that just seemed to energize a person. Apparently more so than pizza and movies on demand. Val was showered and ready to go by the time Aunt Rose and Sally stumbled out of bed, still talking about what a great time they'd had last night, in spite of the heartburn the pepperoni on the pizza had given Aunt Rose. Val sent the two across the street to scrounge breakfast at the diner, while she went over to pick up the car.

It took a little longer than she'd planned. Mike, the mechanic, looked up from under the hood of a green SUV. 'Won't be a minute,' he said, nodding to a panicked woman frantically pacing his Spartan office, glancing at her watch. 'Brakes are acting funny on Mrs Martin's Ford here. Got to get the little darlin's to school on time.' The little darlin's appeared to be making every effort to murder each other in front of the waiting room television, which blared the *Today Show* at full volume while the oldest toyed with the remote he'd just forcefully extricated from his sister's mouth. Val could understand Mrs Martin's urgency. A top up of brake fluid, a reminder of the wisdom of regular check-ups, and the grateful mother and her brood were on their way.

No amount of arguing would convince Mike to let Val pay for the work he'd done on her car. Hawk had settled it and that was the final word on the subject. The mechanic shook her hand with a grip of iron, offered her a broad smile and sent her on her way with her car as good as new.

She had just parked in front of the hotel to pick up the luggage and check out when Aunt Rose and Sally stepped out of the diner with a take-out box. And a biker.

Val did a double-take, her insides gave a little quiver and her pussy clenched with muscle memory. Sure enough, sandwiched in between Aunt Rose and Sally, with a battered rucksack over his shoulder and Aunt Rose gripping one sexy bicep with the claw was Hawk.

Aunt Rose shoved the food at Val. 'You took so long, we decided just to order you an egg muffin. You like egg muffins, don't you? You did when you were a little girl, and I used to make them for you.'

Val took the box and muttered her thanks, but her gaze was locked on Hawk.

'Hawk here agrees with me that it's not safe for three defenceless women to be travelling across the country alone.'

'Oh he does, does he?' Val shoved the hand not holding the take out box against her hip.

He offered her a wolfish grin.

Aunt Rose didn't seem to notice any of the subtext as she continued. 'Especially after our close call yesterday. Instead of such a nice man like Hawk, it could have been a murderer or a rapist or any kind of no-account who stopped out there on the highway seeing us all helpless and broke down. Anyway, keeping our safety in mind and all, and being the gentleman that he is, Hawk has graciously agreed to accompany us in the car for the rest of the journey. Turns out he was headed for Oregon anyway.'

'Oh really?' Val said.

His smile would have melted frozen butter. 'The world is so full of amazing coincidences, isn't it?'

'Isn't it just. Val replied. 'And what about your bike?'

'Mike at the garage will take care of it for me. I leave it here about half the time anyway. No problem really. I have the use of a car in Oregon, and I'll fly home when the time comes.'

186

Before Val could interrogate Hawk further, Aunt Rose shooed him and Sally in to pick up the rest of the luggage and nodded to the box Val had practically forgotten about. Eat your muffin, dear. You'll need your strength.'

Val had a feeling Aunt Rose might be right. Besides, she was ravenous, and very relieved to find a hash brown patty along with the over-stuffed English muffin. Wondering if the gas problem applied to cold hash browns as well as cold French fries, she judiciously ate that first.

Hawk stuffed the remaining luggage into the trunk, while Aunt Rose regaled him with stories of her poor Harry's deviated septum. Sally came out of the hotel with a cardboard take out tray and four enormous cups of coffee.

Aunt Rose took one of the offered cups, heaved a happy sigh and got into the car as Hawk opened the door for her. She called over her shoulder to her nieces. 'Hawk here will take the first shift driving, since he seems all fresh and chipper, and you two can ride in the back. Sally, you can drive next. Val, finish your breakfast, honey, then rest up for your turn.'

As Hawk walked past Val like he owned the world and everything in it, she elbowed him, nearly dropping her muffin. 'Brown-noser,' she whispered. 'You did tell them that you killed Beranger, didn't you?'

'Are you kidding? They'd never believe me after pizza and movies on demand, now would they? Besides ...' he surreptitiously brushed her breast in passing and pressed in just enough to make sure she knew it was no accident. His eyes were suddenly dark and wicked, 'I have ulterior motives.' He sauntered over to the car, got in behind the wheel and pushed the seat back. Way back.

In spite of the heat of his touch and his insinuations, Val felt a tiny frisson of fear in the pit of her stomach. Surely he was joking about Beranger. Had to be. And the way he touched her breast, the heat in his voice, surely she knew what his ulterior motives were. Surely they were safe with him. Surely.

If there could be eye sex, then the glances Hawk was shooting Val in the review mirror had to be the hottest kind of eye-foreplay. She couldn't believe that Sally hadn't noticed, but then for the first hour of the drive, Sally was on the phone with her husband about the "D" Ben Jr. had received in History. After that, she went into lecture mode with Ben, Jr. about the importance of education.

Aunt Rose ignored Sally and just spoke a little louder, talking happily to Hawk, who was ensconced in the driver's seat like he was the king of the world. Sally didn't seem bothered. Neither did Hawk, and the mishmash of conversations made it easy for Val to squirm in the seat without anyone paying attention – though it was a bit more difficult to find the sweet spot in the back. Maybe it had something to do with being farther away from the engine. But the looks Hawk kept flashing her made it pretty clear he knew what she was doing. She wondered if his Cheshire Cat grin meant he'd already found what she was looking for. The thought of all those great vibes from the engine rubbing up against the clench of his tight little asshole and making his cock threaten the integrity of his jeans had her squirming all the more.

In the mirror, Hawk touched just the tip of his luscious pink tongue to his upper lip, then ran his teeth slowly and repeatedly over his bottom one, tugging at its fullness, pulling at it gently, then releasing it. While Aunt Rose went on about high taxes and how the working man just didn't get a break these days, he just kept nodding and tugging, nodding and tugging.

Sally was now giving her husband a detailed description of the films she and Aunt Rose had watched and the pizza they had eaten.

Val raised a hand to rest on her chest, then nonchalantly lowered it to cup her left breast, giving the burgeoning nipple a little pinch through the flimsy summer top she'd worn just because she felt sexy after last night's orgy among the cranes.

Hawk did a double take, offered another lick of his lip and never missed a beat telling Aunt Rose how his uncle had owned a farm in Nebraska when he was a boy and how, when his family went to visit, his uncle let him feed the chickens and gather the eggs, and how there was a rooster who would always chase him. Val was amazed he could talk about chickens and eggs with Aunt Rose and practically fuck her with his eyes all at the same time.

She dug through the ice chest between her and Sally and found a bottle of water. Aunt Rose was now talking about her days as a little girl on a farm in Missouri, and Hawk must have surely been about to dislocate his eyeballs keeping one eye on the road and one on Val. She opened the water bottle and gave the neck of it a good fellating before drinking heavily. Then she pulled back prematurely to let the water spill generously onto her peaking nipple, now clearly visible through her blouse along with the chilled stippling of her areola. She made a fuss about being so sloppy, but the only one who paid any attention was Hawk. As she wiped and caressed and fondled her heavy breast with one of the napkins Sally had nicked from the Starlight Diner, Hawk seemed to be having a little trouble breathing. Aunt Rose asked him if his eyes were OK, because she had some drops for eye-strain if he needed them.

He reassured her that his eyes were fine as Val's hands-on inspection evolved to raking her nipple to new heights with the hard press of her thumb, ensuring that both nipple and areola were as visible as they could possibly be and still be clothed. Then, as though she had only just realised she was being watched, she returned Hawk's hungry gaze from beneath heavy eyelids. All the while Sally and her husband discussed Meg Ryan's best film roles and Aunt Rose got around to talking, once again, about her Harry's deviated septum. No doubt her concern for Hawk's sudden development of breathing problems raised the subject.

Not surprisingly, Hawk pulled into the next rest stop. He waited by the car with a restraining hand on Val's arm until he was sure that Sally, gesticulating wildly as she spoke into her cell phone, and Aunt Rose, anxious to settle in with the newest copy of *Woman's World*, both trotted off to the ladies room. Then he grabbed Val by the arm and hustled her behind the restrooms. This time, it wasn't a wank he had in mind.

There was no talking, just shoving clothing aside far enough to do what needed to be done. And it was amazing how little

189

shoving it took – panties and jeans down far enough for Hawk, with only his condomed cock and his balls jutting from his open fly, to turn her to the wall, bend her over and shove in to her sopping pout. And she was sopping. With one hand on her hip, he steadied her, with the other he groped, first the bounce of her breasts, then the cheeks of her exposed butt. At last the roaming hand came to rest on her heavy clit, causing them both to sigh and groan as though the hand had found its way home, tweaking and stroking and pinching in rhythm to each hard thrust.

'I've gotta come,' he growled between gritted teeth. 'It was all I could do not to come in my jeans when you dumped water on your tit. I can't hold back any longer.'

'Glad you saved it for me,' she breathed, straining as hard as he was. They both came in heavy humid grunts up against the cinder block of the restroom's back wall.

It was only when the shuddering and gasping diminished they realised Sally was watching, cell phone clenched in her tight fist, eyes welling with tears, lower lip trembling.

Before she could turn to leave and before Val could offer any sort of explanation, Hawk, still tucking his tackle, grabbed her none to gently, pushed her up against the wall and landed a heavy kiss on the surprised O of her mouth. It was a deep kiss, a probing kiss with plenty of tongue. To Val's surprise, Sally made no effort to repel his advances. Trembling all over, resting the hand fisted around the mobile on his shoulder, she kissed him back, until at last he pulled away just enough to speak. 'If you wanted to join us, all you had to do was ask.'

His words made Val's insides quiver with a strange mix of emotions. Sex was not something she and Sally had ever talked about. Sally was not someone she could even imagine talking about sex with. And watching the man she had just fucked fondle her married cousin was surreal.

'Join you? Are you crazy?' Sally's voice was thin, high pitched. 'I didn't want to join you. I wouldn't. I couldn't.'

Hawk didn't let her off that easily. 'Don't lie, Sally, you wanted to, didn't you? You wanted me to fuck you like I fucked your cousin, didn't you?' He held her sandwiched tightly between the rub of his body and the abrading rough of the wall. 'It made you wet, what you saw, what we were doing, and you wanted it too, didn't you?'

She shook her head frantically, looking like a frightened deer.

He ran a hand down over her mons and began to stroke the seam of her jeans with a thick finger. When he spoke, his voice was harsh, demanding. 'I know what you need, Sally. I've known from the beginning.' He probed a little harder and Sally dropped her phone with a guttural gasp, wrapped her arms around him and took his mouth like it was food and she was starving. Suddenly she was trembling all over, and Val knew that kind of trembling had nothing to do with fear and everything to do with having the mother of all orgasms. Sally would have collapsed against the wall if Hawk hadn't supported her, held her to him, soothed her. 'There, there.' He brushed his lips gently against the top of her head and held her until she could stand 'That's better, now isn't it?'

Then Sally began to sob in earnest. 'I haven't ... Ben and I don't ... I mean it's not that we ... This is the first time I've ... in ages,' she sobbed against his shoulder.

Hawk shot Val a quick glance, almost as though he needed her approval, then he lifted Sally's chin and held her gaze, as she frantically wiped her nose on the back of her hand. 'Sally, do you love him, your husband?'

'Of course I do,' she blubbered. 'But with the kids and their school and our work and all it's just that we're always so tired and there's never any time.'

He lifted her chin again and made her look at him. 'Two words, sweetheart.'

'Two words?' she whimpered.

Still holding her gaze, he bent, picked up her mobile and handed it back to her. 'Phone sex.'

She blinked. 'Phone sex?'

He nodded. 'You talk to him all the time, take advantage. Trust me on this, Hon.'

'Valerieee! Salleee!' Aunt Rose's voice rose like a siren from in front of the vending machines.

191

Hawk gave Sally a reassuring nod. 'A little sexting in the car, hmmm? And no one is the wiser. And then at the next rest area, well,' he nodded down to her crotch. 'I'm betting I haven't even begun to stoke the flames, have I?'

Val found herself nearly in tears over what had just happened. How had she not seen what was going on in her cousin's life when Hawk so clearly had? She laid a shaky hand on Sally's shoulder. 'Don't worry. I'll drive next, Sweetie. You text.'

They all three emerged from behind the toilets just as Aunt Rose let out another ear splitting bellow.

Chapter Eight

VAL HAD TO ADMIT, it was more peaceful having Hawk along for the ride. After the rest stop, she had taken over the driving and Aunt Rose was happy to browse through her growing stack of magazines, interrupting the quiet on occasion to enlighten Val with the latest shenanigans of some celebrity or politician. All was quiet in the back, with Hawk dozing peacefully in the seat behind Val and Sally texting away like a mad woman.

Every once in a while there was a little moan or a giggle. Wow, Val thought, who'd have guessed something as simple as sexting could bring so much peace to the journey, no more blaring country music, no more Montana ranchers, no more mail order brides, and no more loud phone conversations with misbehaving rug rats.

In their tranquil condition, they managed to put a lot of miles behind them that day. They weren't interrupted by Aunt Rose's sinuses or her hypoglycaemia. She seemed happy to stop when Hawk and Val thought it was a good idea. And by the time they crossed the border into Utah, Sally was positively glowing. There had been no conversations with or about the little darlings in miles, but Val feared there could be some repetitive stress problems in the future for Sally's madly texting fingers. As for what else Sally's fingers got up to at the rest stops and the café restrooms, well Val would really rather not know.

She couldn't help noticing that when he wasn't engaged amicably in conversation with his traveling companions or giving Val the lustful eye when he thought no one was looking, Hawk did his own share of texting and emailing on a Blackberry he pulled from somewhere on his person, not unlike a magician pulling a rabbit from a hat.

Sally had just driven them through Twin Falls, Idaho when Hawk's Blackberry rang. He answered it with, 'Yes. Finally! Perfect. Thanks. Yes it's fine by me if it's made public.' Then he switched it off.

'Is everyone OK to spend the night in Boise,' he said. 'I know a decent hotel and restaurant there. Plus, I have some business I need to take care of when we arrive.'

In Boise, he left them at the little bistro across the street from the hotel. Strangely enough, Aunt Rose's salmon was done to perfection and even the new potatoes satisfied her. She was practically purring over the fresh strawberry pie when Hawk slid into the booth next to Val, and ordered a burger and fries. The waitress was barely gone before Val felt his hand snaking up the inside of her thigh.

'Hope you got all your business taken care of,' Aunt Rose said around a mouthful of pie.

'All sorted,' he replied, dipping the tip of his finger into Val's chocolate mousse and licking it off in a way that definitely made her squirm. 'And faster than I'd expected.'

'A nice hotel you found for us,' Aunt Rose said. 'A bit upscale for our budget, but I reckon we can afford to splurge a little every now and then. And the girls do deserve a treat for driving me all this way.'

'Oh there's no charge,' Hawk said, helping himself to another taste of Val's mousse. 'I know the people who own it, and they owe me a favour. Besides it's off season and the middle of the week. Trust me. They don't mind.'

Val felt the knot in the pit of her stomach tighten again, the one that had been a constant threat since Hawk had arrived on the scene. 'And now we owe you again.'

He offered her a look that made her insides quiver. 'I told you. I like keeping people in my debt.'

Just then Hawk's burger and fries arrived, and the tension was broken as he regaled them with the tale of the unseasonable blizzard he'd ploughed through on the rim of the Grand Canyon with nothing but the hog protecting him from the elements. Not nearly as pleasant, he assured them, as being shanghaied to Oregon by three lovely ladies. And in spite of wondering how much of what he said was true and how much was lies, and feeling unsettled at their mounting debt to the man, Val found that she could no more resist him than the rest of her family could. By the time he'd finished his own chocolate mousse and his fingers were making tight little circles on the inside of her thigh, she convinced herself that none of it mattered as long as his immediate plans involved taking her to bed.

At Aunt Rose's insistence, he did at least allow her pay for dinner, teasing her that if he'd known she was paying he'd have had the prime rib.

Their rooms were down the hall from each other. Val hesitated in front of Hawk's door. 'Auntie, I need to talk to Hawk. I'll be in later, OK?'

Aunt Rose rolled her eyes and shoved her hands against her hips. 'I'm old, Valerie. I'm not stupid.' Then she turned her attention to Hawk. 'You got condoms? 'Cause I'm pretty sure Valerie doesn't since she hasn't had a boyfriend in quite a while, and if you don't have protection then she can just march her little body right on down the hall with us for the night, and that'll be that.'

Before Val could protest, Hawk gently took her hand and pulled her close. 'Don't worry, Aunt Rose, I've got condoms.'

'Well, then. Good night.' Aunt Rose turned on her heel, grabbed Sally's arm with the claw and headed down the hall to their room.

'God,' Val said as he pulled the door shut behind them. 'Did my aunt just give you permission to fuck me?'

'No, silly woman,' he said pushing her up against the door and ravishing her mouth. 'Your aunt just gave me her blessing to make love to you.'

'How do you suppose she knew?' She spoke between kisses and nips, as he helped her out of her blouse and went to work on her bra.

'Did you think she didn't?' He guided her to sit on the bed, his fly right at mouth level. 'All anyone has to do is look at us to know.' He curled his fingers in her hair and held her gaze as she released his straining erection, and it bobbed against her cheek. 'I doubt if they even have to look us really. I bet they can feel the heat. I bet the receptionist knows and the waitress, and the –'

He sucked breath between his teeth as she lifted the cool weightiness of his balls free, still holding his gaze, feeling that same mix of outrageous lust and disquiet in Hawk's presence that she had since she first met him behind the rest area toilets. But the slick twitch of her cunt made it hard to think about her disquiet when the object of her lust was here and now and free for the taking. As she took him into her mouth as deeply as she could, as his fingers tightened in her hair, and he groaned his appreciation of her tongue lapping the underside of his cock, she reminded herself that it actually wasn't free for the taking, and as the debt mounted, she had no idea what the price would actually be.

He pushed her back on the cool slip and slide of the bedding, pulling away long enough to peel her jeans and panties off in one swift move before he began to lick and nibble a sensitive path up the inside of her thigh. By the time he'd arrived at his destination, by the time he slid his tongue up over the tight delicious threshold of her perineum to dip and probe into the back edge of her pout, by the time he tugged and suckled on her swollen labia and nibbled at her clit, she had forgotten all about her mounting debt and was already mounting the first orgasm.

'There,' he breathed, as she shuddered against him. 'That felt good, didn't it?' For a second, he rested his cheek low on her belly, stroking her hip with one hand while he caught his breath. 'You worry too much, Val. You're constantly fearing the worst, constantly dreading what might be. You never let something just be what it is. So for tonight, this is a no worry zone. Tonight is all about getting totally blissed out together.' He offered her his wicked smile, 'And doing it without dried grass poking us in the ass.'

She kissed and licked the taste of herself from his face as he pushed into her, again the condom appearing in place almost as if by magic. The man was good with his hands, she thought. That was her last thought before he rode her to several more orgasms and convulsed his own release until she thought he'd break. In truth, when he was in her, when he touched her and held her and made love to her, she seemed to lose the ability to think, or to do anything really, anything that didn't involve revelling in the pleasure of him.

He smoothed her hair away from her face and curled around her. 'I've been fantasizing about this part more than any of the rest,' he said, pulling her into a spoon position.

'And what part is that?' she asked, wriggling her butt against him.

'Sleeping with you.' He kissed her neck and cupped her breast. 'I mean really sleeping with you and dreaming with you and waking up next to you. That part.'

The knot returned to her stomach with a vengeance, but this time for different reasons. She had never fantasized about sleeping in his arms, waking up next him. She had never allowed herself that. And now here he had brought it up, the one thing that wasn't allowed. But then Hawk wasn't much of a rule keeper, was he? Sleeping with him, dreaming with him, waking up in his arms – the thought felt close and tight and frightening. She might have panicked if he hadn't held her so close, if the tight fit of his body next to hers hadn't, in spite of everything, made her feel safe and cared for. Then last night's lack of sleep settled into her brain like a heavy wool blanket and she slept. She slept in Hawk's arms.

Val woke in the morning with a start, feeling like she was falling. Hawk mumbled something from the dream world, pulled her to him and continued to sleep. Early morning light seeped through the crack in the not completely drawn drapes, and the room was bathed in silence. She wanted to linger there in the smell of their love making and their mutual sleeping and dreaming. She wanted to fall back asleep and let him wake her up in one of the many wonderful ways she could easily imagine him waking her up. She would have loved nothing more than to let the bliss continue a little longer, but the clock on the nightstand read 6:45. Aunt Rose was an early riser, and she was sure the woman would be pounding on their door at any moment now. Plus, she really needed to pee.

Val disentangled herself from Hawk's embrace. He grumbled something incoherent and rolled onto his back, shoving aside the covers and throwing a forearm across his face giving her an exquisite view of the lines of his body and the easy rise and fall of his chest, the slope of his belly and the way his cock rested at half-mast against the soft down below his navel. Her insides melted like warm honey with the overwhelming intimacy of him there so close, so vulnerable. Perhaps she'd wake him for a quickie before Aunt Rose's wake-up bellow, or even just a snuggle, a few more minutes to feel him next to her. It would be worth Aunt Rose's displeasure. That's exactly what she'd do after she peed.

On the way back from the bathroom, she noticed the complimentary newspaper that had been pushed under the door. She should have left it until later, maybe even ignored it altogether. But she didn't. She picked it up, and the bottom dropped out of her world.

Chapter Nine

'WHEN WERE YOU PLANNING on telling me about this?' She tossed the newspaper on the bed next to him and began to pace back and forth, forgetting that she was naked. He stretched his way into wakefulness, rubbing his eyes with the back of his hands before he took the paper and squinted down at it.

The headline read; *Beranger's Loss is Sandhill's Gain.* Underneath was a photo of Hawk, freshly shorn and dressed in an expensive suit. The caption read; '*With Industrialist Tip Beranger still missing, Eco-warrior, Daniel 'Hawk' Mercer, buys acreage earmarked for industrial site. Donates all to Gruid Bird Reserve.*'

He tossed the paper back on the bed. 'Looks like I didn't have to, doesn't it?' He forced a grin, and nodded to the photo. 'I clean up real nice, don't you think?'

She only glared at him.

'Aren't you at least happy for the cranes? I'd hoped you would be.'

She ignored the question, feeling like her heart would explode in her chest. 'You didn't kill him, did you? Beranger.'

'Of course I didn't kill him! For fuck sake, Val, how can you even think such a thing? And this sale, well it's been a battle between Beranger and me for months now. It was a done deal long before he disappeared. I finalised it last night and authorised them to make it public. I was going to tell you after dinner. I was going to celebrate with you, but then,' He nodded to the bed. 'We got a little side tracked and land deals were the last thing on my mind. 'He shoved his way into his jeans. 'I have no idea what happened to the man. He had lots of enemies, you know that.'

199

Val didn't apologise, but she couldn't deny the relief that nearly took her breath away. 'The article says you're heir to a big fortune out east.' She stopped mid pace and jammed her finger at the paper still lying on the bed next to him. 'Is that true?'

He ran a hand through his hair and cursed under his breath. 'Last time I checked what my parents did 36 years ago in a fit of passion wasn't a crime. In fact ...' he fell into step and paced next to her. 'I'm still trying to figure out just what my crime is, and why you're so upset.'

As he reached for her, she shoved him away. 'You made love to me, and you ... you ... you made my family care about you, and you ... you ... you made love to me! Or at least I thought you did.' She gestured at the paper. 'But men like you and Beranger fuck people all the time, don't you? So why should my family and I be any different? You wined us and dined us, and I let you, even though I knew, I knew something wasn't right. But how the hell could I have guessed that we were just the entertainment for a bored rich boy?'

He winced as though she had slapped him and his voice was suddenly cold. 'I have never been bored, Val, and I don't need to use people for my entertainment.' He pulled on his boots. 'I wasn't trying to hide anything from you. You never asked, and I just assumed that you liked me for me.' He stood and walked to the door. 'I never met to hurt you or your family,' he said. 'I like your family, and, well I thought it was obvious how I feel about you. I'm sorry for any misunderstanding between us. Really sorry.' Then he turned and let himself out.

'It's not like him to leave without saying good-bye,' Aunt Rose said as they pulled away from the hotel and headed for the outskirts of Boise. She looked down at the copy of the paper in her lap. It was complimentary, so by the time the three women met for breakfast, Hawk's true identity was common knowledge. 'Course he's a pretty important man. I guess he probably got called away unexpectedly. Rich business men are like that, always off on important business.'

Val did her best to keep the conversation away from Hawk.

She even resorted to finding the whiniest country station she could and cranking it. The newspaper, along with all of her other gossip magazines, kept Aunt Rose occupied, and Sally was busy texting, no doubt sharing with her husband how they had met the rich and famous Daniel, Hawk, Mercer. They were easy, she thought, Aunt Rose and Sally. They were content to believe that some rich high roller actually had time for them, actually had anything for them that wouldn't get him something in return. And really, Val wasn't fooling herself. Her family had nothing to offer someone like Hawk Mercer, and she certainly didn't. She was nobody and not likely to ever be anybody, and it had never mattered as long as she could spend time with her birds. She certainly wasn't the kind of woman Daniel Mercer would want to take home to meet his folks.

So that meant he had to have latched on to them for the entertainment factor. And for some stupid-assed reason, that made her more angry than anything. OK, so they might not be up to his snooty-snoot standards, but they were still her family, damn it, and they deserved to be treated with a little respect.

When they pulled in to a truck stop to refuel the car just across the Oregon state line, Val went in to browse while a friendly woman dressed in a brown cover-all filled her tank. It was hard to enjoy the wander about when the last few wanders-about in truck stops had been done with Hawk sneaking a grope at every opportunity. She forced her thoughts away from his absence and browsed the books and CDs thinking maybe some romance for Aunt Rose might be a good idea. She was trying to decide between The Pirate Captain's Virgin Stowaway, and The Billionaire's Chamber Maid when Sally grabbed her by the arm and dragged her back behind the display of cleaning shammies and waxes for 18-wheelers.

'Enough of this,' she hissed. 'I want to know what happened with you and Hawk, what really happened.'

Val squared her shoulders. 'Daniel Mercer happened, that's what happened.'

Sally blinked.' 'What?'

Val shot a quick glance over at the magazine rack to make

sure Aunt Rose was still well occupied. 'Oh come on, Sally, a rich guy disguised as a biker suddenly wanting to ride shot-gun with us?' She made an inclusive gesture. 'I call it slumming for fun, that's what I call it.'

Sally shook her head and gave Val her disappointed mother's look. 'Here all this time I thought you were the smart one in the family. Was the man ever anything but kind to us?'

Val tried to keep her lower lip from quivering.

'He only agreed to join us because Aunt Rose was so concerned about us traveling alone.' She raised a hand. 'I know, I know, she's a bit neurotic, but it's not like either of us has cornered the market on the well-balanced psyche, is it?' She gave Val's arm an affectionate stroke. 'Hawk was good for us, Val. Good for all of us, and he didn't ask anything in return. He's no more responsible for his birth and his family than we are, is he?'

Val figured the Billionaire's Chamber Maid was a bit too close to home, so, as they headed out across Oregon, they were regaled with tales of bodice ripping pirates. This time the atmosphere in the car was more laid back when the bodice ripping began. There were giggles and rude remarks and a general running commentary for the duration. Lunch was a leisurely picnic shared at a rest area just before they reached the Columbia River. Val figured if she had to feel like she'd just had her heart ripped out, then there were worse places to be, and worse people to be with.

Chapter Ten

THEY DROVE ALONG I84 and the Columbia River Gorge in the late afternoon sun.

'The sign says Multnomah Falls,' Aunt Rose said, pointing out the window, then down at the atlas she had open on her lap. 'Harry told me about that place. He says it's really beautiful. He says it's worth seeing. I think we should stop.'

'Now?' Val shot her aunt a glance from behind the steering wheel. 'But I thought you'd be anxious to get to Harry's.'

'I've heard it's really spectacular,' Sally piped up from the back. 'And there's a lovely gift shop. I might find something for the kids there.'

'Harry says there's a nice view of the falls from the big solarium in the restaurant,' Aunt Rose added. 'He says the food's really good. My Harry has a very discerning palate.' Aunt Rose rubbed her stomach. 'I could eat.'

'But we just ate,' Val said.

'Picnics aren't real meals, are they? Besides my legs ache from being all cramped up in the car.' Aunt Rose massaged one knee. 'The exercise would do us good.'

'I agree,' Sally said. 'We should definitely stop.'

Val knew there was no use arguing, so she pulled into the parking lot off I84, where the falls already dominated the skyline. It was better than a truck stop, she thought, especially since truck stops held painful memories at the moment. A little balm for the soul from the natural world couldn't hurt.

From the viewing deck above the lodge, Aunt Rose pointed to the foot bridge that crossed further up the river and gave a lovely view of both falls and the pool below. 'Shall we?' She trotted off up the footpath toward the bridge. Val was more than a little surprised, since Aunt Rose wasn't noted for anything that involved a lot of footwork. Sure enough, by the time they reached the bridge, the woman was doing her share of heavy breathing, but strangely she didn't complain or even reach for her inhaler.

The bridge was crowded with people making their way back down the steep path from the top as the late afternoon light faded. The view was breath taking, and romantic, which did little to ease Val's aching emptiness. How could she feel such pain for someone she'd known such a short time? The light breeze bathed the viewers in a bracing mist from the lower fall as they all raised their heads to view the top of the neck-cricking upper fall, ooohing and awing their appreciation.

'It's the highest waterfall in Oregon.' A familiar voice came soft and humid against her ear.

'Six hundred and twenty feet. Fed by underground springs on Larch Mountain. That and spring run off.' Hawk moved in closer and folded his arms around her making her feel weak-kneed and giddy.

'That huge boulder down there in the pool, it weighs 400 tons and fell from the face of the cliff in 1995.' He nipped her earlobe. 'Can you imagine the splash?'

She tried to laugh, but couldn't quite manage it, and the sudden mist in front of her eyes had nothing to do with the waterfall. 'So what are you, a tour guide now?'

'Can be, if I need to be.' He tightened his embrace. 'Wanna see the top?'

'Of course she wants to see the top,' Aunt Rose said. 'Mind you, Harry'll be here in an hour and a half, and I'll be starving by then, so if you two poke around up there, we'll eat without you, don't think we won't.'

'Harry? Harry's coming?' Val asked.

'Just in case you two get side-tracked. I'm too old to hitchhike, and Sally won't show a little cheesecake to anyone but her Ben, so how else are we going to get on to Portland.' Aunt Rose stood on her toes and gave Hawk a kiss on his cheek, then she did the same to Val, offering her a smile that was almost tender.

'Come on, Sally,' she said, shooing her niece back down the path toward the lodge. 'Let's find that gift shop.'

For a second Hawk and Val stood watching the two women saunter down the path like ladies of the manor, then they turned and headed toward the top of the falls in silence, getting curious looks from the mass exodus heading the other way. At last he spoke. 'I'm sorry, Val. I'm sorry for running out like I did this morning, but I was angry. I admit, I should have told you I was the spoilt little rich boy. I'm sure it was a shock to find out from the paper.' He reached for her hand, but she pulled it away.

'I don't care how rich you are. What I care about is that you manipulated all of us, and now you've got my aunt and my cousin manipulating me.' She jerked her head in the direction Aunt Rose and Sally had disappeared. 'I can only assume you were all in this together.'

'Oh come on, Val, I couldn't have manipulated them if I'd wanted to. Your aunt would have seen through it with her eyes closed.' Hawk grabbed her by the arm and pulled her out of the way, forcing a smile and a nod to a handful of Chinese tourists who passed them on their way down. When they were out of hearing distance he turned his attention back to her, speaking in a forced whisper as they continued their ascent. 'Sally flat out said on the phone that Aunt Rose wouldn't have let me near you if –'

'Wait a minute,' she turned on him, 'Sally has your cell number too?'

'Yes. Both she and Aunt Rose.'

'Oh that's just perfect!' She headed off up the trail at a fast trot. 'You give my cousin and my aunt your cell phone number but can't be bothered to give it to me, the woman you're fucking! That's just great!'

'The woman I'm fucking never asked for my number, damn it!' he said, practically running to catch up with her.

A couple coming down with a toddler papoosed on the father's shoulders gave them a wide berth and hurried on past.

Hawk caught up with her and grabbed her arm forcing her to walk next to him. 'Do you think Aunt Rose would have let

205

me anywhere near you in Gruid if she hadn't interrogated me to within an inch of my life first?'

'What?'

'Did you really think she'd hang out in the hotel room watching *Sleepless in Seattle* for the millionth time while you went missing for most of the night? You really don't give your family much credit, do you? Would you slow the fuck down! This is not a footrace, and you're missing the views.' He pulled her to a stop as they rounded the next hairpin curve overlooking the broad expanse of the Columbia River, now bronzing in the fading light. It was shouldered on the Washington side by shaggy forested bluffs. To their left Upper Multnomah Fall spilled noisily over the breast of Larch Mountain into the abyss they couldn't see the bottom of for the growth of evergreens rising up around them.

'Christ, Val, why do you have to make it so hard? Why can't you just let things be what they are?' He lifted her chin and forced her to meet his gaze. 'I followed you to Oregon. That wasn't my plan, you know? I was heading for New Mexico. But I followed you to Oregon, and now that I have, now that I know you, I'll follow you back to Missouri if I have to.' He chuckled softly and stepped back. 'That makes me sound like a stalker, doesn't it?'

This time, she let him take her hand as they turned back up the path. 'So I was the only one who didn't know what was going on?' she asked.

'You were pretty oblivious.'

'Was that all an act, then – Sally and Aunt Rose thinking you were a cannibal biker who killed Beranger?'

'Oh they thought that all right. They didn't know anything about us until Aunt Rose saw me kissing you by Bill's truck at the truck stop. The woman has eagle eyes. Then while you were over at Mike's garage, Aunt Rose gave me the royal once-over. When she was convinced I wasn't going to kill you and eat you, she ordered me to take you to see those silly birds you were always going on about.' He glanced at her and offered her a mischievous smile. 'That's what I had in mind anyway, but I think she'd have been after me with the Walther if I'd tried it without her blessing.'

'She told you about that, did she?'

'She told me about a lot of things. Val, my point is that they both love you and want you happy. And they're hoping, and I'm certainly hoping that your happiness will at least in part involve me.'

Suddenly they found themselves on the viewing platform at the top of the falls, surprisingly invisible from below. 'Oh my God!' She spoke over the roar of the falls, as they took in the dizzying view of the Columbia River and the world beneath that now looked miniature and toy-like.

She leaned out over the metal railing into nothingness. Her insides quivered low in her pelvic girdle and her stomach flip-flopped. 'You feel that?' she breathed, as he moved in behind her and slid his arms around her waist. 'I love that feeling of almost falling, almost flying, you know, the way it feels to be up so high and looking down. I wonder if that's what birds feel. I dream about that sometimes, flying like they fly.'

'Oh yes, I feel it,' he said, 'But that's not nearly all I'm feeling, Val, not nearly.' He started by nibbling the nape of her neck, and as he moved in close enough that she could feel the tight undulation of his groin, the delirious free-falling sensation intensified until she shuddered and quivered against him, feeling goose flesh tickle up her spine. She guided his hand down inside her tank top to her breasts, cupping him to her until her nipple caressed his fingertips and he gasped against her ear. 'God woman, I wouldn't trade this. I wouldn't trade this for the best thing any bird might feel.'

She wore a light summer skirt, and though easy access hadn't been her plan at the beginning of the day, she was certainly happy for it now as his fingers scrunched the fabric until they made contact with bare skin, and the squirmy falling, flying feeling was joined by the thrum of ravenous arousal. She shifted her hips and opened her stance, taking care to rake herself hard against him as she did so. He gave a low belly-grunt in response, and she caught her breath in a little whimper as his hand slid over the crotch of her panties teasing the landscape below to full, humid attention. He thumbed the rise of her clit and drew a heavy finger up the length of her pout, pressing the soft gusset deep along the folds of her until he found her hole, wet and grasping. Then he wriggled and burrowed into it, fabric and all, making her squirm and bear down until the fabric was drenched and clinging. 'You're so soft and warm,' he whispered against her nape. 'And you smell like honey, hot and sticky and so ready.'

She heard his fly open, but as she reached around behind to grasp his heavy smoothness, he pushed her hand a way with a tight groan. 'Don't do that. I'm so full I'm not sure I can control myself and I don't want to come in your hand. I want to come inside you.'

She heard the rattle of the condom wrapper as the hand stroking her through her panties at last slipped the crotch aside. She pulled a tight breath and rubbed herself against the flat of his palm.

'Grab the rail.' His voice came in tight staccato bursts. 'That's it. That's my girl. Push your butt back. Open your legs for me.'

She did as he commanded, feeling the giddy clench of the height as she looked over the edge of the fall. The cool caress of evening air bathed her bottom as he lifted her skirt up over her hips, worried her panties until they were uselessly stretched over one butt cheek then he shoved into her with a trembling moan. 'Oh God,' he breathed. 'Oh my God.' Then he pushed in close, and she could tell by his gasp that they both felt the vertigo of the view into nothingness. The tingling gripping sensation was made all the more exquisite because it culminated in the place that already buzzed with excitement, the place where his cock pushed into her cunt.

And suddenly, they had company.

Fortunately, the couple wasn't quiet in their approach. Val and Hawk heard them coming down the path talking happily about the lovely drive they'd had down the Gorge. Hawk placed a pussy-scented hand over Val's lips in warning. 'Don't move.' His words came out in a whispered rush. 'I'm not about to take my cock out of your sweet cunt for polite company or otherwise, so stand still and let me take care of this.' Careful to keep her pressed up tight against him, he straightened, smoothed her skirt in front then wriggled in very close. She arched her back, shifted her hips and pushed her bottom out to keep his cock from dislodging. He quickly straightened her skirt around his open fly and shoved his groin forward to settle himself still deeper in her pussy. Then he carefully rested a hand either side of her on the metal railing. 'Now,' he breathed. 'Just act like you're enjoying the view.'

She gave a nervous clench with her cunt lips and he gasped. 'Stop that, or I'll fuck you hard right here in front of them. I'll grab your tits and hump and grunt and make such a scene that they'll send for security.' He nipped her earlobe enough to make it sting. 'But you'd like that, wouldn't you?'

Just then the woman came to the rail beside them. Fortunately her full attention was on the view. 'Lovely, isn't it?' she said.

'Mmm. Lovely.' Hawk managed. His voice vibrated down through his cock and made Val's breath hitch, but she disguised it with a cough, which did nothing to ease the tight, tetchy sensation growing where her pussy gripped his cock.

'You two here on vacation?' the man asked.

'Mmm. Vacation, yes,' Val replied, fighting the overpowering urge to thrust.

'Us too,' the woman said, taking her husband's hand. 'Well honeymoon, actually.'

'Congratulations,' both Val and Hawk managed in unison. Val noticed Hawk was white-knuckling the railing, and her toes were curled so hard that she feared she'd dig holes through her sandals.

As the couple moved around the platform to view Little Multnomah Fall flowing into the deep pool beneath, Hawk's hand migrated under the front of Val's skirt to stroke her mons. Then he gave a subtle but deep thrust and tweaked Val's clit until her knees nearly gave with the thrum of animal lust and vertigo pulsing up through her. 'Feels good being sneaky, doesn't it? Makes you even wetter, doesn't it?' He nuzzled her ear. 'Makes my cock feel like iron.'

Fortunately the couple didn't linger over the view, but

turned and disappeared back down the path.

In spite of himself, Hawk burst into laughter, a feeling that was anything but unpleasant vibrating through Val's pussy, 'Woman, you're gonna get me in trouble yet. Can you imagine the headline on the front of your Aunt's next copy of *The National Enquirer*; 'Eco-warrior caught with his pants down porking sexy ornithologist.''

She wriggled against him and tightened her grip. 'The question is, does your ass look as good on the front page as that smug face of yours?'

'You've seen my bare ass, honey,' Hawk breathed. 'You be the judge.' Then he began to thrust in earnest, with Val braced against the rail, the view sending delicious prickly shivers up her spine.

'Can you feel that,' she gasped. 'Oh my God, can you feel that? Feels like I'm gonna explode, all of me, and just drift away on the breeze out across the Columbia.'

'Then let's do it together,' he breathed. 'Let's make the biggest explosion ever.' And they did. They came in quakes and tremors that felt like they were falling, that felt like they were flying, that felt like all of Multnomah Falls was happening inside their joined bodies. Then they collapsed against the rail of the viewing platform in bursts of laughter and gasps for breath as the last rays of sun stained the waters of the Columbia mauve.

When they could breathe again, there was frantic straightening and smoothing of clothing, then with one hand holding Val's and the other holding his Blackberry to his ear, Hawk called Aunt Rose. 'Harry arrived OK? Good. Yes, we're on our way down. Yes, go ahead and order for us. Some nice, juicy red meat would be good.' He winked at Val. 'We trust your judgement. See you soon.'

He shoved the Blackberry in his pocket. 'Aunt Rose is ordering us prime rib, and she says there are some nice Oregon wines on the menu. And afterwards.' He squeezed her hand and gave her a fleeting, almost shy glance. 'Well what happens afterwards all depends on you.'

She could feel her pulse hammering in her throat as though

it were about to jump out. She took a deep breath and found it was suddenly difficult to speak. 'Well, actually, I was kind of hoping that, since it's so important to my family and all. Well, I was hoping that maybe my happiness might, to some degree, involve you, I mean if you're all right with that, and you don't need to rush off to New Mexico or do important business stuff that spoilt rich kids are required to do. Only if you're all right with that.'

There was a long moment of silence, and she was just beginning to wonder if she'd misread the whole situation when he kissed her hard, then gathered her to him and held her close to the rapid thud, thud of his heart. 'I could be,' he said. His voice sounded tight in his throat. 'I could be very, very all right with that. If it's acceptable to a burgeoning young ornithologist, that is, and it won't cramp her lifestyle too much.'

They stood for a long moment, wrapped in each other's arms, bathed in the deepening shadows, then Val spoke in a breathless giggle. 'Come on, we don't want to keep Aunt Rose waiting. She has hypoglycaemia, you know. Besides I'm starving. I'm looking forward to lots and lots of juicy, succulent red meat.'

He gave her one last sloppy kiss, and they turned and continued down the path picking up speed as they went.

More great titles in
The Secret Library

Silk Stockings
9781908262042

One Long Hot Summer
9781908262066

The Thousand and One Nights
9781908262080

The Game
9781908262103

Hungarian Rhapsody
9781908262127

Silk Stockings – Constance Munday

When Michael Levenstein meets Imogen, an exotic dancer at a Berlin nightclub, a passionate and intense love story develops. Michael becomes obsessed by mysterious Imogen and falls into a world of intense sexual fantasy and desire. But Imogen is determined to protect a personal, dark secret at all costs and because of this she has forbidden herself love.

With Imogen afraid of committing and afraid of losing what she has fought for so desperately, can Michael break down her barriers and discover a solution to his lover's deep dark secret, thus freeing the enigmatic Imogen to truly love him?

The Lord of Summer – Jenna Bright

Banished to the back of beyond, in the middle of a long, hot summer, Gem and Dan Parker find their marriage filling up with secrets. As they work to reopen the Green Man pub, tensions and unacknowledged desires come between them. From their first night, when Gem sees someone watching them make love from the edge of the woods, her fantasies of having two men at once start to grow and consume her. As the temperature rises, she becomes fixated by her imaginings of an impossible, gorgeous, otherworldly man in the forest. A man who could make her dreams come true – and maybe save her marriage.

Off the Shelf – Lucy Felthouse

At 35, travel writer Annalise is fed up with insensitive comments about being left "on the shelf". It's not as if she doesn't *want* a man, but her busy career doesn't leave her much time for relationships. Sexy liaisons with passing acquaintances give Annalise physical satisfaction but she needs more than that. She wants a man who will satisfy her mind as well as her body. But where will she find someone like that?

It seems Annalise may be in luck when a new member of staff starts working in the bookshop at the airport she regularly travels through. Damien appears to tick all the boxes – he's gorgeous, funny and intelligent, and he shares Annalise's love of books and travel.

The trouble is, Damien's shy and Annalise is terrified of rejection. Can they overcome their fears and admit their feelings, or are they doomed to remain on the shelf?

One Long Hot Summer – Elizabeth Coldwell

Lily's looking after her friend, Amanda's, home on the Dorset coast, hoping it will ease her writer's block and help her get over her ex, Alex. What she doesn't expect is that Amanda's 21-year-old son Ryan will arrive at the house, planning to spend the summer surfing and partying – or that he'll have grown up quite so nicely. Ryan's as attracted to her as she is to him – but surely acting on her feelings for a man 14 years her junior is inappropriate? And when Alex makes a sudden reappearance in her life, wanting to get back together, should she follow her head or her heart? How can she resolve this case of summer madness?

Just Another Lady – Penelope Friday

Regency lady Elinor has fallen on hard times. The death of her father and the entail of their house put Elinor and her mother in difficulty; and her mother's illness has brought doctor's bills that they cannot pay. Lucius Crozier was Elinor's childhood friend and adversary; and there has always been a spark of attraction between the pair. Now renowned as a womaniser, he offers a marriage of convenience (for him!) in return for the payment of Elinor's mother's medical bills. Reluctantly, she agrees. But Lucius has made enemies of other gentlemen of the upper echelon by playing fast and loose with their mistresses, and one man is determined to take his revenge through Lucius's new wife ...

Safe Haven – Shanna Germain

Kallie Peters has finally made her dream come true – she's turned the family farm into Safe Haven, an animal sanctuary. But financial woes are pressing in on her, and she's worried that the only way to keep the farm is to allow her rich ex-boyfriend back into her life. When a sexy stranger shows up in her driveway with a wiggling puppy in his arms, she knows it's her chance for a hot rendezvous before she gives up her freedom. The sex is hot, wild and passionate – the perfect interim before returning to the pressures of real life – but something else is happening between them. Can they find a way to save their dreams, their passions and their hearts, or will they have to say goodbye to all they've come to love?

The Thousand and One Nights – Kitti Bernetti

When Breeze Monaghan gets caught red-handed by her millionaire boss she knows she's in trouble. Big time. Because Breeze needs to keep her job more than anything else in the world. Sebastian Dark is used to getting exactly what he wants and now he has a hold over Breeze, he makes her an offer she can't refuse. Like Scheherazade in The 1001 Nights Seb demands that Breeze entertain him to save her skin. Can she employ all her ingenuity and sensuality in order to satisfy him and stop her world crashing about her? Or, like the ruthless businessman he is, will Seb go back on the deal?

Out of Focus – Primula Bond

Eloise Stokes's first professional photography assignment seems to be a straightforward family portrait. But the rich, colourful Epsom family – father Cedric, step-mother Mimi, twin sons Rick and Jake, and sister Honey – are intrigued by her understated talent and she is soon sucked into their wild world. As the initial portrait sitting becomes an extended photo diary of the family over an intense, hot weekend, Eloise gradually blossoms until she is equally happy in front of the lens.

The Highest Bidder – Sommer Marsden

Recent widow Casey Briggs is all about her upcoming charity bachelor auction. She doesn't have time for dating. Her heart isn't strong enough yet. But when one of their bachelors is arrested and she finds herself a hunky guy short, she employs her best friend Annie to find her a new guy pronto.

Enter Nick Murphy – handsome, kind, and not very hard to look at, thank you very much. And he quickly makes her feel things she hasn't felt in a while. A very long while. Casey's not sure if she's ready for it – the whole moving on thing. But as she prepares to auction Nick off, she's discovering that her first hunch was correct – he's damn near priceless.

The Game – Jeff Cott

The Game is the story of Ellie's bid to change from sexy, biddable housewife to sexy dominant goddess.

Ellie and Jake are a happily married couple who play a bedroom game. Having lost the last Game Ellie must start the new one where she left off – bound and gagged on the bed. As she figures out how to tie herself up before Jake's return from work, Ellie remembers the last Game and has ideas for the new one. Jake is immensely strong and loving and has seemingly endless sexual stamina so the chances of Ellie truly gaining control look slim. Although she has won the Game on occasions, she suspects he lets her win just so he can overwhelm her in the next. She has to find a way to break this pattern.

But does she succeed?

One of Us – Antonia Adams

Successful artist Natalie Crane is midway through a summer exhibition with friend and agent Anton when Will Falcon strolls tantalisingly into her life. After a messy divorce, a relationship is not Natalie's priority. Anton takes an immediate dislike to the shaven-headed composer, but Natalie is captivated. He is everything she is not: free, impulsive and seemingly with no thought for the future. He introduces her to Dorset's beautiful coves and stunning countryside and their time together is magical.

Things get complicated when her most famous painting, a nude self-portrait, is stolen and there are no signs of a break-in. When it's time for her return to London, Will doesn't turn up to say goodbye, and she cannot trace him. Anton tells her to forget him, but she cannot. Then she discovers the stakes are much higher than they first appeared.

Taste It – Sommer Marsden

Jill and Cole are competing for the title of *Best Chef*. The spicy, sizzling and heated televised contest fuels a lust in Jill she'd rather keep buried. She can't be staring at the man's muscles ... he's her competition! During a quick cooking throwdown things start to simmer and it becomes harder and harder for Jill to ignore that she's smitten in the kitchen. Cole's suggestive glances and sly smiles aren't helping her any. When fate puts her in his shower and then his chivalrous nature puts her in his borrowed clothes, there's no way to deny the natural heat between them.

Hungarian Rhapsody – Justine Elyot

Ruby had no idea what to expect from her trip to Budapest, but a strange man in her bed on her first night probably wasn't it. Once the mistake is ironed out, though, and introductions made, she finds herself strangely drawn to the handsome Hungarian, despite her vow of holiday celibacy. Does Janos have what it takes to break her resolve and discover the secrets she is hiding, or will she be able to resist his increasingly wild seduction tactics? Against the romantic backdrop of a city made for lovers, personalities clash. They also bump. And grind.

Restraint – Charlotte Stein

Marnie Lewis is certain that one of her friends – handsome but awkward Brandon – hates her guts. The last thing she wants to do is go on a luscious weekend away with him and a few other buddies, to a cabin in the woods. But when she catches Brandon doing something very dirty after a night spent listening to her relate some of her *sexcapades* to everyone, she can't resist pushing his buttons a little harder. He might seem like a prude, but Marnie suspects he likes a little dirty talk. And Marnie has no problems inciting his long dormant desires.

A Sticky Situation – Kay Jaybee

If there is a paving stone to trip over, or a drink to knock over, then Sally Briers will trip over it or spill it. Yet somehow Sally is the successful face of marketing for a major pharmaceutical company; much to the disbelief of her new boss, Cameron James.

Forced to work together on a week-long conference in an Oxford hotel, Sally is dreading spending so much time with arrogant new boy Cameron, whose presence somehow makes her even clumsier than usual.

Cameron, on the other hand, just hopes he'll be able to stay professional, and keep his irrational desire to lick up all the accidentally split food and drink that is permanently to be found down Sally's temptingly curvy body, all to himself.

The
Secret Library

Essential sensual reading

www.TheSecretLibrary.co.uk